**Critics cheer for master mystery-writer Earl Emerson
and his feisty detective.**

"This is an expert . . . job with a likable hero. May he return."
— Newgate Callendar,
The New York Times Book Review

"This new novel . . . laces firefighting lore—the danger, the grisly
humor—with corruption, elusive identities and haunting images. . . .
Emerson paints characters and images that stay with you after you
put down the book."
— *Chicago Sun-Times*

"A high-combustion thriller . . . Emerson's style is muscular and
active. . . . It's always a pleasure to read an author who is indubitably
authoritative."
— *Los Angeles Times*

"Fontana is sympathetic and charming. . . . A first-rate crime story"
— *UPI International*

"Emerson's lean, lucid, and picturesque prose masterfully describes
Mac's abrasive encounters with renegade arsonists and a greedy real
estate developer. Easily as good as Elmore Leonard's *Glitz*"
— *Library Journal*

"A gripping mix of tensions and humor"
— *Publishers Weekly*

"A solid entry for readers partial to rough-stuff and offbeat ambience"
— *Kirkus Reviews*

"Emerson . . . is ready to emerge as one of the most distinctive writers
among the new wave of crime novelists."
— *Booklist*

PENGUIN CRIME FICTION

BLACK HEARTS AND SLOW DANCING

Earl W. Emerson is a lieutenant with the Seattle
Fire Department. He has written five previous mys-
teries: *The Rainy City*, *Poverty Bay* (Edgar Award
nominee and Shamus Award winner), *Nervous
Laughter*, *Fat Tuesday*, and *Deviant Behavior*.

STAIRCASE is a fictional town, as are the people therein. While the procedures and the equipment depicted in the Seattle Fire Department are accurate, the characters and incidents in this book are imaginary. I have nothing but the highest regard for firefighters—as friends, co-workers, and professionals in a dirty, dangerous, and frequently tedious job—and for the Seattle Fire Department, one of the finest in the nation.

BLACK HEARTS AND SLOW DANCING

EARL W. EMERSON

PENGUIN BOOKS

PENGUIN BOOKS
Published by the Penguin Group
Viking Penguin Inc., 40 West 23rd Street,
New York, New York 10010, U.S.A.
Penguin Books Ltd, 27 Wrights Lane,
London W8 5TZ, England
Penguin Books Australia Ltd, Ringwood,
Victoria, Australia
Penguin Books Canada Ltd, 2801 John Street,
Markham, Ontario, Canada L3R 1B4
Penguin Books (N.Z.) Ltd, 182–190 Wairau Road,
Auckland 10, New Zealand

Penguin Books Ltd, Registered Offices:
Harmondsworth, Middlesex, England

First published in the United States of America by
William Morrow and Company, Inc. 1988
Reprinted by arrangement with William Morrow and Company, Inc.
Published in Penguin Books 1989

3   5   7   9   10   8   6   4   2

LIBRARY OF CONGRESS CATALOGING IN PUBLICATION DATA
Emerson, Earl W.
Black hearts and slow dancing/Earl W. Emerson.
p.   cm.—(Penguin crime fiction)
ISBN 0 14 01.1732 6 (pbk.)
I. Title.
[PS3555.M39B56   1989]
813'.54—dc19   88–23784

Printed in the United States of America
Set in Times Roman

Whom Fortune wishes to destroy she first makes mad.

—PUBLILIUS SYRUS, *Moral sayings* (1st c. B.C.)

When a man tells the truth, he best have one foot in the stirrup.

—ANCIENT PROVERB

BLACK HEARTS AND SLOW DANCING

1

A Dog Named Booger

FONTANA LIKED TO THINK he wasn't a murderer. There was a subtle distinction between the words *kill* and *murder*, one he found himself reviewing until it became a catechism. It was only one of many problems resulting from having carried a badge. Now the mayor was pestering him to be sheriff.

"That is the ugliest dog in the world," Fontana said.

"Really, he's not bad," said the mayor. "If you look at him. Take a good look."

Fontana choked on a halfhearted laugh.

"Watch my eyes, lady. I am looking at the Dugan. He was the only male dog left, the species would go extinct. A bitch in heat would jump under a speeding locomotive if she saw him round the corner."

"He comes with the truck. I can't help that," said the mayor, tugging her aquamarine sweatshirt against her heavy breasts. They had been haggling on the parking strip for five minutes.

"Not when I'm driving, he doesn't."

"They trained him in Germany. He wouldn't hurt a fly—unless of course you told him to. You're only being contrary."

"Being honest, lady. Get him outa there." The truck was a palomino, a faded burnt-rose against white, and MacKinley

Fontana, for some peculiar reason, fancied it, curb feelers, dust vanes, suicide knob, and all. A two-door 1960 GMC, it had seen its share of wilderness, though it was well taken care of. Original paint. Seat cushions. A cargo space in the back easily large enough to haul four bales of hay. A three-quarter-width bench behind the front seat.

In the backseat hunkered the major drawback, the largest, most flyblown German shepherd he had ever laid eyes on. Shaggy, scarred, the beast had a cunning, lupine aspect to him that made Mac nervous.

"Sheriff Bounty hauled him around everywhere he went," explained the mayor. "He thinks this is his truck. He knows you're going somewhere and he won't budge."

"In the first place," Fontana said disgustedly, "I never wanted to play sheriff for a day."

"No welshing. You're the perfect candidate. With all your experience. You made a commitment. You *have* to."

Stroking his neatly cropped beard, Fontana locked his blue eyes on the mayor, looked her up and down, and spat into the grass beside the sidewalk. "I don't *have* to do anything."

Though she was under thirty, her voice was throaty, as if roughed up by cigarettes, alcohol, and sinful living. On the phone, people invariably thought she was a man. Shorter than average, she had a buxom figure, wide hips clad in work-worn jeans. But her hands were tiny and delicate as bird claws and gave the impression that in a strong light you would see through the skin.

Inexplicably, Maureen Costigan had been elected mayor of Staircase in a landslide five years before. She reigned with a curious mixture of glee and authority.

Funneling her fleshy lips into a horn, she blew a tube of air at her bangs. "He's not a bad dog. Look at it from his point of view."

"Lady, I haven't spent forty years blundering around the surface of this planet so I can think like a dog. A dog is a moron and so is anybody who tries to think like one."

"You don't look nearly that old. Anybody ever tell you that?"

"He's out or the deal's off."

"I can't. He frightens me."

"Thought you said he wouldn't hurt a fly. Listen. I got a rock out by the river needs sitting on real bad. I get a notion, I might even drop a hook into the water and see if the coho are feeling frisky."

"I'd move him, but you're making him nervous."

"Godsakes."

Popping open the door on the passenger side, Fontana folded the seat forward against the glove box and said, "Whew! He smells like he slept on a pile of dead cats." He motioned for the dog to exit. Fontana hadn't kept a dog since he was a kid, and he made a point of scrubbing his hands after touching one.

Eyes alert, the dog roosted on a well-worn slab of mauve carpet. When Fontana reached inside, the dog's good ear got pointy and his eyes lit up. A dollop of slobber spattered the floor. He didn't move. Didn't even shift.

"Come on, doggie. Get your ass outa there. Out, Booger."

"Booger's not his name."

"Move your bones!"

As Mac reached for the collar around his matted neck, the dog let out the merest hint of a growl, a decibel or two of warning. Fontana jerked his hand back and glared at the mayor.

"It won't hurt you to drive around with a passenger in back," said the mayor.

"A growling passenger, lady."

"And stop calling me lady. Folks around here call me Mo. I didn't hear him growl. Nobody heard that but you. And you know what I think? I think a man who doesn't like animals is a poor excuse for a human being."

"You already bamboozled me into wearing the fire chief's

hat for a couple months. Ten grand a year ain't much, but the work is easy and I like it just fine. But as for bein' sheriff? Stuff it."

"It's only for one day, goddammit."

She seemed to have trouble controlling the muscles in her face. Anybody would have thought she was a BB stacker in a brain rehabilitation center. Yet, three months earlier he'd been startled to learn she ran a successful CPA business in Bellevue and earned enough to drive a spanking new candy–apple-red Porsche. Several locals said she was borderline screwy. Next time somebody reiterated that tired local saw, he'd ask them to omit the "borderline."

"If this town wasn't so tight they'd hire a full-time law officer."

"You know we don't have a large enough tax base to pay for both full-time jobs. Warren was sheriff and fire chief simultaneously. It wasn't so rough on him."

"So go fetch Warren."

"He had a nervous breakdown." She added quickly, "It didn't have anything to do with the job. Warren was a good man."

"So what kind of dog is he? A guard dog? A rat catcher?"

It took Mac a moment to realize she wasn't going to answer. She couldn't move the dog and neither could he. The game was over.

He pivoted and strode half a block to the post office. There he waited for a cadaverous Seth to finish bragging up this year's tomato crop and scoot a block of stamps across the counter while he casually surveyed Alice Street, the fire station, and Mo, the disgruntled mayor who was pestering him to be sheriff. She couldn't possibly know what the contemplation of getting back into law enforcement did to him. Yet it was only on the loneliest nights that Fontana thought of himself as a murderer.

She remained in front of the town hall, a modern brick and glass building that contained a bay wide enough for three emergency vehicles. It was one of the few all-new buildings in the one-horse town. Inside were two Seagrave pumpers; parked behind was a twenty-two-hundred-gallon tanker. Until recently, the sheriff's ancient GMC had been slotted in the third stall, but the Staircase council had purchased a new aid unit, and it now occupied that position.

Off the minuscule sheriff's office in back, they had rigged up a small cell, though in a town this size nobody except the occasional drunk sleeping off a binge ever dirtied the sheets. They said the ex-sheriff used to take naps on the narrow bunk. Three or four snoozes a day. Before he went bughouse.

Despite Mo's claims that he'd had a nervous breakdown, Fontana knew he'd nearly died with the D.T.'s. The state police had caught him shooting invisible fanged gerbils off his ceiling with an Ithaca over-and-under.

As he watched Mo's chicken-hearted attempts to coax the dog out of the truck, Fontana's beard dented into a slow smile.

Then the whole complexion of the morning changed.

Fontana saw a redhead emerge from the hole-in-the-wall sheriff's office to buttonhole Mo.

Directing her gaze up the street toward the post office, Mo yakked with the overwrought redhead, jittery the both of them—water about to boil. From Fontana's vantage point, the redhead looked more athletic than pretty. Mo ushered the stranger back into the sheriff's office, then returned to the sidewalk alone, casting furtive looks in his direction.

Suddenly Fontana sensed the morning's charade with Mo had been a ruse to get him to execute some grubby sheriff's job she didn't want to handle.

When he returned to the truck, Fontana positioned himself so that he could peep through the chink in the curtains of the sheriff's office; the redhead was fidgeting on the padded bench along the wall below the collection of yellowed wanted posters. At twenty feet she was prettier than she had been at two hundred: broad cheekbones, straight

17

nose, the mouth vaguely Scandinavian and teeming with big white teeth. Her hair was clasped in a short, bobbing ponytail, braided into one thick strand. She had something on her mind that kept her eyes as blank as those in a taxidermist's drawer.

"What's she doing?"

"Who?"

"Don't play games with me, Mo."

"She has a minor problem." Minor, perhaps, but his words had caused the color to drain from the mayor's face. "Business with the sheriff. I thought you might wanna take a crack at it, but I guess it wouldn't interest the likes of you."

"Says who?"

"Wouldn't want you to have a nervous breakdown."

They pondered that for a moment, just the two of them. No traffic marred the small-town street. A pair of starlings on a nearby phone pole scratched the morning with their cries. The low sun began to radiate heat off the GMC.

Fontana said, "I'll have a chat with her."

Her voice weighted with sarcasm, Mo replied, "You do that."

2

Hocus-Pocus in Hot Pink

"What can I do for you?"

The redhead's words were clipped, stamped out through stark lips. In her lap was a handbill for the Friday-night dance at the Bedouin. "I have a friend who lives up here. I'm worried about him. He hasn't been around much."

"Those dances are nice," said Fontana. "I thought it was hicksville when I first got here, but they're fun."

"I might try one sometime." Outside she'd seemed shaken, almost demoralized, but here she was a little calmer. She was young; a naïveté in her eyes that made him doubt she got into trouble often. She wore obscenely brief hot-pink shorts and a snug white T-shirt that had nothing under it but herself. It was September, breezy, yet still warm enough to forgive such foolishness. "You the sheriff of Staircase?" she asked.

For a second, she ran her gray eyes over him, gave him a look that was a hell of a lot more than citizen to law officer, the ratchety breath-robbing look a single woman gives to someone who's piqued her interest. Against his will, the moment eroded and she lapsed into formality, her eyes refreezing. The whole thing was over as if it had never happened.

"Why don't you go look for this friend yourself?"

"I did. I came up yesterday. Things didn't seem right. I was worried something might have happened to him."

"Such as?"

"I couldn't even hazard a guess. Something serious."

"So you drove up today to ask me to go over and take a look?"

"Yeah."

"What didn't look right?"

"I dunno. Just . . ." She shrugged. "I dunno."

"Give me your name, address, and phone number." He got out a pen and a notebook he'd already cluttered with jottings.

"April. April Smith." Though it was cool in the office, her lightly bronzed arms and legs seemed to have a sheen of sweat on them. Or was it suntan oil? He couldn't know without touching it.

"Tell me about it."

"Steve Zajac is his name. He moved up here a few months ago. Lives in a cabin over on Burdock Road, across the highway, last one before the creek. He's a real good-looking fella. Taller than you. Steve bought the place from some old guy they put into a nursing home. I guess the old man lived there eighty years or something. There's a mailbox with a hand-carved blue jay on it. I'm worried. Of course I am, or I wouldn't be here. Am I making any sense? I haven't seen him in a couple of days."

"Generally bump into him more often?"

"Daily. Or we'll phone. He hasn't been answering his phone. I even called the operator to see if it was working."

"Your boyfriend?"

"I don't like that term. It's patronizing, don't you feel?"

Cynicism tortured his reply. "Sorry."

"We're lovers."

She rose, edged backward a step at a time, and ran her bottom into the tall counter in front of the sheriff's desk. Bracing both palms on opposite ends of the high, heavily shellacked elm crosspiece, she formed a lazy human cross. Her tanned physique flexed in unexpected and mildly intriguing ways. Something about the conversation was jarring to her, something he mistakenly assumed was the residue of their earlier mutual attraction.

Had Fontana tackled anything more formidable than skipping flat stones on the river the last three months, he might have been suspicious. But he hadn't. And he wasn't.

She obviously pumped serious iron. Somehow, it hadn't gummed up her looks, had enhanced all of it, including a chest small enough and hard enough to appear adolescent. For her body weight, she'd be hellfire in a tussle.

"I've been busy. I called a couple of times. Then I drove up early yesterday morning. No answer. His truck is there, but I couldn't raise him. He doesn't have another vehicle. I don't know. Maybe this is all stupid. But he's gotta be around somewhere."

"And it scared you?"

"A little bit."

"You have a key to his place?"

She dug a single chrome house key out of the front pocket of her hot-pink shorts and tossed it at him. It was still warm.

"You use this yesterday?"

She shook her head.

"Why not?"

Again, she shrugged. It was something that could go on all morning. Her shrugging. Him watching. It occurred to him that he hadn't slept with a woman in a coon's age.

"Zajac in some sort of trouble?"

"It's nothing like that. Nothing serious, anyway. He's a firefighter. He works in Seattle."

"What do you mean, nothing serious? Is he in trouble?"

"He had a dispute on the job. Nothing to do with his personal affairs."

"You sure?"

"Yeah."

"I'll take a look, April. Wait here until I get back."

"I've got nothing else to do."

Fontana smiled in a weak effort to resurrect that first relatively torrid trafficking of glances, but all he gained for his effort was blankness. She had bags under her eyes, and their ice gray was coated with a rheumy, watery look. Maybe she hadn't slept in a couple of nights.

"I'll check it out."

"Don't you want his address?"

"Burdock Road. Blue jay on the mailbox. I know the one."

"One last thing?"

"Yeah?"

"If he's up there, you might be a little careful. He's taken to carrying a gun. Don't ask me why. He just does. Sometimes he gets a little cocky."

"Not in trouble, but he's armed?"

"Don't look at me like that. I don't know why he carries one. It's just, you might wanna be careful."

" 'Preciate the warning."

"Anytime."

Outside on the sidewalk, Mo was hoisting an oversize policeman's coat replete with emblazoned shoulder patches, silver-plated badge, cigarette scars, and a frazzled name tag: "Sheriff Bounty."

"You going to do it?"

"You knew about the missing boyfriend?"

"Lovers. They're lovers." Mo winked broadly in a conspiracy of satire. It occurred to him she was about as sarcastic a woman as he'd ever met.

"What can I say? Talked me into it."

"I'll bet. I suppose you gave her a pint of blood, too? Here, put this on and the dog'll stop grumbling." Mo gave him another one of her cockeyed looks, one he didn't attempt to decipher. Reeking of tobacco, three sizes too large, the sheriff's jacket was an eyesore. But he took to it.

"Gimme a gun and I'd stop the growling."

"You talk tough," she said, stepping into the truck beside him.

"Booger," he said.

"Keep it up." She sang the next. "He won't like you."

The GMC was a four-speed, ancient enough to require double-clutching on the way down the gears, but not up. Having driven fire trucks for eight years prior to his stint in Fire Investigation, it posed no problem. He'd heard Mo wheeling it around town earlier in the morning, rounding off the gears. The truck's off-road tires purred. Curtains were strung up on brass rings on a rod over the windows.

Staircase was laid out in a small valley dwarfed by absurdly steep foothills and bisected east to west by a state highway snaking into the Cascades in lazy S's. He was infatuated with the picture-postcard hamlet. One of the finest ski resorts in the state lay twenty minutes higher in the hills. To the west, an hour away, was Seattle, on the Puget Sound. Above the northeastern corner of the town loomed Mount Gadd, a four-thousand-foot-high ridge as steep as a cake and draped in evergreens. Tattooed with hiking trails and rock-climbing tracks, it had an overlook at the flat, rocky top that was frequently used as a launch pad by hang-glider aficionados. Over the years three had been killed, though none in recent memory.

When he settled in Staircase several months earlier, Fontana was presumed a natural for the office of fire chief. He'd been a captain in a large metropolitan fire department in the East. Most recently, he'd worked in the fire investigation section, toting a gun and a badge, then was promoted into administration and paperwork the last year. The administrative experience had been the clincher. Maureen was determined to shoehorn him into the role of chief-cum-sheriff.

Sure, he said. Chief of a one-horse fire department. Chief was fine and dandy. Sheriff was something he wouldn't touch with rubber gloves and a tetanus shot.

On the jaunt through town and across the main highway to

Burdock Road, Fontana marveled at how Mo had gulled him. She'd given him a feeble dodge about the town losing its insurance rating because the insurance inspector was visiting today and mustn't discover they had lost their sheriff.

Wouldn't Fontana please stand in for one day? Pin the badge on, take the truck for a spin, make himself visible. She offered a hundred bucks out of the council's miscellaneous expenses for one day of goofing around with a badge on his chest. It had been a swindle all along. The redhead was already cooling her heels in the office.

Had the mayor played straight and trotted April Smith out in the beginning, he might not have quibbled. But then, too, Mo was gulling the redhead, who imagined he was a real sheriff.

Something was disturbing about April, something more than a boyfriend she couldn't contact, and Fontana should have called her bluff. He should have made her fess up. Better still, he should have dragged her along. Had it not been for the dog, he might have. He was afraid if he put her in back she'd get bit. He was afraid if Mo didn't come along, *he'd* get bit.

Mo'd been feeding and de-fleaing Bounty's German shepherd since Bounty had gotten himself slung into a straight-jacket and trundled off to the asylum. Actually, Fontana didn't believe for an instant she couldn't get the beast out. It was some sort of police-trained dog. She undoubtedly felt more comfortable with it along. He presumed that Mo had been up at Burdock Road already this morning, had driven up with April and been spooked.

The nearest neighbor to the little shanty on the creek with the blue jay mailbox lived half a mile up a narrow tarmac country road.

As April Smith had claimed, a three-year-old Bronco sat in the gravel outside the house, which itself was a good fifty yards from the road. The spread had been carved out of the forest that spilled across the foot of Mount Gadd. The forest was situated among a scree of slate-colored boulders, brooks, and ancient geologic rubble.

Fontana blockaded the mouth of the driveway by parking across it. They trooped in, the twenty-four-hour sheriff, the mayor in aquamarine, and the dog, sniffing the ground in a zigzag pattern as if he were actually good for something. Businesslike and cagey, the dog circled the house, disappeared.

The first thing Mac saw was a shattered window on the Bronco in the driveway. Three days earlier, he recalled, it had rained, yet the papers inside hadn't gotten wet. Some Dugan had burglarized it within the last two days, sometime after that rain.

Strolling to the house across a blanket of crisp yellow and auburn leaves, Fontana shouted, thumped on the door, and, when nobody replied, turned the key in the lock.

When he saw the room an ominous feeling crept over him. He'd been screwed.

3

Bend Over, We're Not Finished

HAD FONTANA THOUGHT to circle the house and peek into the windows, he might have seen the havoc and been forewarned. But he hadn't. And he wasn't.

The house was quaint and simple.

The name "Zajac" was burned into a wooden plaque on the front door. If Maureen and April had been up there earlier, they could hardly have missed the salad of belongings.

"Must have been a hurricane in here," said the mayor tentatively. An actress she was not.

Newspapers, magazines, furniture, clothing, and bric-a-brac from drawers were thrown helter-skelter. Pictures had been ripped off the walls and shattered. Glass from the frames glittered in rhinestone aerials across the hodgepodge. A thorough and destructive search.

"You've been here before. You and Legs. What? An hour ago?"

"That's a lousy term. Legs."

"You lied to me. This is all a con."

"Don't get steamed. We needed your help. And I knew how you felt about sheriffing."

"Don't move your butt or I'll nail your shoes to the floor."

Alone, Fontana made a quick reconnaissance of the looted house.

It was minuscule.

Three rooms and a hot plate.

Beyond the sacked living room was a bedroom, a bath, and a kitchen almost large enough for two people. Every drawer and cupboard was eviscerated. Yet it was not a typical burglary.

On a table in the living room lay a .357 revolver, loaded. A shotgun, also loaded, was propped behind the door. An expensive brother to the .357 lay on the disheveled couch. Several boxes of ammunition were scattered throughout. Usually, weapons were the first things a burglar stuffed into the gunnysack.

"He expecting WW Three?"

"Gosh."

"Don't give me that dizzy-dame routine. You were up here earlier. You and Little Red Riding Hood. Insurance inspector, my ass. Why didn't you tell me there was a man missing and his place had been ransacked? I get pissed off when people run cons on me, Mo."

Mo kept her eyes on the shambles. "What would you have said?"

"Would have told you to call the goddamn county police. Now go call the goddamn county police!"

"You're angry."

"Pissed is what I said."

"Last year the county took two days to show up on Mrs. Hansen's burglary. This guy's a firefighter. You were a firefighter."

"*Were* is the operative word here. I *were* a firefighter."

"Don't you care what happened?"

"I know what happened. Somebody broke in and trashed this place. You need a real cop for this. Somebody who likes to write reports."

Fontana picked up the phone and discovered it was dead. Tracing the line, he found the jack had been rooted out of the wall. In the brittle colored leaves outside, the dog, who had been barking during his tirade, now stood staring at them through the open door. His legs were inexplicably wet, his tongue lolling like a thin pink dishrag.

"Go chase a stick, Booger."

The dog barked.

"That's not his name," said Mo. "He's got a name, and it hasn't anything to do with boogers."

"Christ."

"That's not it, either. Warren Bounty revered that dog."

"So what's his goddamn name?"

"Satan. His name is Satan."

"Good grief." Fontana, moving toward the dog with the intention of following him, didn't know why but he had the feeling the animal was trying to show him something.

Tracing the little finger of her left hand nervously around her wet lips, Maureen Costigan said, "You're not mad at me, are you?"

"Stay here."

"You *are* mad."

"Don't whine. You're whining. I don't like whiners."

He halted and stared her down. For a moment she looked innocuous and klutzy, managed to take on the air of the injured party. He could see the hurt in her brown eyes. When he was a kid they'd had a cow named Rosie with black-brown eyes like that. An unreliable animal, she'd give you that same look right before she put her mucked-up foot into the milk bucket.

As if to even the score, she blurted, "We called your old department back there. We know the whole story. We know why you're out here. I thought you'd be grateful. This is a second chance for you. Don't look at me like that. Somebody who's been in the kind of trouble you've been in, I'd think you'd appreciate a chance to redeem yourself."

Towering over her in the doorway, Fontana felt his ears burn and hoped it didn't show. He ground his teeth, stone-walled, and tried to clear his mind.

"Just out of curiosity, sweetheart, what did they tell you?"

"They said you beat a man to death." Her gravelly voice began dropping. "Said you quit because they were going to fire you. Not over the beating but because of your overall performance. They said you'd been good once, but you had some sort of problem knuckling down. They said your attitude turned sour. They claimed you beat that man to death with your fists. Said we'd be crazy to hire you. That you'd seen psychiatrists. They said you couldn't be trusted."

"If you're going to call back East, at least get somebody who'll give you the straight poop."

"That wasn't it?"

Fontana grinned a sour grin, turned and followed the dog, who'd been waiting patiently. He stopped in the yard, heeled around, and glanced at Costigan, who had not taken her eyes off him.

He'd known he would never be able to hide that episode, never be able to embalm the memory. It was bound to boomerang. His life, which had been on a steady upward track until he was thirty, had degenerated into a succession of downward spirals. Surely Staircase was to be the end of it.

Cripes. Sheriffing, even a few hours, was bound to produce mishaps. His whole aim in coming out West had been to keep from getting crowded in—to earn a subsistence living and sit on a rock until he got his bearings. Holding down a job meant getting elbowed every day. He could handle being sheriff the way a mosquito could fly off with a bowling ball.

Beat a man to death?

Why would they tell her he beat a man to death? Whether she said she was mayor or not, they had no right telling her anything. Any bean planter could call up and say he was mayor. And why tell her it had been a man? Somehow the

29

legend had gotten twisted. He had never beaten any man to death. Well, he'd tried a couple of times.

A woman.

It had been a woman he'd slugged and killed.

And he hadn't exactly slugged her. Slapped. Six times. Six whacks and she was down for the count. Broken neck. The worst part, the intimidating part—if he had it to do over again, the part that scared the soup out of him—was that he'd replay it precisely as he had, word for word, whack for whack. And the second time he might not go to court and skate.

It scared him so badly that he would wake up in the middle of the night with the heebie-jeebies; lips dry and numb, hands tingling.

The house was situated in front of a narrow creek, six feet across, which gurgled merrily until it joined the same river Fontana's property abutted, which river was a tributary to another, larger one that oozed across the state into Puget Sound. Folks were always talking about going to Staircase for steelhead.

He and the German shepherd trekked through the birch trees and crossed the creek, Fontana using rocks as stepping-stones, the dog plunging into the shallow drink. The dog roved far in front, cocking his head every once in a while to be sure Fontana hadn't strayed, led him three hundred fifty yards around a curve at the base of a hill at the foot of Mount Gadd.

The slope wasn't steep.

Semiclad autumnal trees stood in ranks close enough to blot out most of the sunlight. They were deciduous at this elevation; farther up the slopes, evergreens flourished.

The ground crunched with early autumn.

Fontana was muttering when suddenly the beast pulled up and squatted, ears up, one pointed, one scarred and floppy.

Still fuming against the mayor's espionage, Fontana wasn't ready for the sight that greeted him in the shadowy forest.

They had used a deadfall wedged into the notch of a living tree. It slanted toward Mount Gadd at a low angle. Thick as a fat man's torso, it was also rotten, the underside bearded in thick shaggy moss.

Tying his limbs with twine, they had lashed his hands and feet separately.

It was a man.

At least, it had been a man.

Now he was just a specimen for an eight-foot stainless-steel tray. Some Dugan had dragged him out here and tied him up where nobody could hear his cries. Suddenly, Fontana felt as alone as he'd ever felt, as if he were the only man left on the face of the earth.

They had spent some time with him. Fontana guessed it had started with fists, perhaps sticks or clubs. Indisputably, it had ended with a knife, because there it was, jutting out the center of his back, a thin-bladed kitchen knife. Possibly from a drawer in the shanty. They had tied him face down against the bole of the dead tree, beaten him, tortured him, then stabbed him.

"Nice work, Booger."

Fontana sat on his haunches beside the dog, scratched his beard, and absently watched a pair of ants battling over the carapace of a dead bug. "Nice fucking work."

The dog didn't budge.

Neither did Fontana, not for a long while, just squatted, listened to the fluctuations in the dog's panting, to a chicka-dee's whirring call that sounded like a snake's rattles, to the rhythmic thumping of his own heartbeat.

"Yeah, buddy boy, you're worth your weight in gold. I wouldn't have missed this for a date with Jane Pauley. Might have been years before I was invited to see another man killed with so much loving attention to detail. Fucking dog."

Rabinowitz

This Dugan had been dead a couple of days.

Damn it all to hell.

Life wasn't fair.

Certainly not from the point of view of the man lashed to the tree.

He thought of Rabinowitz back East who had mustered into the department in the same class as Fontana. The slaughterhouse they called it, where more than half washed out in boot camp. Rabinowitz, after gutting out the last few weeks of training with a badly sprained ankle, rode Engine 47 to a woman's suicide on his first alarm one stormy night. Drunk and despondent, having just stumbled from a tavern and a fracas with her boyfriend, she'd leaped in front of a speeding garbage truck, been run over by the front wheels, and, before the driver could stop, gotten picked up by the rear duals and gone round and round the way a towel spins in a washer. It was ugly.

Engine 47 was dispatched to clean it up. Scoop shovels. Even the hard-core black-humor artists puked, some for the first time in their careers.

Rabinowitz went home the next morning and never returned to Engine 47. Tendered his resignation. Mac thought about Rabinowitz a lot over the years, Rabinowitz who went back to college, was awarded a degree, and became a librarian. The fire service changed people, and Rabinowitz, once he glimpsed that mutation, determined not to let it happen to him.

It was a kitchen knife, buried smack to the hilt. Mac didn't touch it. In the back pocket he found a fat wallet, carefully pried it out of the jeans, tossed it near the dog, then took off the sheriff's jacket and removed his outer shirt, gently draping it over the man's head and face.

"Wish we could have met under different circumstances, Pilgrim," he said.

The dog let loose something that sounded like humming.

Mac walked back, picked up the wallet, and sorted through the contents. He riffled the bills. Three hundred eighty-six bucks in cash. A MasterCard and several other major credit cards. They had not been out to pillage. Same as the house. These ghouls had been after other booty.

The Washington State driver's license showed a harsh photo of a ruggedly handsome man, identified him as Zajac, Steven Paul.

Fontana didn't have any reason to doubt the man on the tree belonged to the wallet. The height, six three, and the weight, one ninety-five, seemed to confirm that, along with the eye color, BRN, and the black hair in the picture. It was endorsed for motorcycles. He had been born 12/13/51; hadn't done nearly enough damage to this world before his ungainly exit.

In a plastic fold-out section of the wallet Mac discovered pictures of a smiling, outgoing man, chesty, with longish black hair, a mustache. Two toothy kids stood alongside in most of the photos. You could tell he was divorced. Conspicuously lacking were photos of the children's mother.

Before he tucked it into his own back pocket, Fontana spent a good while putting the wallet back in order, stalling.

By that time, Maureen Costigan had arrived.

Fontana said, "It's not mine. I'll have nothing to do with it."

"Whatever are you talking about?"

"Not getting flimflammed into anything. Understand?"

"You all right, Mac?"

"Get out of here."

"What are you doing?" she asked, bypassing him and approaching the dog.

"Stay where you are, Mo."

"I'm tired of taking orders from you."

"You'll be sorry."

"You think I'm not fit to see what the hell you're doing out here? You think a woman mayor's—"

Without a moment's hesitation, she hunched up her back, tethered her chin-length brown hair at the nape of her neck, and barfed into the leaves.

As she coughed and hacked, she tried to talk but couldn't. Mac hoped she hadn't eaten a large breakfast. She mouthed something garbled about never seeing a dead body before, that she was sorry she'd come out here, that she was even sorrier she'd deceived him this morning, and was that really a man over there with a knife in his back? When she'd straightened up, she spoke through a mouth that had lost its definition, lips moist and formless. "That the man we were looking for?"

"Near as I can tell."

"I didn't know about it. I didn't."

"I'd have trouble not believing that, darlin'. Just tell me about this morning."

"She came up and wanted the police."

"Legs?"

"She has a name. April Smith. I tried to help her, and we came out here—not here, to the house—and it was a little creepy. You saw that much. The truck. The inside of the cabin. For some reason, I thought of you."

"Yeah, we've been through your reasoning."

At this point Maureen Costigan hunched up and let loose another salvo. When she was finished she spoke in a phlegmy voice. "I'm sorry."

Fontana patted her on the back in a fatherly way, massaging between her clammy shoulder blades. He couldn't help noting her brassiere strap felt thick as a gun belt. "Quite all right."

"I feel like such a twit."

Fontana held her by the shoulders and walked her back toward the burgled cottage.

"Don't even think about it. No more than if you had food poisoning, eaten a bad jelly roll." Arm around her shoulder, he walked her along the rolling path. He sat her down on a bench outside Zajac's shanty, went in, and wet a washrag without letting any water flush down the trap. He knelt in front of her, cleaned her up, wiped her mouth, her sweaty brow, the rest of her face, then chucked her gently under the chin. She let him doctor her wan face. "People die every day. You just saw one, that's all."

"Not like that. It surprised me. Even with your shirt over him."

He patted her knee. "I'll be gone a minute. Gonna run out and use the radio in the truck."

When he came back, she was in the same position, the stare stamped into her eyes. He reached across to brush a strand of hair out of her face, and she came alive.

"Why did I do that? Why did I? Gosh, you must think I'm a complete simp. I trick you into coming out here and then I go to pieces like a five-year-old. Do you? Think I'm a simp?"

He didn't reply.

"Who would ever do such a thing? You think it was somebody we know? I've taken advantage of you, and now it's worked out so badly. I'm sorry, Mac. Can you forgive me?" Fontana stood up and ironed the wrinkles out of his jeans with his knuckles. "Can you? Please?"

Fontana went inside. The wood stove was cold. Ashes had

dribbled outside the mouth onto the grate. The house smelled of smoke, of a structure fire, not a wood stove. After a bit, he realized the origin was a heap of bunking clothes in one corner, a Janesville coat and pants fitted around the boots, a yellow Seattle Fire Department helmet with a "6" inside a white circle on either side.

Engine 6.

Engine numbers were placed in circles. Ladder numerals were painted on triangular patches.

Fontana figured somebody had knocked at the door, caught Zajac off guard, then dragged him out to the woods, no doubt trying to extract information, or wreak revenge. Then they'd returned and sacked the cottage.

But what were they looking for? Then he saw something under the couch. He moved it to examine them.

Three pieces of paper.

Two of them were crisp hundred-dollar bills. The third paper was a thick, stapled King County Medical Examiner Division Autopsy Report. The subject was a four-year-old girl named Kim Sung.

On the first page under "Pathological Findings" he read the cause of death: "Asphyxia due to inhalation of products of combustion: (a) Soot throughout conducting airway system. (b) Pulmonary congestion and edema, mild, with focal intra-alveolar hemorrhage."

Fontana had perused similar reports. The child had expired in a fire, from smoke inhalation, not from burns, though in later pages of the report burn injuries, all sustained after death, were described in clinical detail. He set the sofa back into the permanent indentations in the rug.

Two other items were noteworthy. One, a picture that had been thumbtacked to a door, a photo of Zajac with his arm thrown around the shoulders of another man who was older, balding, and strapped into wire-rimmed glasses. Manly smirks on their faces, the two of them hoisted a string of fish. Outside, just before the arrival of the first uniformed county cops, he found the footprint. It was small, a waffle pattern. It was set up in the hard clay. It had been made during or right after the rain three days earlier. He tried to recall what type of shoes April Smith had been wearing.

"Mac? Can you ever forgive me?"

"Forget it, Mo."

"No. I mean it. This is all so ghastly."

"Forget it."

"Does that mean you've forgiven me?"

"Means shut up."

The county people seemed efficient, if not diffident.

"He yours?" a pudgy officer asked, slapping the dog's hide. The dog's coat soiled the surrounding air with dust.

Fontana took them on a tour of the house, the burglarized Bronco, the footprint, the hundred-dollar bills, and the autopsy report, then escorted them out to the woods.

Eight of them participated in the glum hike, including Maureen Costigan. When they got there, somebody said, "Jesus H. Christ." Somebody else wheezed. Then it grew quiet. They stood in a ragged cluster and rubbernecked for a while before anybody else spoke.

When some of the watchers started rustling, Fontana pulled out the wallet and handed it to a washed-out redhaired man with fat lips and a paunch over his belt. He was in charge of the investigation. Charles Dummelow.

Chuck was all business.

"Shouldn't have touched it."

"I know."

"What made you come out here? I mean after this April Smith told you she was worried. Out here. To this part of the woods. It's a good ways from the house."

"The dog."

"Bounty's old animal? I heard he had that thing pretty well trained."

Maureen gave Mac a knowing look.

Dummelow shook his head. He had yet to take his eyes off the corpse. "Hell of a way to say adios. I mean, he had to have been tied down for a while. Look at the marks on his wrists where he tried to get out of it. And he probably knew they were going to kill him. Had to know. Makes me sick. We'll take our pictures in a minute, then you two can go. Poor bastard."

"I'll be poking into this," announced Fontana.

The statement surprised him almost as much as it did the others. In fact, it took him a split second to realize it had come out of his mouth. Stupefied, Dummelow and Maureen turned to Fontana. They spoke in concert. "You?"

"I *am* sheriff."

"I don't think you will," said Dummelow.

Maureen shook her head. "You leave this to the professionals. Warren never would get into anything like this."

"Warren was a drunk."

"Stay out of it. I'm telling you," said Dummelow.

"The body's in my jurisdiction. I'll cooperate with you, and I expect you to reciprocate. You'll do the lab work, and I'll get started on some background color. In a day or two we'll get together and swap notes."

As he watched them leaving, Dummelow didn't quite know what to say. Finally, he shouted, "You ever handle a murder case before?"

"At least one," said Fontana without turning his head, but only Maureen, goose-stepping beside him, heard it.

In the GMC, Maureen, winded from the pace and consequently silent for the entire walk, said, "That was a woman's shoe print back there, wasn't it?"

"A boy, maybe."

"You didn't tell them about April waiting back in town."

"They can have her when I'm finished."

After he parked on Alice Street in front of the sheriff's small office, Fontana reached across and opened Maureen's door for her, then tipped the seat forward. "Come on, Booger, you big bad body-finder."

"That's not funny," said the mayor.

"I know."

"Mind if I don't come in? I'm still feeling a little green around the gills."

"You did a number on your gastrointestinal tract, that's for sure. I was waiting for your shoelaces to come up." She turned pink. "By the way—ever see April before this morning?"

"Never heard of her before this morning. I was in the office here doing paperwork when she wandered in. We were only out on Burdock Road a minute before we both got antsy and left. We thought maybe somebody was still out there." Fontana didn't see how that could jibe with April's assertion that she'd been out the day before. Surely, it had all happened at least two days ago. And surely April was aware the perpetrators would not be loitering around. "I guess, somehow, we sensed there was something fishy."

The sheriff's office was empty. Fontana looked her name up in his notebook and dialed the Seattle prefix. A recording announced the number was bogus.

Outside, Maureen shrugged, gave a sorry look, and said, "Mac?"

"What?"

"You don't have to pursue this. I didn't know it was going to be anything like this. The county always handled this sort of thing for Warren."

"Get a lot of craziness out here?"

"I was thinking more of the highway accidents. When there's an investigation, the state patrol usually does it. You don't have to mess with it. In fact, I wish you wouldn't."

"I'd feel like I was playing hooky."

She'd verbally appointed him interim sheriff, and she was going to pay hell firing him if he didn't want to be fired. Three months earlier, when the council had first approached him about being sheriff, he'd studied the city charter, along with the Staircase civil service rules: It would take a full vote of the city council, and he knew two of the five members were vacationing out of town. A quorum was four. It would be a week before she could depose him. He could cause a lot of havoc with a badge in a week.

"Mac?"

"Uh."

"You were very nice to me out there."

"Don't worry about it."

"I'm sorry I even called those people back East."

"That makes two of us."

He traipsed through the sheriff's office, through the interior door, and down a long, waxed corridor into the beanery of the fire station to ask the crew if they'd seen April Smith.

In the office he could still smell traces of her perfume, as if it were the fragrance of a barely remembered girlfriend.

5

Keep Dancing, Son

THE REGULARS IN the Staircase Fire Department were led by fat Ray Allan, who walked like a tottering bowling pin. He was resented by the majority of the volunteers for his prissy mannerisms and know-it-all attitude. As lieutenant he took in a hundred twenty bucks a month more than the other two regulars. Over the past three months there had been strong indications that he was afraid of flame.

If Fontana had had his way he'd have fired the man.

Next in seniority was Kingsley Pierpont, one of the few blacks in town. He wore heavy diamond rings and kept his hair conked and greased as if it were 1958. Positioned in the middle of the seat directly under the mink-lined mirror in his pink '74 Caddy, he tucked a different gaudily painted woman up against his hip each week. An untraveled twenty-year-old screenwriter from Minnesota couldn't have turned out a better stereotype, and Fontana had said as much, jokingly, to Kingsley, but he didn't care. He was the way he was and he didn't apologize for it.

A thin, almost emaciated lad, Peter Daugherty was the newest member of the regulars, having been hired three years earlier. In his spare time he sketched. He was the only one of the three with even a thimbleful of ambition, which was fine with Fontana.

"You guys see that redhead in the sheriff's office?"

"One with the little pink shorts and the little brown legs?" Ray Allan asked, all teeth. Talking was an aerobic exercise for Ray. He had a way of describing strange women that hinted he'd already been intimate with them, or would be shortly.

Kingsley said, "She left the minute you taken off widda major. Sixty seconds, she scoot." He scuffed one palm against the other and it made a noise like a loud kiss. "She be gone. She sure is a fine-lookin' thing."

"She was that all right," said Fontana. Kingsley, of all the regulars and volunteers, was his favorite.

"She's drivin' a 'vette," Kingsley added.

"Color?"

"Yellow. Can't miss it. Don't know the license. Din't know she was runnin' out on you. What's you got goin' widda major?" Pierpont invariably called the mayor "the major."

"How'd she look when she was leaving? Scared? Bored? Late for an appointment?"

"All the above. She be movin'."

The three full-time firefighters anchored an eight-hour shift Monday through Friday. Eager volunteers within hailing distance of the tower siren would dash into the streets when an alarm sounded, to fill empty positions on the rigs. At night the engines and aid car were manned by volunteers.

Twice last year Mel Howard's chicken house had been rescued from an arsonist before it finally burned to the ground in a rather festive conflagration the whole town turned out for. Mel liked to boast that it made KOMO-TV news in Seattle, but that was sheer hyperbole and he never made the brag if he hadn't already surrounded a beer or two. The only thing about Staircase that always made the big-city news was when a hunter found another set of anonymous bones scattered in the hills.

Afterward, they discovered Mel Howard's teenage daughter had set the blazes after he'd placed her on restriction for becoming pregnant by a boy in the army. Later, she married the boy and the two of them moved to Portland to live with his folks. Even months after, the chitchat at the Saturday-morning training sessions at the firehouse centered on the smell of Mel Howard's fried chickens, all ten thousand of them. Scorched feathers and fried drumsticks.

For some reason Fontana let the dog tag along when he drove the GMC to his rented house on the river. He went inside, put on a shirt, then jogged down the path along the river to ask a favor of his landlord, Mrs. Gilliam.

Elderly, jolly, she had incredible blue eyes and was built like a dumpling. Having lived in Scotland as a child, she spoke with the slightest trace of a Scottish brogue, which thickened when she got excited. She spotted Warren Bounty's jacket first thing.

"You sheriff now?"

"Not if I can help it."

In the center of town he parked alongside a block-long cyclone fence that encompassed the playground at Staircase Elementary.

Recess. Children's unabashed laughter.

He climbed out, stood on the sidewalk, watched the kids caterwauling, listened to the yips of delight. It was a sound he could listen to all day. He inserted his fingers into the fencing, and before he knew it was squeezing so hard the wire gouged his flesh. After a few minutes a small mop-haired boy separated himself from a group on the monkey bars and ran to the fence.

"Hey, rug rat."

"Hey, old man. What's happenin', Mac?"

"Might be a little late tonight, Brendan." Fontana squat-ted. "Mrs. Gilliam'll be there after school. If I'm going to be real late, like after dark, I'll phone somebody and have them run a message over."

"Mac?"

"Yeah?"

"Are we righteous dudes?"

The question caught Fontana's attention. "What makes you ask that?"

"I heard bachelors are sometimes righteous dudes."

"You could say we were righteous dudes."

"See ya, Mac."

"I love you, Brendan."

"Me too."

Traffic was sparse; it was not yet noon, and he hoped to get to Seattle before the crunch. There was nothing Fontana hated more than sitting in an idling vehicle behind several thousand other idling vehicles. He hated it so much he'd sold his car, had survived the last three months without any engines in his household, a feat unheard of in this country of four-wheel-drive buggies, dirt bikes, chain saws, snowmobiles, gas-powered blowers, and ATV's. People in Staircase thought he was afflicted. The lack of phone and TV added to the misconception.

The house was close enough to town that he and Brendan could hike in for grub and supplies. Mrs. Gilliam had chauffeured them to Bellevue for Brendan's school clothes. He'd ridden the bus to Seattle once. He was beginning to think he'd never own another car, although this truck might be worth keeping, even if it did sound like an earthquake in a chopsticks factory every time he hit a pothole.

This trip to the city would be a vaccination, a booster shot against the rat race. He wasn't sure why he was making it. Maybe it was because the killers had spent too much time with Steve Zajac. He kept visualizing those smiling boys in the dead man's wallet.

From time to time rage would suck him up and spit him out. He'd always had a temper, even as a child, yet it was only during the last few years that he began regularly losing control of it. The best way to divest himself of this particular furor, he figured, was to flow with this sheriff mumbo jumbo, solve the puzzle, or hope the county beat him to it. Keep busy. Keep dancing, son. Maybe the inevitable boredom of the investigation would settle him down.

A rust-brown smudge ballooned over Seattle, end to end, a thousand feet thick. Mac knew the locals were telling themselves that if they were getting headaches and their eyes were bloodshot and their noses ran, it must be something else. Seattleites had a stunning town, but it grew dirtier by the minute. It was only Northwest vanity that kept people calling it fog. But he'd seen it in the East. Fog didn't have a taste and it didn't wipe off the hood of a clean car in black streaks. Given the inversion layers the Puget Basin was prone to, things might get almost as smoggy as L.A. It was a pity. That's why he'd opted for the hills an hour east. People thought he was bonkers. Maybe he was.

When it came to clean air and open spaces, Fontana was a fanatic, should have been living in Antarctica. His first week in town he'd sat in on a city council meeting—much as he detested meetings—while a developer proposed putting up a twenty-unit condominium near Galer Road. It would mean revenue for the town.

In a losing bid, Fontana spoke against it.

Before it was over, he asked the mayor in a heated exchange why they didn't start laying concrete between Staircase and Seattle. "Pave the damn state end to end!" he'd shouted, to everybody's amazement, including his own. Then he turned and snapped at the developer, "And put out that cigar. Can't you see the No Smoking signs?"

The cigar went out. The condos went up. The audience tittered at his antics. Yeah, they thought he was a nut. He thought so too, but he didn't know what to do about it.

He'd pulled other stunts in that vein, and it made him wonder why Maureen Costigan had thought of him for sheriff. But then, she was something of an eccentric herself.

Most days Staircase had a strong south wind ripping through it, a wind that kept people from moving to the area.

Too windy. Takes down your TV antenna two or three times a year. Blows your hat off. Inside-outs your umbrella. But windswept air was pure. After smothering in a big eastern city for eighteen years, it was a whole new way of life for Mac.

He called it idling. Yeah, he was weird, he thought, and this laid-back life-style in Staircase might be contributing to it, but at least he hadn't backhanded any women in a while. Hadn't slapped anyone to death.

Now this foofaraw with Zajac. The trick was to keep your days from cannibalizing your life.

He had visions of himself six months from now, sitting on the rock by the river, fly pole in hand, wondering who'd killed Zajac. Even if the county found the killers first, he had to be in on it. Killers. That was funny. For the first time he was counting them. Two or more of them had done in Zajac.

⑥

Chief Crews

SEATTLE FIRE DEPARTMENT headquarters was situated upstairs in a working fire station, Station Ten at Second and Main in Pioneer Square. The area was frequented by pigeons and panhandlers, crowded with renovated buildings from the early 1900's, parking lots, and the original-style street lamps that resembled huge white fruit on stubby trees.

Heavy construction trucks traversed the area hourly, inking the air with dust and soot and clouds of blue-black diesel exhaust. Seattle seemed to be eternally rebuilding.

This year the headline project was a series of four skyscrapers in the south end of town: the Attwood Towers. For months the papers had been full of hoopla. The first one was already up and, at ninety-six floors, dwarfed the seventy-six–story Columbia Center, which had been the tallest skyscraper in the state. Environmentalists and Lesser Seattleites had picketed the project, but it went up anyway.

Parking the GMC in an "Official Vehicles Only" space, he looked at the dog.

"Booger. I suppose I leave you cooped up in here you'll wee-wee all over my maps and chew up my Chuck Yeager aviator sunglasses, and when you're finished with that you'll pull the ashtray out and eat butts." Somebody had trained this dog to withstand virtually any insult. Fontana let him out and the mutt did some business on the front tire of a chief's buggy, then obediently hopped back in.

"Chief Crews saw that, he'd have a myocardial infarction." A firefighter grinned at him from the east doorway of the station. He had a raggedy gray mop in one hand, a galvanized bucket in the other.

"Damn dog. I'm going to have it put to sleep right after lunch. Looking for a guy named Steve Zajac."

"Works out of Sixes. Twenty-five percent shot at it but you got the right shift. Wrong station." Tall and ungainly, about twenty-five, the firefighter was betrayed by a gold tooth in the front of his mouth.

Fontana wandered into the watch office on the first floor behind the man and inveigled him into a conversation as he mopped. It all came back to Fontana, and he loved it. Every big-city fire station in the world smelled the same from years of spilled diesel fuel, cleaning fluids, bleach, cigarettes, and men. In ten minutes he had gleaned the general layout of the station, the department, and the shifts—Seattle worked four separate twenty-four-hour shifts.

An engine, aid car, chief, and a ladder truck all responded out of Station Ten. In addition, the city's hazardous materials team was comprised of the men who rode the engine and truck. The firemen's quarters were on the second floor. The third and fourth floors of the gray concrete monolith were taken up by administrative offices.

The chief he wanted to see had an office upstairs. Chief Frederick Crews.

"By the way," said Fontana, "you know this guy Zajac?"

The firefighter looked as if somebody had farted in an elevator. "Seen him around."

"Sixes." Fontana knew from an earlier trip into town that the Seattle people referred to their stations in the plural. "He told me that much but he didn't give me a home phone. Got it handy?"

48

The gangly firefighter went to a short console against the wall, pulled a slate-colored binder out, and sorted through the department directory. He gave Fontana a home phone number, which had a Staircase prefix, and used an intercom to call somebody to escort him up to Crews's office. The escort turned out to be a female, husky and sullen in her navy-blue uniform. As they ascended the stairs, Fontana recalled that Seattle had more women firefighters than any other department in the country.

Over six feet tall, saturnine, hulking, Chief Crews met him in an office cluttered with charts and graphs. Fontana was five-feet ten and forty years old, although he looked younger, but he felt like a boy beside Crews.

Crews had dark hair, olive skin, tea bags under his eyes, and hound-dog jowls waggling below each cheek. He had obviously been an immensely strong man at one time. His chest had slipped until the only thing keeping it out of his crotch was a belt. The muscles of his arms sagged. Yet he was still fierce. Downstairs the man with the mop had advised Fontana that Crews had played pro football as a kid, had been a head-knocker.

"Can I do for you?" Crews asked. His eyes were dark and tight, the type that you had to look at twice to see the difference between pupil and cornea.

"Excuse the coat. Belonged to my predecessor. I'm new on the job. Sheriff out in Staircase. Name's MacKinley Fontana."

"Oh," said Chief Crews, managing to turn the simple phrase into an accusation. It was apparent he had Fontana pegged for a hick. Mac decided not to mention his years in the department back East, decided to play it stupid. Some instinct told him to do it. He could have simply told him Zajac was dead, but word would spread fast and spoil his advantage. No, he would take a chance.

"I'm here to find out what I can about Steven Zajac. Lives up in my neck of the woods. I'm not at liberty to go into the whys and wherefores right now. I need to talk to some of the man's co-workers, get an idea of what he's about. If your department's like any of the others I've run across, I need your permission to do that."

"He begging for employment up there in your department?"

"I'm not at liberty to say. Believe he works out of Station Six."

"Sixes. I'd say so. Yes, that's right."

"He's not at work today, and I thought if I could get permission I'd take advantage of that and interview a few of his co-workers."

Crews slipped a pencil behind his ear, ignited a Camel, sucked on it, made a show of examining the face of his watch, then ran his tongue around the inside of his mouth, between his teeth and cheeks. He knew how to make others wait, relied on the tactic to keep inferiors in their slots.

"Zajac's not at work *any* day. He's been in rather a speck of trouble lately. Been suspended."

"For how long?"

"That's up to Mr. Zajac. Entirely up to him. The ball, as they say, is in his court."

Fontana felt bad about pulling the wool over Crews's eyes, seemed almost an offense against Zajac's memory and disrespectful of Crews's authority, but he'd decided and stuck with it. Knowing Zajac had been murdered would color people's answers. This advantage would be available only a few more hours. The county guys weren't going to see any of it.

"Must be important, Sheriff Fontana."

"There's not a lot for me to do in Staircase. I get a chance to get out like this, I jump on it with both feet."

"What sort of questions are you planning to ask?"

"More or less a general background interview. Who his friends are, hobbies, what type of guy. You know."

"No, I don't. That's why I'm asking."

"Pardon."

"Uh, I'm sorry, but I doubt it's in the best interests of the fire department or the city of Seattle to have outside law-enforcement agencies taking field trips through our stations because they have nothing better to do. You want to appeal, be my guest. See my boss. He's out of town just now, but feel free to write a letter."

"I see." Fontana strode to the door, opened it. "What have you got against Zajac?"

"He never should have gotten into the department, that's all. He wasn't a firefighter, and now that he's left, the city's better off without him. I actually doubt if he'll be able to get back into combat."

"I sense there's something personal going on. What's Zajac to you?"

"You saying I'm not totally truthful in this matter?"

"I'm just wondering what it is about Zajac that's being left unsaid."

Crews considered that, pursing his lips, sucking on the cigarette, squinting until the tea bags under his eyes puckered. "We were forced to suspend him two weeks ago. Erratic behavior. Two-twenty. You know what that means?"

"Radio slang. Means he was stark raving mad."

"That's about the gist of it. In fact, that's what I'd call an accurate description of it. Zajac was stark raving mad. Don't quote me."

"Wouldn't dream of it."

7

Kissing Concrete

THE CREASES IN Chief Crews's starched white shirt and black wool trousers were blade-sharp. "Sad truth of the matter is," continued Crews, "Mr. Zajac had some serious mental problems he had to get straightened out before he came back to work. He'd gotten to the point—I guess I don't know all the technical jargon for such things, but he'd gotten to the point where he seemed to be confusing reality with things that were going on in his head. Deeply troubled. Isn't that right, Ring?"

A dough-faced firefighter in glasses so thick the lenses looked bulletproof had come into the room. A bilious type. Mac guessed he was Chief Crews's gofer. "Ring" read the tattered name cloth over his heart.

"Damn right he was troubled," said Ring. "That's putting it mildly."

"So you threw him out?" Mac asked.

"No choice. Left me no choice," said Crews. "Don't try to ferret out the particulars—they're a department matter. He needed psychiatric counseling. I told him flat out, until he gets a certificate of some sort from our department doctors that says he's seen a qualified psychiatrist and gotten whatever it is that's disturbing him out of his system, until such a time, uh, he's no longer a contributing member of this department.

He was just too far gone to squeak by without seeing a psychiatrist. It was that simple."

Fontana noted Ring had been nodding throughout all of this.

"What did Zajac say at the time?"

"I'm afraid that's not for public disclosure."

"He on drugs?"

Crews turned it over as if the thought had occurred to him before. "I really don't know."

"I'd like to ask again your permission to do some interviews in fire stations. In the end I'll talk to all of these people anyway. It would be simpler if I could get them all in one place."

Crews stared at him for a long while, his pale gray eyes fixed and unblinking, the Camel smoke curling up around his thick eyebrows and balding brow. He had no intention of caving in. The pause was for dramatic effect, coming from a man whose idea of sport would be trout fishing with hand grenades.

"Ring? Show Mr. Fontana out."

The woman had brought him up three dim flights of concrete stairs as if she took any excuse to get a little exercise, but now Ring led him to an elevator and pushed a button. There was a long wait. Fontana took in the hustle and bustle of the third floor. A man in gray slacks and a white shirt went into Crews's office and closed the door, which had been ajar. The clicking latch was a signal to Ring.

"Zajac was a real shit. You guys thinking about hiring him out there, you're making a mistake. Big troublemaker."

"In what way?"

Ring chortled and faced Fontana. He was a head taller, and his doughy skin looked as if it had never been exposed to the sun. "Every way. Just was. There been chiefs trying to get rid of Zajac since the day he signed on."

"Rabble-rouser? Incompetent? What?"

"I suppose you couldn't say he ever really stirred things

up among the men out in the companies. He was just . . ." Ring pulled his tortoiseshell glasses off, pushed the elevator button again, even though it was still lit, then polished his lenses on a flag of shirttail. "I guess you'd have to call Zajac a misfit. Yeah, I guess that's what you'd have to call him. Wasn't a team type of player, you know. I don't care if he was fireman of the year once. In this job you have to play ball with the team."

The elevator doors opened and they stepped inside.

"Been around a long time. Fifteen years in the department. Came in the class in front of mine. Shame to get suspended like that. Downright humiliating."

"How did it happen?"

"I don't think Crews'd appreciate my delving into that."

"It'd be too bad if Zajac edged out some other guy for a job when he really didn't deserve it."

"Crews is not the kind of guy you want to cross."

"Neither am I." Mac didn't know why he said that.

Snorting derisively, Ring said, "Crews is tougher than the nut sack on a crocodile. Taught in my drill school. He was a lieutenant back then. We have this concrete room about eight by ten they put us in. We call it the smoke room. Stoke up a mattress fire on the floor in the corner and then throw us in there for a couple of minutes at a time to see what we're made of. Every Friday afternoon we'd get the smoke room. You come to dread it.

"I was in there one Friday afternoon coughing and choking, my eyes watering so bad I can't hardly see. You crouch down low. The heat and the worst of the smoke is high. Get low enough you can find a layer of cold air about an inch above the floor.

"You end up kissing that concrete slab. Awful tough if the recruit in front of you's spit or upchucked. Anyways, I'm in there, and in one corner I see the glow of the burning mattress all choked down cause there's no oxygen, and in the other corner I see this ember lit up all by itself, about head

54

height. Little bitty thang. I can't figure out what it is so I crawl over there and feel around. It's a man standing in the corner smoking a cigarette. Bloody fucking Crews standing in the corner watching me. And goddammit, he was smoking a fucking cigarette. Don't come any tougher than that old bird."

Mac walked out of the elevator past the trophy case in the lobby. "Your chief had troubles with Zajac before his suspension?"

Linked to Fontana by the thread of their conversation, Ring followed.

"Years ago. I guess I can tell you this. One time Zajac was off-shift downtown in his civvies and Chief Crews ran into him. Zajac was down at Twos picking up his check or something. The chief had been on Zajac to get his hair trimmed. We got regs. So he's bawling Zajac out and following him out to his car, and there's Zajac's car with his wife and kids in it and Crews getting a little wild, I guess—that hair thing really griped him—and Zajac ignoring him and walking along as if he's not there and Crews getting redder and redder and beginning to yell now, and Zajac just gets into his car and starts driving away.

"Somehow, I guess, the chief got his hand caught in Zajac's door handle because Zajac dragged him about half a block. Ruined his shoes. Probably never would have stopped if he hadn't hit a red light. Crews knew Zajac knew he was there. Hell, he was screaming at him. Zajac claimed he didn't see him."

"So the chief had a personal vendetta?"

"One thing about Crews, he forgives and forgets. Zajac brought this other all on hisself. Didn't have nothin' to do with ancient history. Zajac just lost his marbles. You can ask anyone. Well, I guess you can't. But he did. Went flaky on us." As Mac walked down the short hallway to the sidewalk, Ring shouted, the lampoon evident in his voice, "By the way, nice coat."

"Thanks."

Fontana's intention had been to collect whatever information and permission he could from the brass in the SFD, then use up the rest of the day searching for April Smith. Instead, he made a beeline for Sixes, which, according to the huge wall map in the watch office of headquarters, was situated on Twenty-third and Yesler. He found Yesler and headed up the hill.

Back East they'd had their own version of the smoke room when he'd come into the department. Suck up the filthy smoke in the little concrete dungeon for as long as you could take it, blacken your lungs and breed headaches for the next day or two; the ripping pains in your chest would last a while longer. The instructors stood outside the door and clocked them with stopwatches. While answering questions from a masked instructor, the smart ones held their breath for as long as they dared, then inhaled through their clothing.

Masked, Lieutenant Jersey went in with him once and emerged telling the other lieutenants he had doubts about Fontana, that Fontana had been holding his breath. By sheer coincidence, Fontana had ridden to his first fire in the companies with Lieutenant Jersey. Knowing he'd been such a strict taskmaster in boot school, Fontana thought he was going to be a hellion with a fire hose.

They were first through the doorway of a vacant tenement apartment, and the heat and the billowing smoke knocked them to their knees. In those days, though they carried them on the rigs, nobody wore masks at fires; you went for one, you were labeled a pussy and shunned. Fontana had dreaded it, anticipating an endurance contest with the hard-line Jersey. Leather-lungs. They were inside twenty seconds when Jersey slapped him on the back and said, "Let's go take a blow, kid."

It sent Mac into a rage. Two weeks earlier in training, if he'd backed out after twenty seconds, Jersey would have written him a "recommendation to terminate."

"Take a blow? Like hell," he'd replied. It turned out Jersey had a reputation for backing out of fires.

The weather was beginning to grow muggy, cloud cover sliding in from the south, not rainy so much as just dark and ponderous. It was the sort of weather he always senselessly blamed for inviting earthquakes and aid alarms one never forgot.

8

Don't Scare the Horses

Sixes was a compact little building, its appearance vaguely Spanish: pink concrete, chipped walls, and funky lightning bolts on the windows over the apparatus doors.

Fontana manhandled the GMC through a rutted gravel drive to the rear and let the dog patrol the dirt parking area behind the station.

There were two dangerously narrow apparatus doors in front. The ladder truck would have only an inch or two on either side for mistakes. Speeding to an alarm, any compartment doors left open would be ripped off. Over the north door was written "Engine Co. No. 6." Over the south, "Ladder Co. No. 3." The ladder was not in evidence.

Inside he encountered a short, desiccated lieutenant wearing a lake-blue shirt and a scowl. He had gray hair and looked uncomfortable. The nameplate on his shirt read "Lt. Grady."

"Steven Paul Zajac work here?"

"Yeah, but he ain't in."

"Got suspended, didn't he?"

"Actually, he don't work here no more. He's on indefinite detail to Twenty-sixes. South. Out by the city limits. I'll show you on the map."

"This is his old stomping ground? Dropped by to ask a few questions."

Tarping his lap with a section of that morning's *Post-Intelligencer*, Lieutenant Grady sank into a chair that sported a burst cushion. "Got nothing but time. Just don't scare the horses."

They were in a high-ceilinged room that had three inside doors leading off it, all of them propped open with small wooden sprinkler wedges or hooked with twisted coat hangers. One door led to a pair of offices, with a desk and a tall bed in each. The other two doors opened onto the apparatus floor. Engine 6 was a tall red '64 Mack. Both the Seagraves they ran out of Staircase were '82's.

"That your regular rig?" Grady nodded. "The city holding a grudge against this station? A '64 Mack doesn't even hold four hundred gallons, does it?"

"Little over two hundred. Get fifteen hundred runs a year on that pig. There are newer rigs in companies that don't get five hundred a year. But that's the city for you. Must be some politics in it. It's all I can figure."

"I neglected to introduce myself. Sheriff Fontana, from Staircase."

"Great steelheading country." Though he managed to sound tough and outdoorsy, Fontana guessed he was a feckless and rather harmless man. He'd be unlikely to let loose anything important, or to be any more accurate than a drunk with a handgun when he did let loose.

"Why was he suspended?"

"Zajac? I dunno. I can't give you nothin' more than rumor 'cause I wasn't there. It didn't happen out of Sixes. Steve was working out in South Park out of Twenty-sixes. Pissant place. Never gets any runs. All I got is rumors."

"But you know what happened?"

"Heard he botched things at a fire and lipped off to Chief Crews. Crews had placed him out there at Twenty-sixes more or less as a favor. Moved him out there as a disciplinary action. The favor was he probably could have fired him. They could have suspended him months ago, but Crews was bending over backward to give the boy the benefit of a doubt."

"That still in the city? Twenty-sixes?"

"Some people think so. Got a little high in the britches, Steve did."

"Yeah?"

"Insubordination, we called it."

"You talking about Steven Zajac?" The man in the doorway wore a firefighter's navy-blue uniform, and wire-rim spectacles that made him appear older than mid-forties, which was what Fontana calculated he was. His thinning black and gray hair was slicked straight back so that his head resembled some sort of wet vegetable. According to the tag on his shirt his name was Reinholt. Fontana recognized him as the same man he had seen holding up fish with Zajac in the photo at the cabin.

"Sheriff of Staircase," said Lieutenant Grady. "Wants to ask some questions about Zajac."

Reinholt put on a cat-smug smile, adjusting his glasses with both hands, hitched at his trousers Popeye style, and strode across the watch office, hand outstretched. He had a chesty stance. His massive tattooed forearms made his grip formidable.

"Don's the name. Don Reinholt. Come on down in the basement and I'll fill you in. I got something on the stove in the beanery, otherwise . . ." He turned, giving Fontana a wink when the lieutenant couldn't observe.

Fontana sensed an immediate rapport with Reinholt. Perhaps it was the dry humor he saw burning in Reinholt's eyes, eyes the color of silver coins. Reinholt took Fontana down a flight of concrete stairs, past a narrow beanery.

They stopped in a large room along the south wall of the basement where a high row of windows looked out onto the parking area. Satan was outside sitting obediently beside the GMC, his good ear flicking this way and that at the sounds of traffic.

A weight bench striped with duct tape stood in one corner next to a stationary bicycle. A pop machine. An old refrigerator. In one corner was a TV, another firefighter snoring in a chair in front of it.

"I ain't got nothing on the stove," said Reinholt.

"Didn't figure you did."

"Listen. 'Bout ten minutes before you got here our platoon chief phoned and asked for the lieut. I told him he was in the crapper like I always tell him. He was in his office but fuck him. Chief said there might be some copper coming around asking questions about Zajac and we weren't to talk. Whatadya want to know?"

"Just like that?"

"I figure if Crews's agin it, then it must be something good for Steve. And that old cunt upstairs—Grady? Wouldn't say shit if he had a mouthful."

"Didn't seem to know much."

"Only worked with Steve five years. Knows him better than he knows his own son. That your dog out there next to that junker truck?" Don Reinholt was fencing until he could size up Fontana.

"Belongs to the city of Staircase."

"Glad he ain't yours, 'cause I was going to say he looks about like you throw him into a threshing machine once a week just for the sheer-de hell of it."

"He's no beauty."

"Sit down."

Scraping a battered black chair across the floor, Fontana sat and teetered it backward on its squared chrome legs. Reinholt moved a chair three feet away to face him and did the same, cigarette dangling from a pair of thin, colorless lips.

Reinholt said, "What do you want? Just background bullshit?"

Fontana was thinking he really should be telling him his

friend was being trundled around by the medical examiner's staff right now, put into a cooler for tomorrow morning's scalpel hijinks. "You were pretty good friends?"

"Me and Steve. Worked together twelve years. No major squabbles. Fact, I'd say right now he's about the best friend I got in the department. Hell of a firefighter. Gone through some hard times in his personal life the past couple of years. Wife abandoned him and took the two boys to Montana, so he don't get to see them much. To make it worse she remarried some guy used to be one of his best friends. That just about killed him. Loves them boys. Then he's had some more recent woman trouble."

"He remarry?"

"Naw. For a while after she left him he was runnin' around pretty good. Woulda fucked a wet stump if he could of found one. Then he was living with some hellacious gal. Goldang-dest thing. None of us ever got to see her. Fact, for a while there we wanted to sneak around and find out who she was. We figured she was some big old blimp. All I know for sure is he had every sort of trouble with her. Calling him here at work every shift. Really messed with his head. He kept trying to get rid of her, but she wouldn't get the message. Then for a while there right at the end before he went to Twenty-sixes, they seemed to be getting along again."

"Where'd they live?"

"Over by Greenlake someplace. He moved out on her about six months ago. Up to Staircase. In the middle of the night, from what I gathered. She was pissed because he didn't tell her where he'd moved to. Didn't even tell her he was moving. She'd call here and ask for him, and he'd hide out downstairs and hiss at us to tell her the engine was out on a run, anything.

"Anytime we went hunting together or something, why, we'd meet here at the station instead of picking him up at home. When he was still with Susan he used to tell me everything. They have a spat, I'd hear about it, blow by blow.

Never could figure out what was going on with this other woman. Must have been ugly as a broke-dick dog."

"Think so?"

"Maybe not. He's always had pretty fair taste in women. Susan was a looker. Steve's never known how good-looking he is. He'll go into a store or someplace and turn all kinds of women's heads and never notice."

"When was the last time he saw this girlfriend?"

"Didn't know there was a last time. Haven't been in touch with Steve much since he got shipped down to Twenty-sixes. I know she was still on his back the night he left here 'cause I took a call from her right after. Sounded like a bitchy thing at times, then other times she'd phone and be sweet as sugar."

"Why'd he get kicked out of the department?"

"You should talk to a guy named Bill Kite."

They teetered on the chrome legs of their chairs for a few moments. Reinholt's eyes grew unfocused.

"Who's he?"

Reinholt took a minute to answer. "Sorry 'bout that—I was thinking about Zajac. Kite worked a debit here a while back."

"Debit?"

"Payback days. Our normal schedule only gives us forty-two hours a week, but we're bound by contract to work forty-six. Every two months we come in and work a day on some other shift to bring our total hours up. Kind of a pain in the butt."

"I worked the Detroit system back East."

"Fire service?"

"Eighteen years. Till I came to my senses."

"I got a year to fill in my twenty-five. Then I'm history. Anyway, Kite's a young black kid. Got to laughing the other night when he was here telling all the things he'd heard about Zajac before he met him, and how scared he was of him. The story that stood out in his mind was the time Zajac and us got an alarm on Empire Way—they've renamed it Martin Luther King Junior Way South. Try saying that at three o'clock in the morning on the rig radio. Peter Piper. Mostly we call it MLK.

"Anyway, somebody ran his goldanged car into the back of a flatbed truck was hauling lumber. Only this guy didn't have a stack of lumber hanging off the end of his flatbed. Just had one two-by-four about twelve feet long sticking out.

"And this car came along and rammed into it. Speared the poor fucker. Came out in the seat behind his back. Didn't even break the two-by-four. We got there and there was nothing for us to do. Had a blood pressure and everything. But we all knew the minute we moved him he'd bleed out. Only thing keeping him alive was the fact that the two-by-four hadn't been moved and neither had he.

"Guy had guts. Gotta give him that. Said he couldn't feel nothing and he knew he was going to die in a few minutes and would we please just let him do it in peace. He asked for a cigarette and we gave it to him. Left us a message for each member of his family, sucked on the butt, and died.

"Somebody heard Zajac muttering as he walked away, 'When are they going to learn? Smoking kills.' "

Reinholt let out a hoot and the sleeping fireman changed position.

"That story's followed Zajac everywhere he goes. Was tidbits like that had Bill Kite buffaloed. Scared of the legend. In the old days the department was fulla characters like Steve."

9

The Knucklehead Factor

"KITE WAS THERE THE NIGHT Steve got into hot water with Crews. You best get the story from him. Or Steve. I'd fuck it up."

Reinholt cracked a smile and stubbed out his half-consumed cigarette in an ashtray jury-rigged from a tin can, then fired up another in his cupped hands. He basked in the gunmetal-blue smoke.

"Steve's always been in hot water with the brass. Not a lot, because he's a damn fine firefighter and they know it. He got into some sort of beef with Chief Crews over a fire in South Park where he was first-in."

"This where he got suspended?"

"Got suspended just a couple of weeks ago. That was Crews, too. No, this other was early last spring. Hell of a deal. You know, for a while there they had Crews locked in a closet in the FMO sorting the pepper from the fly shit. Why they ever let him back into combat, I'll never know.

"Anyways, Steve's out inspecting with Bill Kite in a department car. They'd hired too many floaters again and didn't know what to do with them, so Chief Boyd here in the Fifth, he had these two out together doing night hotels. And I guess they were maybe a little farther south than they

65

should have been. Hell, they was five or six miles away from where they shoulda been. So they spot smoke rising up off Des Moines Way South out there beyond South Park over by Boeings.

"Just to find out what's going on, they mosey on out. Turns out it's an apartment house fire. Goin' pretty good. About a quarter mile outside the city limits."

"That raise problems of jurisdiction for Seattle?"

"We got a mutual-aid program where we go in if there's life endangerment and the county's not on the scene. So Steve sizes it up, gets on the blower to the dispatcher, and tells them to send a full response, that they have a fully involved two-story apartment house and there aren't any county units within shooting distance. Also, two trapped victims. Kids."

"He told them it was out of the city?"

"They would have known in the alarm office when he gave the intersection. But he told 'em."

"Go on."

" 'Bout six years ago, Steve and me had four kids burn up on us in a house fire down on the lake. It tore us up. Zajac, especially. Things like that haunt a guy."

"They do," said Fontana.

"Down in South Park he figures Engine 26 is about two minutes away and they can unhook the aluminum thirty-footer off the side of the rig, raise it up, and make a quick save."

As he listened, Fontana regarded the dapper tattooed man teetering on the chair in front of him. There was something cranky about this old war-horse, something about the way he spun yarns that implied he'd never uttered them to another soul, so you and he were in some elaborate conspiracy against the rest of the unsympathetic world.

"Turns out Chief Crews is visiting the fire-alarm center at the very moment Steve turns in this alarm. Pretty bizarre coincidence, huh? In any mutual-aid stuff, the on-duty platoon chief has the final say. So he recognizes Zajac's voice, realizes Zajac's way the hell out of his district, which he is, and tells the dispatcher to call County. County says they're sending but all their units are tied up at that big tanker fire they had on the freeway last spring. Remember that?"

"Wasn't in the area last spring."

"So here's Zajac listening to these kids upstairs screaming in this blaze, and downtown Crews is tryin' to decide if he should punish Zajac by not sending. Show him who's boss. Shit, just a single engine would have been common courtesy, even if there hadn't been any trapped victims."

The story was beginning to make Fontana's skin prickle. Chief Crews, the man who needed so desperately to impress rookies that he'd show up in the smoke room with a cigarette. A man who had denied Mac access to the fire stations, seemingly on a whim. "What happened?"

"Crews decides no. We ain't sending. Now Steve felt sure it was because of the long-standing hard feelings between them, that Chief Crews was just flexing his muscles. Upshot of it was, Steve and Kite stood there in the parking lot and watched these kids die."

"Must have hit him hard."

"Hit *me* hard, and I wasn't there. Tell you right now he wasn't good for diddly-squat after that. Took him maybe two months to pull out of the worst of it. You seen him lately? How's he look?"

"Not too good. These Asian kids?"

"Why do you ask that?"

"I was thinking there might be some reason he would have an autopsy report of a young Asian child."

Slamming his chair down, Reinholt rose and strode to the high window, took a drag on his cigarette, then pushed the window open to expel the smoke into the Seattle humidity. "The folks weren't home when the fire started. Just the two kids. Folks came by here one day. Little short people . . . boat people . . . could barely speak a word of English.

Cambodian, I think. Mountain people. Out of the boonies.

"Steve got burned trying to get inside and they knew that. Valiant effort and all. Steve figured, what the hell, he hadn't gotten them out. That was what mattered. The county tried to give him an award but he told them to go to hell. Anyways, the parents thanked him. Very polite. Lots of bowing. Would hardly look you in the eye they were so scared to come in here. Mother had a baby on her hip wrapped in one of those big scarf thingamajigs." The memories were beginning to put tremors in his voice. "Don't know why Steve would have an autopsy report. That's a strange one. We can call and ask him."

"Not right now."

"You never did tell me what this was about."

"Nothing that'll injure Steve, if that's what you're implying." Mac rubbed his face with both hands. Zajac was so far beyond injury he didn't even want to think about it.

"Don't know why, but I trusted you the minute I seen you pull up in that truck with that there dog. And the phone call from Chief Crews telling us to keep our yaps shut . . ."

"You hate Crews."

"He just better damn well watch it when he walks under a fire building. Somebody's just apt to drop a hunk of rafter or something."

Fontana remembered back East when he'd first gotten into the department. A chief had narrowly escaped death when unknown assailants had dropped a garbage can loaded with sopping-wet carpet pieces from a five-story window. The can, weighing a couple of hundred pounds, landed beside the chief and exploded like an aerial bomb. Old-time firefighters were a rough bunch.

"What sort of trouble went on between Crews and Zajac? I talked to Crews this morning and his tone of voice made it seem personal."

"I was on vacation, and when I came back most of it had

died down. Never even got the gist. Kite might know. Steve wasn't talking. And things were hectic around here. Word had been passed down to badger Steve any way they could. Our battalion chief is a climber, so all he needs is a hint. And Grady, upstairs—you saw that spineless whore. They was like kids pulling the legs off a spider.

"Everything was by the book. Drilled us two, sometimes three hours a day. Add that to three hours of inspections, an hour or two of paperwork, half hour wiping down the rig, hour doing housework around the station, four or five runs a shift. Took us down to Fourteens and ran Steve to the top of the tower every drill. Seven stories. At night the chief would come up here and give Steve ten or twenty pages of typing to do.

"We're not allowed to wear crew-neck undershirts. Steve showed up with one. Before he had a chance to get a paper clip and snag it down, Grady wrote him up. Wrong color of socks. You name it. They suspended him a shift. Gave him every dirty detail rolled down the pike. Arson patrols. Fire watches. Mind you, this was all while Steve still felt like hell about losing those two kids."

"How'd he manage?"

"One tough son of a bitch. The trouble was, I was beginning to get into as much trouble as Steve. I think what he did to the watch office was because of me. Was scared I'd get myself in trouble." Reinholt grinned. "Dry-hose drill. It was raining, so we weren't going to charge the line. Grady was sitting up there reading the paper and scarfing up dinner, but me and Steve were supposed to drill. Even the guys on the ladder here were getting PO'ed with Grady. I mean, we've made the joke for years: Grady's so department-oriented, if the chief came out and issued a four-fingered glove, Grady would break out the hatchets . . .

"Knuckleheads and disciples of knuckleheads. So I pull the rig out into the rain and Steve masks up and coils two hundred feet of dry preconnect in front of the door there between the apparatus floor and the watch office. The ladder crew was eating. Grady was eating and checking his stock portfolio in the paper. Me and Steve was drilling. We had two fires that day and about six aid runs and we were bushed, but Grady was scared shitless Crews would drive by to see if we'd drilled yet.

"Steve stood there in the doorway in his Survivair, opened the bale on the Wooster, and hollered for water. Hell, I give it to him. I hear water, I give it. Can't be second-guessing the man on the pipe, now, can I?" Reinholt jabbed the Marlboro between his lips and gleefully rubbed his knuckles. "Should have seen it. Grady sitting there, half cocked around as the air is being forced out of the hose and it's coughing. Grady saying, 'No . . . wha . . . no . . . wha?' It was crazy. People jumping out the windows and doors. Steve washed it down like a man hosing out a henhouse.

"When it was all over Grady was sitting in a puddle about two feet deep. His dentures had been knocked out."

"Zajac didn't get suspended for that?"

"There was an alternate B-One working that night."

"B-One? That's your platoon chief?"

"Yeah. Some battalion chief from the north end. He was 'fraid to do anything drastic, so together he and Chief Boyd shipped Steve to Twenty-sixes on an indefinite detail. Sent us that in return." Reinholt nodded at the firefighter sleeping in front of the Playboy Channel. "By the time Crews got back from his vacation or whatever, it was too late to suspend Steve. But he got him in the end. Been suspended about two weeks now. I know what it is. Steve's suing. Right?"

Before Fontana could reply, the chimes went off, sounding like a doorbell in a hurry, and he was suddenly alone in the room.

Jogging upstairs behind the two Seattle firefighters, he heard the last of the three rounds of dispatch information on the station amplifier, watched through a cloud of steel-gray exhaust as the '64 Mack roared out onto Twenty-third, red lights flashing, siren howling. The man on the tailboard had donned a heavy yellow bunking coat and helmet.

Listening to Engine 6 take the aid run brought to mind a plethora of memories. As in Seattle, his old department had relied heavily on first-aid work for citizen support and good-will, had instituted a full-fledged paramedic program shortly after Seattle had.

Fontana sometimes regretted having gone into investigations, despite his knack for the work; regretted giving up the simplicity, the camaraderie, and the occasional razzle-dazzle of a firefighter's days.

On the scanner in the watch office, he heard Engine 6 get the address, repeat the address, then arrive. A few minutes later Grady's voice came across, crackling and weak. "Engine 6. Code green Medic ten and give us one red ambulance."

He vividly remembered the very last aid run he'd handled in the company. It had been a panicked man with pain in his chest—one of the major symptoms of a myocardial infarction is said to be a sudden sense of impending death, a deep, black foreboding. The man absolutely knew he was going to die. It was the EMT's job to reassure the patient. Fright alone could put a person into shock.

"I'm dyin', ain't I?" the man had asked, balling up the lapel of Fontana's coat in his fist. "I'm dyin'. Tell me I'm not dyin'! I don't want to die."

"You won't die. You're in the best hands you could be in. We're sending you to the hospital. They'll patch you up. Going to be just dandy. Now relax and enjoy the ride."

"Tell me I'm not going to die," he repeated. "I know I'm gonna die. Tell me I'm not. Gawd, I don't wanna die tonight. Tell me."

"Not the slightest chance," Fontana reassured. "Seen a

million cases like yours. Not one chance in a hundred you'll
die."

"Sure?"

"Positive, man."

"Thanks."

On the way to the hospital the man stopped breathing for
good.

10

The Third Rail

IT WAS ONLY WHEN the apparatus door closed on its automatic timer that Fontana realized he had the station to himself.

An eerie, almost sensuous feeling flooded him, as if he had signed on again, with a big city department with its reams of paperwork, forms, practical jokes, petty politics, and sheer, unmitigated bullshit. For a moment he felt as if he actually was pulling a check every other Thursday.

Staircase didn't count. In Staircase, with just two 911 lines, they were only tinkering at firefighter, just as he was only tinkering at sheriff. Why kid himself? He had been good. But that had been another world.

When the bell hit in Staircase, it rang for chicken-coop fires ignited by pregnant teenagers, cow carcasses on the highway—allegedly left by UFOs—or maybe the occasional, very occasional, house fire. The aid car paid a visit to Mrs. Armbruster once a month after she belted her live-in boyfriend with a skillet or a ball-peen hammer.

Here they battled flames and saved lives. A torrent of nostalgia oozed through him. Sometimes when he mulled over the decision to move West, he found himself remarkably close to regret.

He was beginning to empathize with Zajac, who had held many of the same iconoclastic attitudes he had.

He looked up Bill Kite in Station Six's directory, which was organized according to battalions, after that by stations. Reinholt had told him Kite worked at Thirteens, but he wasn't certain which battalion Thirteens was in. He found it in the Fifth; same as Sixes.

Penning Kite's number in his notebook, he tucked the Seattle Fire Department directory under his jacket, jammed three inches of it into his belt, and zipped the coat.

Mac used the telephone beside the watch console—an outside line referred to in department lingo as the third rail—and as he waited for Kite to answer he stared at the wall and noticed a list of the station members, their home addresses typed alongside their names. Zajac's name was crossed out, but the address was the house on Burdock Road in Staircase. He needed Zajac's address when he'd been chummy with the mystery woman, the woman he hadn't wanted anybody to see.

"Bill Kite?"

"Yeah?" He could hear small children chattering in the background.

"Sheriff Fontana from Staircase."

"Didn't know they had a sheriff out there."

"All the police powers any other agency has. Even let me tote a gun if the rats get too bad in the city dump." He was drawing on stories he'd heard about fat Warren Bounty getting drunk and potting rodents for hours on end—had even, right before he was committed, driven through town with the carcass of a Norwegian rat strapped across the hood of the GMC as if it were an elk. "Need to talk to you."

"What is it? I haven't been out that direction in months." A note of alarm corroded Kite's voice.

"Nothing serious. Need to discuss somebody you know from work."

They made an appointment for that afternoon, and Mac

got directions to Kite's place in Issaquah, a burgeoning bedroom community between Seattle and Staircase. Kite assured him it didn't matter what time he arrived, that his wife was working overtime and he was stuck baby-sitting.

Fontana rummaged through a scarred pinewood desk in the engine officer's room, found no address rosters.

In the disciplinary section of the captain's journal Zajac had been written up on disciplinary charges eight times in the last six months for crimes ranging from improper attire to insubordination. Don Reinholt had been written up once. Insubordination. Nobody else in the station had so much as a mark against him, which showed how often the department resorted to charges.

While he waited for the engine company to put itself in service and return, he found a black-and-white photograph on one wall, a photo that must have been taken in the late sixties. It was of Station Six, snapped from the street with some sort of special camera built to take exceptionally wide photographs. In the picture the apparatus doors were open and in front of the rigs were lined up pridefully two crews, legs picketed apart, arms locked rigidly behind their backs, all wearing old-fashioned black hats with silver badges.

It was very military, and they looked as if they put ground glass in their chewing gum. He recognized a younger, hairier Don Reinholt, that same conspiratorial grin. Zajac wasn't in the photo. But Crews was, holding the rank of lieutenant and looking haughty and grave and stiff-necked. He looked a trifle ulcerous as well. It happened that way, Mac knew that from bitter experience. The higher he had climbed, the unhappier he'd grown.

After the engine roared down Twenty-third and backed on to the ramp, he asked Reinholt if he had Zajac's previous address at Green Lake.

"Sorry," Reinholt replied.

"Steve be likely to have a bunch of hundred-dollar bills around?"

"Sure."

"Really?"

"Maybe."

"Ever deal drugs?"

"Did marijuana in Nam. Never heard him talk about anything else, though. We see enough in this job, I doubt he was tempted."

"Yeah."

"Hey," said Reinholt, uncoiling a garden hose to squirt inside the wheel wells.

"Yeah?"

"Tell Steve to quit making himself so scarce. We need to see that old buckaroo."

Fontana bunched up one cheek in an awkward smile. "Sure."

11

The Annotated Guide to Big-City Dames: Their Quirks, Foibles, Faux Pas

MAC WALKED AROUND BACK, let the dog into the truck, and drove the GMC downtown. He was not a complete stranger to Seattle's streets; in his salad days he had gone to the University of Washington for a year, had driven a cab to make ends meet. That was before the army, before the job in the East.

The layout hadn't changed; the main library was precisely where he remembered it, sandwiched between Fourth and Fifth avenues, smack in the middle of downtown. But now there was the constant barrage of construction trucks and cement mixers. The Columbia Center rose black and sleek, looking otherworldly against the cumulus clouds. Beyond that stood the Attwood Towers project.

They were erecting a city of shadows.

In the main library he asked a dour woman librarian with a peach-down mustache to direct him to the second floor so he could peruse old phone books.

In last year's white pages he located Zajac's former number and address off Woodlawn Avenue, a block from Greenlake. Unless the town had drained the lake and thrown up a pile of strip malls and overpriced condominiums, it was prime jogging and sunning territory.

Next, he traced an index finger slowly through the listings for "Smith." There were a million of the Dugans and none seemed to be named April.

Fontana got off the northbound freeway at Ravenna Boulevard, and the street, with its wide, grassy medians and yellowing trees, was just as parklike and crawling with joggers and bicyclists as he remembered.

Zajac's former address was half a block off Woodlawn behind a church, and had the pristine look of a rental owned and watched over by a fussy old man. A yardless gingerbread house, it was small and homey, parking on the street. He and Linda had lived in a similar place when they were first married.

Cupping his hands, he peered through the front-porch windows. Vacant. When he rounded the corner and headed for the backyard, a chubby man came bustling from the rear of the church. He had short dun-colored hair, a broad face, and plum-blue eyes set deep into his cheeks. His skin was as poreless and waxy-looking as a banana peel. His hands were busy.

"May I be of service?" he yelled, as he walked closer in a high-stepping canter. "Pastor Coburn. You looking to rent?"

"Trying to find some former tenants. Church rent this?"

"Mrs. Seely left it in '74. Pancreas went out on her. She didn't even belong to the congregation. She just bequeathed it. She didn't have any relatives and thought it'd be of use to us."

"Looks like it's been vacant."

"Not too long. We had a couple of unfortunates in here and they put a stigma on the place."

"A fireman?"

"Two young women who turned out to be ladies of the evening. We were forced to evict them a couple of months ago. It took me until last week to get it cleaned up the way it should be. Interested?"

78

Coburn did not look like a man who could evict someone—even a prostitute—without losing a night's sleep.

"Remember a fireman?"

"Yeah, sure. Fella named Zajac. He was fireman of the year one time, I heard. He lived here almost twelve months. Good tenant. He was always very polite."

"Somebody living with him?"

Pastor Coburn colored and his hands buzzed around his face like huge fat bumblebees. The two hookers had been a problem of logistics, but Zajac's girlfriend was something else entirely, something that erased the cordiality from his eyes and replaced it with a troubled look.

"I was just wondering if he lived with somebody?"

"As a matter of fact, he did. A young woman."

"What'd she look like?"

"I can't recall."

"This is important."

He ticked off the items as if it were a grocery list. "Pretty. Redhead. Vigorous girl." His pig-pink face went almost maroon. "Extraordinarily robust, vigorous. I didn't know her at all."

"An athlete?"

He nodded and hemmed and hawed. "I know Zajac was. He used to jog down by the lake. I'd see him down there sometimes during my own run. I do the lake in twenty minutes now."

"How about her?"

"You mean was she an athlete?"

"Yeah."

"I might have seen her lifting weights in a bikini in the backyard once or twice. Come to think of it, I might have."

Fontana smiled at the pastor's discomposure and at his own discovery. It was probably April. And the pastor was concealing nothing more exotic or unhealthy than simple lust. "Know her name?"

79

"No, why I, uh, never did get formally introduced to the young woman."

"Got any of their old mail? Anything like that? They friendly with any neighbors? Happen to know where I could find either of them?"

"I really don't. I couldn't help you there. They moved out quite a while ago. About nine months, I believe. I may be wrong, but I don't think they socialized with any of the neighbors."

"Anyone in the congregation know either of them?"

"We got him from a blind ad in the paper. I invited him to attend services. He was polite, but it was clear he wasn't interested."

"And her?"

"She moved in later. At least, that's my recollection."

Fontana thanked him, whistled to the dog, and drove downtown again. Parking at the central post office was a mess, and it took him fifteen minutes to get the slot in front of the hydrant. Inside, he paid his fee, flashed his shield, and asked for a new address for Zajac. He got it easily enough. Burdock Road in Staircase. Then he asked for another new forwarding address from the same house, for an April Smith. The clerk took a long time finding that one, eventually came back with an address on Capitol Hill for "Sumner."

A. Sumner.

"Sure it wasn't Smith?" said Fontana.

"Our records indicate Sumner," replied the clerk. "Both addresses, the old one and the new, Sumner."

Mac fought his way through the beginnings of the downtown rush-hour clamor and located her apartment house on East Jefferson, on Capitol Hill near the hospitals. The sidewalks were thronged with kids coming home from school. Nurses in white walked to and from work. The threat of rain had lifted, and portions of the sky were blue and sunny, the clouds roly-poly.

Three stories, brick, it was a security building that had once been very posh. Now it was clean but a bit run-down. The name was on a label over a buzzer in a column of buzzers: "A. Sumner." He might have rung the manager and told them he was official, but some uniformed kids coming home from a Catholic school let him in.

The apartment was on the top floor.

Fontana had no idea how he was going to handle this. It might not even be her. Then there was the off chance that she'd been perfectly sincere this morning, that she'd had to leave for an appointment, been ill, whatever. The thought was nearly enough to take his mind off the discomfiting realization that he was going to have to tell her her boyfriend was dead.

Apartment 312.

He knocked, heard some rustling inside, then, after a bit, knocked again. A woman's voice, unrecognizable through the door.

"Who is it?"

"Sheriff Fontana."

The door swung open cautiously and made an ugly thunk at the end of a reinforced chain. A face moved into the backlighted chink, poised at an angle, cheekbones wide, hair red and dripping, as if she'd just bailed out of a shower. He guessed she'd either play it very meek or absurdly outraged. He could smell sweat mingling with the perfume.

"April Smith, I presume?"

"You?"

"Let's talk."

The door wavered like a water witch, as if she were thinking about slamming it in his face. "What about?"

"I thought you wanted to find out where Zajac was."

"Where?" The query had been filed to a needle-sharp point by anxiety. Then she got another notion from her toolbox of notions. "Did you see the bastard? Does he know how worried I've been? Just like always, he never thinks about anybody but himself. He's always been that way. So what's his sad story?"

"It's complicated. I'd like to come in and tell it."

Nervousness muzzled her voice. Her dry mouth made clicking sounds. She was talking to the law.

"I would have stayed and waited for you," she admitted. "I remembered something I had to do."

He was thinking her story was a sorry thing, but then, what he was about to tell her was a whole lot sorrier. She hadn't driven all the way out to Staircase to find out what happened to her boyfriend and then left because she suddenly remembered she had to sweep the dead flies off the window-sill. The way he figured it, she had taken off for one of two reasons: She was implicated in Zajac's death and already knew what Mac would find. Since she was living here in town under the name of April Sumner, she thought he wouldn't be able to locate her. The second choice was that she simply grew so fearful waiting that she couldn't stand the suspense. After all, she had seen the havoc at the cabin. The Bronco was still there, windows shattered. In her place, Mac would have been worried, too.

Although on opposite sides of the door, their heads were inches apart, close enough to sniff each other's breath. Hers smacked of licorice.

"Well," he said, waiting for her to let him in.

"We can talk like this."

Like a shill working in concert with him, a woman in her fifties emerged from another unit and walked the corridor past Fontana.

"If you want all your neighbors to hear, we can."

April closed the door, unlatched the chain, and swung it wide. Clearly, she hadn't been expecting visitors. She wore shiny black Lycra tights and a raggedy sweatshirt that must have been around since the Eisenhower era. The sleeves were sawed off and it was pitted with holes. She was sweating profusely. She wore nothing underneath either garment, but he was too preoccupied with his mission and the rest of the place to stare.

"I guess it's all right," she said. "You can come in."

12

A Brother to Dragons

APRIL SCANNED HIS BELT for a gun or cuffs. Mac wore neither.

He stepped inside the room and gently snapped the door shut behind him. They were alone. The chain on the door pendulumed, tapping the wood. Her wet hair hung in darker-than-red ringlets almost to her shoulders. Beads of sweat dotted her brow. She wore a yellow sweatband around her forehead. She had stepped backward upon his entry, almost to the other side of the room.

A worn beige rug was the tackiest object in the room, except, perhaps, for his sheriff's jacket. An old lady's rug for an old lady's apartment. Except that somebody had stuffed this old lady's apartment chock full of weight benches, weight bars, wall mirrors, and similar gizmos. There was no furniture, just stacks of weights, pulleys, and contraptions he would have had a hard time guessing the uses of.

Her physique resembled the sculpted shapeliness of a Valkyrie on a sci-fi paperback, powerful and sexy. It looked like something she had honed for long hours each week over a period of years. She had been in the middle of a weight workout when he knocked.

"This'll take a while," he said.

"I don't see why. Just tell me what you found. Was

he shacked up with some bimbo down the road?"

"It was quite a bit more complicated."

A bead of sweat marched down her forehead and clung precariously to the tip of her nose. She flicked it off expertly with one finger. "So what was it?"

"Maybe you'd better make yourself comfortable."

Glaring, she turned and strode from the room, stumped down a short corridor, and vanished. In a few minutes he would tell her that he'd found her longtime lover tied to a tree in the woods, stabbed to death. An image intruded itself: the doctor who had told Mac Linda was dead. The melding of compassion and ghoulish curiosity on the doctor's face had been a revelation. Mac felt a bubble of nausea in his throat. Maybe he should have let the King County police do this? Maybe he should have stayed out of the whole mess? Maybe his soul already had enough rents.

He waited in an off-white dining room set up with wicker furniture, the only furniture he could see in any of the rooms, an off-white rug laid over the in-house carpet. A stereo component system was thrown together in one corner, a massive television and VCR combination in another.

He could smell supper in the oven—baking fish. Fish, sweat, perfume, talc, incense. The books on the coffee table were pictorials penned by and starring famous bodybuilders.

Barefoot, clad in filmy chartreuse running shorts and a peekaboo tangerine tank top too loose at the ribs, she walked down the corridor. The tank top adhered damply. Judging by her face, she was twenty-eight, twenty-nine. All the pumping had edited her body into the stuff of adolescent wet dreams. She didn't seem to have body hair anywhere. No fuzz on the backs of her arms, everything bare as a head of lettuce.

"A. Sumner?" he said, challenging.

She hesitated, stammered. "April. It's April Sumner. Not Smith. Okay. I admit it."

"You weren't lying about everything?"

"Of course I wasn't."

"Just most things."

"Don't push it. Only the name. I used Smith because I was afraid of what you'd find up there. I didn't need my name connected to it if it was awful. Was it?"

"If you'll bear with me, I'd like to ask a few questions about Zajac before I answer that."

"Why can't you answer now?"

"Just want to ask a few questions."

"I guess."

"Why do you think somebody broke into his place?"

"I've no idea. I really don't."

"They get tougher. Why didn't you tell me his place had been burgled when you asked me to go up there?"

"The mayor."

"What?"

"Maureen Costigan told me not to. She said you were a crackpot and you'd help us, but we had to play you like a weasel on a string."

"She said that? Like a weasel on a string?"

"Yeah. I thought it was a little funny. I mean, you're the sheriff and everything. But you did look a little eccentric."

"A weasel on a string?"

"You still do, look a little . . . I like it. That coat looks like a car cover."

He fingered the zipper on the jacket. He'd grown rather attached to it, as he had to the truck, and as much as he hated to admit it, her comments stung. Maybe he was a bit of an eccentric, but he'd never thought of the word as an insult until she uttered it.

13

Tuition for a
Private Hell

"I WENT UP the day before like I told you," April said. "And I also went up there this morning with the mayor. We got a little fright and came back. Then she got you."

"Was Zajac in some sort of fix?"

"By the way, how'd you find me?" Her cheeks went stiff and the plump flesh began twittering. It was the only plumpness on her body. Her damp hair hung limply, frizzed a bit around the edges where it had partially dried, forming a corona around her from the low sun outside the window.

"I don't like being duped. I don't like it when people gull me, hand me dummy phone numbers and addresses that don't exist. Puts me on edge, you know. What I found up there? A burgled Bronco. Couldn't tell what was missing, but the tape deck was intact and it should have been on its way to a swap meet. Found a cabin that had been thoroughly searched and ransacked but, as far as I could discern, not robbed. Don't see that often. Loaded guns all over the place, a TV, you name it. It had all the signs of a meticulous search. Now, as to what they were looking for, I thought you might tell me."

"Steve wasn't . . . ?"

"Wasn't in the house. Wasn't in the Bronco. Wasn't on the lot."

She exhaled so forcefully he could feel the wind from it across the room. "You didn't see any evidence he'd been seeing a woman?"

"Which woman did you have in mind?"

"No one."

"No other women. No makeup kits. No used prophylactics stuck to the floor." She blushed. "You used to live with him?"

"In north Seattle."

"And you're still lovers?"

That one required contemplation, not because she didn't know the answer, but because she evidently wanted to frame it correctly.

"Sometimes we're lovers. Sometimes just colleagues. He calls me if he gets lonely. Lots of times he calls me." According to Reinholt, it had been the other way around. "Lovers? Yeah, I guess that's the appropriate term. You couldn't say we're having an affair. That's more of an illicit thing. We're both free to go our own way. Lovers. From time to time.

"You have to understand some things. Steve is going through a lot of problems. He is a paranoiac, did you know that? Thought people were after him. Everywhere we went he thought people were after him. We went out to the Rusty Pelican one night and a car U-turned behind us out of the lot, made a couple of the same turns we did, so Steve slammed on his brakes. It was raining and the way he did it he sort of trapped this other driver. The guy rolled his window down when Steve approached. For godsakes, he was some middle-age salesman, had picked up some woman with yellow hair. Yellow! They were looking for a motel with adult movies and water beds."

Her gray eyes glistened, took on a moony look.

He prompted her with a nod.

"Steve? He smashed his face in. He beat the hell out of

the poor guy right through the window. Steve works out with a heavy bag. He can really hit. You wouldn't want to get into it with him. He thought this guy was following him, working for some combine or something."

"Combine?"

"A crime syndicate. Some big organization."

"Is that why all the guns?"

"Yeah. He thought he was on to something in this city. Something really really big."

"Was he always so paranoid?"

"Since last spring. He had some trouble on the job. It gave him fits. And he just sort of wigged out. He rammed tailgaters. Twice I saw him do that. He thought people were following him. Where we used to live . . . We lived together until he flipped. We got broken into. Kids or something. He thought it was a conspiracy."

"Ramming tailgaters doesn't sound so bad," Fontana said. "Some of these drivers around here need a lesson in manners."

"He hurt people, though. Everybody tailgates during rush hour, but he couldn't stand it. He'd slam his brakes on. I was riding with him when he caused a really big accident on the freeway one night in the rain. I almost called the police on him. I read in the paper the next day nobody got killed. Thank God. He was just . . . moody."

"Tell me about this crime syndicate."

"There's nothing to tell. He made it all up."

"Sure?"

"As sure as anyone can be about anything." But somehow she didn't look confident.

"Why did you end up getting separate digs?"

"He couldn't sleep at night. And being a fireman, it really galled him. I mean, there were two, three nights a week at work he wasn't sleeping anyway, because that was his job. You wouldn't know what it was like. It drove him up a wall."

"I've been there."

"You couldn't know. So then when he did come home, he'd be dog tired, exhausted by evening, and he'd go to bed at nine, maybe ten if there was something on TV, and a couple of hours later he'd be up, roaming around the house. Or he'd wake up in a sweat and the sheets would be soaking wet. He was going through a private hell.

"And the thing about Steve, he wouldn't talk. He would never talk about it. Everything was always such a secret." It was the same word Don Reinholt at Station Six had used. Secret. Except that Reinholt had applied it to the woman with whom Zajac had been cohabiting. April. He still couldn't figure out why their affair had been under wraps. And for some reason, he didn't ask her.

"You ever meet his co-workers on Engine 6?"

"How'd you know he worked on Engine 6?"

"Bunking stuff was up at the house."

"His friends. Yeah, I guess I've met them."

"A guy named Reinholt? Don?"

"He must about have his twenty-five in right now. He's a crusty old guy. Surprisingly strong. He works off-shift for a contractor wrestling boulders and lumber and stuff. He and Steve were pretty good friends. They went hunting and fishing a lot."

She knew Reinholt, but Reinholt didn't have a clue who she was. Fontana would figure it out, but now wasn't the time. In a few moments he was going to tell her about Zajac, and when he did, he figured he'd have a situation on his hands.

"April, was there some reason Zajac would have an autopsy report around?"

A fleeting look of guilt. She had a lot of traits in common with Mo Costigan, except that April was prettier, fitter, and, he imagined, a good deal trickier. But one thing—she and Mo, neither of them seemed to be much of an actor. Either that, or they were so good they could look bad convincingly.

"Autopsy report? Yes, maybe. Steve went to a fire last

spring. I don't know all the precise details, but I do know two kids died."

"In South Park? That why he wasn't sleeping?"

"That and a chief in the department who was giving him a hard time."

"Crews?"

"You already know all this, or what?"

"Piecing things together as I go along. Tell me about this fire."

"I wish I could. It was months after it happened that I even knew he'd been. It was big news in town because there'd been some mix-up dispatching—was splashed all over the television for a week or so. The crux of the matter is he had a run-in with this chief—yes, Crews.

"And after a while he began seeing Crews behind every little thing that went wrong in his life. We applied for a loan to buy a house. We were going to buy it together, and something went wrong and he blamed that on this chief. I told him he needed some sort of psychiatric help. Bad. He was getting real paranoid. And talking about this imaginary crime syndicate. But he wouldn't listen. He never listens."

"The way I understand it, Crews was harassing him at work."

"That was going on. Everybody knew that was going on. But this went a lot deeper. Steve concocted this theory that Crews had had some sort of personal interest in that fire in South Park . . . Steve thought Crews had derailed Seattle's response on purpose. It was a totally wigged-out theory. And he was spending all day going around researching it. Followed Chief Crews around for weeks and weeks."

"He what?"

"Crews and Sam Ring. Followed them both. For absolutely weeks."

14

Slow Dancing Without the Music

"You TALKING ABOUT big-time corruption in the Seattle Fire Department?"

"That's what he thinks. He has this conspiracy theory built up in his head. He thinks fire department personnel are making money off fires and helping to cover up afterward. Crazy as a hoot owl."

April Sumner went off on a long riff, told him as much as she knew. Huge chunks of Zajac's recent life and thinking were either incomprehensible to her, or simply missing. She also intertwined Zajac's theories with irrelevant facts and fantasies about their life together. In her version, they had *never* squabbled. Steve dutifully phoned her from work every night and they gabbed for hours on the third rail. Selective amnesia.

She forgot her fits of jealousy. She gave no rational explanation as to why they'd broken up. And, whereas Reinholt's version had Zajac moving out on the sly, she reported it had been a mature decision in which they'd both participated. The troubles had all been on Steve's side, and those spurred by the Seattle Fire Department. Had it not been for his career, they would be married. If Reinholt was telling the truth, and Fontana thought he was, April was rounding off the sharp corners of reality.

Fontana wandered around the apartment as she spoke.

Twice she bounded out of the wicker chair to check on her dinner, each time gulping down a slug of vitamins from a cupboard teeming with brown vials.

It took her almost ten minutes to wind down. When she began a despairing monologue about what she was going to say to Steve when she next saw him, Fontana decided it was time to tie the string to the tooth and slam the door. He watched her switch off the oven, watched the hem of her shorts rise on her derriere as she bent over. He felt wretched. He should have done this first thing.

"Maybe I better tell you something." He was aware that his tone had betrayed the mission.

She swerved around and a tear glistened in the corner of one almond-shaped eye. Intuitively, she had known he was the bearer of bad news, or at least, now that he'd spoken, she knew.

"It's about Steve, isn't it?"

"The house was torn up. You saw that."

"Yesterday and again today. You told me you didn't see him."

"I told you he wasn't in the house and he wasn't on the lot. I wanted to hear you talk about him. I made a mistake. And I've been putting this off. It's not easy. Somebody took him out across the creek. He's dead, April. I'm sorry. I really am."

"What?"

"He's dead."

"That was the dirtiest trick."

"I wasn't sure you weren't implicated."

Her lip quivered. "Are you sure now, you bastard?"

"Of course," he lied.

"That bastard."

"I said I was sorry."

"Not you. Steve. Why did he do this to me?"

Fontana hesitated. "I doubt if he planned it to get at you."

"It was his fault. He should have . . . Oh, shit!"

Without discarding the oven mitt, she padded barefoot across the room and circled behind him, stripped Warren Bounty's voluminous foul-weather jacket off him, then draped it over a white wicker rocker. Underneath, he wore a short-sleeved lavender polo shirt and he could feel her damp hair brush the bare skin of his arm as she bent over with the coat. Then she came around and stood in front of him, tears in her eyes.

"What happened?" she asked.

"Somebody killed him."

"Why?"

"That's what I was hoping you could tell me, April."

"He can't be."

"I'm sorry, but he is."

"It doesn't add up, because of the way you've been talking to me."

"I saw his wallet. It was Steve."

She shook her head.

"Be stubborn. It won't bring him back. I'm sorry. You don't know how sorry I am." For a split second he remembered vividly what it'd been like when Linda passed away: the shock, the disbelief, the grim sense that his world had altered inescapably, along with the helpless sensation that nothing was going to change for anybody except him—that the earth would continue to revolve, rain would continue to drop, and Linda would continue to be dead.

Her eyes were filmy. "He can't be dead. You wouldn't have let me jabber on like that. You would have come to the door and said, 'I have some very sad news for you, miss.' And then you would have told me. You wouldn't have interrogated me. You wouldn't have let me jabber on making a fool of myself."

"I'm not good around death. I used to be, but not anymore. I should have told you first thing, but I couldn't bring myself to it."

"Yeah, and you wanted to get your information. I don't think much of you, Sheriff Fontana. I really don't. And Steve, that jerk-off. Why did he do this to me?"

He didn't have a reply for that. He'd slipped into the role of heel without really trying, and things were turning out worse than he could have guessed. What made it even trickier was that he was beginning to think she might be acting.

Spinning around on one bare heel, she moved into the kitchen, perfunctorily checked the oven, unscrewed the cap on a pill bottle of B_{12}, popped one, neatened up the counter, took off her mitt, put her mitt back on, then strode across the room to slouch in defeat in front of him. She took off the mitt, picked at it, and slipped it back on a second time. Teardrops scuffled down her face. She sniffled, lost some of it onto her upper lip, and unthinkingly wiped the result across the back of the mitt.

"I'm sorry, darlin'. Sorry about Steve. Sorry about the way I told you."

He reached across the space between their bodies and held her shoulders, fussed with an orphaned thread of her tangerine tank top, watched her unfocused eyes blink and bat. He caressed her hair, moved a strand out of her face. He slipped the mitt off her hand and, using a scorched spot on it, dabbed at her nose.

Slowly, he pulled her against him. She came, unwillingly at first. As she sobbed against his chest, her red mane smothered his face. Strands of hair Velcroed themselves to his beard. They stood that way until his shoulder began to go to sleep, until the wet had soaked through his shirt and run down inside the shirt. As they tilted against each other, her sobs gradually grew louder, until she was wailing so loud he imagined they could hear it all the way to Missouri. Legs wobbly, arms shivering.

It took a while for her to begin interspersing the sobs with a commentary, chopped up and stretched out by further weeping. Nonsensically, she droned on about a discussion she and Steve had had before purchasing the massive TV in the corner. It wasn't until a cloud scudded across the setting sun and the room suddenly dipped into deep shadow that she stopped and rubbed her plump cheeks against Mac's polo shirt.

He cradled her face between his hands and kissed her on each cheek, realizing suddenly that his taut body was carrying a cargo of lust. Just what she didn't need. She shuddered against him. She was very hot. He was sweaty.

"I've got to meet somebody," he said, glancing at a numberless clock on the kitchen wall. He'd been with her almost two hours. "Will you be all right?"

"Stay with me?"

The pleading in her voice was painful to listen to, reminded him of a Gloria Swanson line out of *Sunset Boulevard*. In fact, there was something Norma Desmond about April, an anomaly he'd noticed before he told her Zajac was dead. Yet she'd taken it better than he had when Linda died. April had moxie in her eyes, a ripple in her jaw, and enough strength still in her legs to walk a mile.

"I'd like to stay for the next week," Mac said. "But I can't. I'm not the person to do it. You should have a friend here, a sister or something. Besides, he was murdered. And it was pretty bad. Bad enough to make me go after them "

"Stay?"

"Do you have a friend who could come over?"

"No."

"Must be somebody."

"Nobody. Steve was my whole life. Besides, I have to get to work in a little while." Inhaling deeply, she stepped back. Her tank top was saturated. "Will I see you?"

"Looking forward to it. Leave a message at the fire station out there anytime. Day or night. I mean that. Need to talk or see someone, I'm available. As a person, not a sheriff. Somebody to talk to."

"Thanks, I just might do that."

"Take care."

She sniffled, entombed in grief. "Taking care of myself is something I'm good at."

15

Interviews with the Last Dog in America

On the street a Toyota, nosing snug up against his rear bumper, had blocked the GMC. A scant two feet of play.

"Damn yo-yo!" Fontana's vehemence surprised himself and aroused the dog.

After he'd grappled with the wheel five minutes and realized he had not freed the truck, he jammed it into reverse and let the clutch in with a jerk. Pedestrians on both sides of the street gaped. The sheet metal on the Toyota let out a squawk.

He climbed out, smiled, nodded at the citizenry, penciled a note on a piece of stationery from his notebook, and slipped it under a wiper blade on the Toyota. The grille, one headlight, and one fender had been re-formed. When he looked up the spectators had dispersed, satisfied he'd left his name and phone number. "To whom it may concern. Next time you block me in I'll tear you limb from limb and dump you and your gas-saver into the bay. You got off lucky. Signed, a crippled grandmother."

On Broadway Fontana found a service station, gassed the truck, slopped cool water into a bowl, then scooted it into the cargo space in back. The dog vaulted the backseat and lapped rhythmically.

Farther up Broadway he turned into the lot at Dick's Drive-In, parked the unwieldly GMC, and let the dog oil hubcaps. In Dick's he spoke to a reedy, blue-eyed girl working behind the counter at what must have been her first job.

"Dick's Deluxe, a root beer, and eight hamburgers."

"Thatforhereortogo?"

Fontana clambered into the truck, brushed the sniffing animal away, and tipped the end of the bench seat forward on the far side by the passenger door. He laid out a sheet of wrapping paper and began dumping meat patties onto the wrapper. The dog only looked at him.

"Eat, Booger." Nothing. Perhaps he was waiting for Mac to say grace.

"Satan. Eat."

As if pricked by a bee, the dog lurched into action, tore into the hill of beef. Mac could hose the floorboards later.

One leg dangling out the door, Mac sat and chewed his Deluxe, gazed out at the evening troops on the sidewalk. Two leather-clad men strolled by, clasping hands. Directly behind followed two women in denim and paisley, lovers also. Much had changed in the twenty years since he'd hacked a cab through these streets.

He realized his meeting with April had been a bizarre transaction from beginning to end. He had blown it. He never should have taken up the badge.

"What do you think, Booger? April and Mo stumbling around at the cabin this morning? She tells me Zajac was conducting an investigation into Chief Crews, that he thought Crews and Ring were into something suspicious. I don't know whether to believe her. She was hiding something. Had that feeling the whole time I was there. Yeah, I should have come right out and told her Zajac had been offed. But she was hiding something. Even after all our talking and crying she was hiding something."

Two teenage girls walked through the parking lot and got into a Subaru. They noticed he was talking to himself.

"It's the dog," Fontana said to them, grinning. "Name's Booger. A talking dog." The dog looked up for a moment, espied the girls, licked his chops, and went back to business. "I'm teaching him Esperanto."

The girls didn't know whether to laugh or burn rubber. They did both, neither very convincingly.

"Booger. So what do you think about this Zajac character? Moved up into the woods, so he couldn't be all bad. Big strapping firefighter. So, what's going on here? He had a fire. Went hooly-gooly. Started thinking people were following him. Began some sort of investigation. Got suspended; suspended by the guy he was trying to expose. Then there was this morning. April's little disappearing act. Maybe she just wanted me to find the body. Booger, are you listening?"

The dog continued scarfing up hamburgers.

It was a '66 Mustang, primer gray and burning oil, which was why Mac noticed it. Awash in neon, the area was bright enough that when the man turned his head, Fontana got a glimpse of his profile.

Pock-marked. Bug-eyed. Tall. Erect, as though he had a steel rod down his neck. Tough-looking. The sort who collected beer bottles so he could break them in a sandbox. He was impressive, even from a distance.

The Mustang parked on the street but the driver didn't get out. The lot had had spots but he'd parked on the street after going through the lot twice.

On an impulse Mac went back for two blackberry sundaes. The dog slurped his on the sidewalk outside.

Fontana was beyond Bellevue on I-90 before he knew for certain the Mustang was tailing him. It lagged far enough back so that all he could see was the occasional shot of its headlights and low-slung silhouette mingling among the other cars. They were the only two vehicles on the road doing the speed limit. With trouble brewing, he wished now that he had a weapon.

Following Bill Kite's instructions, he took the Issaquah

exit and wended his way through the boxy new houses ricked up along Lake Sammamish. Years ago it had been all woods and trees. From the highway the ticky-tacky aspects of the development disgraced the countryside. A yuppy ghetto where hucksters got rich peddling Cuisinarts and aerobic dance classes door to door.

Bill Kite lived near the lake. His lot, not yet planted in sod, was child-packed dirt. Plastic milk bottles dotted the yard to keep stray dogs off. The curtains in the kids' rooms were sheets. Two children's bicycles were chained to the iron railing on a front porch. Kite hadn't saved up enough cash to live up to community standards quite yet, but there were other nearby houses in the same state. Young couples stretching their budgets.

Mac thumbed the buzzer and scanned the street for the Mustang, but his seedy GMC was the only warm vehicle in sight.

"Bill Kite?"

"Must be Sheriff Fontana. Come on in. Excuse the mess, but the wife's been working overtime all week and I'm afraid I can't handle it all myself." He grinned sheepishly. He was the shade of rich chocolate, and his voice had that rumbling quality of a soul singer, deep, stentorian. Authority might have come naturally with such an instrument, but something or someone had drummed the authority out of him.

Kite led him past a room in which three small children were clustered around a television.

The living room was better furnished than the outside of the house hinted. The place smelled new; lumber, carpets, paint. Fontana sat on a davenport.

Bill Kite had friendly yet troubled eyes. Slender and wiry, he had a narrow head and a mustache that might have been a paste-on, along with a tiny matching triangle of untrimmed whiskers below his lower lip. Had he been dressed in a starched white shirt and a black frock coat, he could have passed for an old-fashioned fundamentalist Baptist preacher.

In the dark room, his brilliant teeth looked almost fluorescent.

"How long you been in?" Fontana asked when Kite had seated himself in an armchair and turned up the lamp.

"Two years. Well, almost. I guess you came to talk about Zajac? I almost have two years. It'll be two in December. Steve Zajac? That's what I thought you said this afternoon."

"Yeah."

"I don't, uh, really know him that well."

"Understand you went to a fire with him last spring. Some kids got killed?"

Kite cleared the phlegm from his throat and stared at the carpet. Fontana checked the street again through a chink in the curtains. Kite skated his palms to and fro over the padded edge of his easy chair, blotting up perspiration.

"You like it out here?"

"Issaquah? It's got its good points. We've only been here six months. Trouble is, to make the house payments Sheila had to go back to full-time. Don't know if it's worth the trade-off. Ya know?"

"I know."

"With my shift, I'm home a lot. But it hurts Sheila to miss out on so many things with the kids. Still, uh, it was her idea. She was raised in the CD and could hardly wait to get out of there. CD's the Central District, if you don't know Seattle."

"The south end of Capitol Hill."

"Sheila calls it the sorry side of town. I guess you wanna hear about that fire we had. See, the trouble is, I have a sticky time talking about it."

"It's important or I wouldn't ask."

"Zajac do something? That why you're here?" It had been on the radio, but apparently Kite hadn't tuned in.

"You know he was suspended from the department?"

"I know. I was there that morning. Funny. Both those fires I was there. The one last spring. And the one where he

102

got suspended. He used to make jokes I was bad luck for him. But then, I thought maybe he was bad luck for me."

"What happened last spring, Bill?"

"I'll tell you about it because you're asking and you're a sheriff and all. But it won't be easy."

"Take your time."

"Smoke. We saw this heavy black smoke and drove out there to investigate. We were in the extra car, s'posed to be doing night hotels. We were mostly done, so Zajac drives us out to Twenty-sixes to talk to this friend of his about fishin'. We're about four miles from where we're s'posed to be. He thought it was funny 'cause I was so nervous. Bein' new and all, I try to just do my job and not take any chances. Know what I mean?"

"That's usually the best way."

"Zajac don't think like that. Anyways, we're there talkin' to this guy at Twenty-sixes and we spot this smoke off in the distance. Dirty black stuff. Rising fast like a hot fire. So we took off to investigate. It's this apartment house, the Eldorado Arms, just outside the city going like a five-cent firecracker. Zajac, he's a funny dude. Told me a joke on the way. They never dispatched us, but we were running red lights and siren, illegal as hell, and he tells me this joke. Know how to make a cat bark?"

"Pour gasoline on him, light a match. Woof. It's been around a while."

"You heard it, huh? So I was laughing when we got there and there's some ladies runnin' around in the lot sayin' there's kids trapped upstairs. Steve got on the horn and told the dispatcher we were outside the city but they'd better send somethin' real quick. You could see their heads as these two kids were runnin' around under the windows in the apartment. It made me sick in my stomach, you know?

"We put our coats and helmets on and ran around to where the stairs were, but we couldn't get in. Steve burned himself good gettin' halfway up the stairs, but then he hadda come back down. Gutsy guy. They always said you weren't gonna find a firefighter in the city any better than Zajac. Been to a couple of good flame-ups with him now, and I believe it."

The kids started a commotion in the other room. Kite excused himself, got up, and tended to it. He returned three minutes later, a bottle of Jack Daniel's in one hand, a pair of cut-glass tumblers in the other.

"Care for a drink?"

"I'm driving," Fontana said, but he was thinking about the Mustang that had been following him.

"Mind if I have one? Where was I?"

"You called for help. You couldn't get inside."

"You have all these ideas about what firefighting is going to be all about, then when you get in, it's actually—for the most part—not that big a deal. The house is on fire. You get your equipment and run in. It's a matter of doing it, and doing it enough times that you get smooth at it. Hell, after you've done it a couple of times, what you're scared of isn't the fire. You're scared of screwing up in front of everybody. Or maybe some freak accident. Well, Zajac was smoother than any of us. He got probably twenty feet farther up those stairs than I did. And *I* got burned.

"We went back and he got on the radio again. The dispatcher told him flat out they weren't sending anybody. Persons trapped, Zajac said. The dispatcher said the county was sending and the county could handle it. We told them the county wasn't anywhere around. Didn't make no difference. The dispatcher wasn't going to send. Zajac swore on the radio. It was the first time I ever heard anybody do that. I like to died standing out there watching that place go up."

"I know you won't believe this, but I think I can imagine," said Fontana.

"So did Zajac. We both did. Like to died."

16

Crispy Critters

FROM THE OTHER END of the house children's giggles pierced the muggy stillness.

"So when did the county show up?"

"Oh, they got there. Just seems like forever when nothing's being done and you're standin' with your thumb up your . . . ear. When we couldn't fight our way up the stairs, we went back round to the front. The trouble was, we couldn't see their heads bobbing in the window anymore."

It grew quiet as Kite unscrewed the cap on the Jack Daniel's, poured himself a couple of fingers, and gulped.

"When County finally showed, we went into the unit with the first-in guys. That was really a mistake. Never saw anybody burned before. Killed me, man. Really slayed me. Just a few minutes before they'd been running around under the windows. It was awful."

"How'd Zajac take it?"

"He was the one found 'em. Couldn't tell at first. Never said a word. He stood around for a while. Then, after it was over, we packed up and he drove to the Fire Alarm Center. Under the Space Needle. He wouldn't tell me where we were going, and it was kinda scary 'cause Chief Crews was calling us on the radio sayin' we were supposed to meet him at Tens.

'Cept Steve wasn't going to Tens. He parked in the lot behind the FAC, walked inside, and about tore Lieutenant Frazier's head off. Took three of us to pull him off. Spilled coffee all over the console and everything."

"He figured the lieutenant in the Fire Alarm Center was responsible for not sending help?"

"And the thing was, Twenty-sixes could have been there inside of two minutes. It was a cryin' shame."

"What happened?"

"Zajac's a big dude. The only reason we dragged him off Frazier was Frazier yelled real quick that he'd wanted to send help, that Chief Crews had been there and wouldn't let him."

"So where were the county units all this time?" The momentum of the tragedy and of Kite's reliving it was beginning to affect Fontana. He'd seen his share of dead children.

"County had a deal on the freeway. They were tied up six ways from Sunday. Don't think it was anyone's fault, really. But Zajac did. Hoo, he was hot. He went straight from the FAC to Tens and 'bout got into a fistfight with Crews. Zajac called him every name in the book. Murderer. Motherfucker. You name it. It's a wonder they didn't start throwing fists."

"How did Crews react?"

"He told Steve to cool off. What else could he do? But everybody up there heard. Everybody on Ladder One, Engine 10, the whole shitteree. I thought Crews was going to suspend him then and there."

"So what happened?"

"After Zajac shot his wad and Crews was done yelling back at him, Steve drove me back to Sixes. I never felt that bad. Not about anything. Not even when my mother died. I shouldn't say that, but there was something . . . I don't know . . . inevitable about my mother. She had the big C. Those kids . . . we were so close to saving them."

"You were there at this other fire, where he got suspended?"

"It was just a couple weeks ago at Twenty-sixes. I got detailed there one shift. Was a bunch of arson fires in the area. Piddly things. We had eight or ten runs during the day. Then about four in the morning we got the big one. Twenty-sixes was first in. Zajac said on the way out there, this is an arson, watch your butt. Don't ask me how he knew.

"Told me not to go inside, that he thought the place was booby-trapped. It was a vacant house down in South Park, and we were there a long time before help came and I heard these voices in the back of the building. Later it turned out to be a tape recording the arsonist left. Sounded just like kids."

"Seems like an awfully elaborate trap."

"They were trying to hurt somebody."

"That sort of thing common in Seattle?"

"Never had it before. Steve told me to just hit it from the doorway. That's not how we usually fight fires in Seattle. We usually crawl right to the seat. We get done with a fire and find water on the floor, we screwed up. We lay on just enough to black out the fire, no more, no less."

"You heard voices?"

"I was amped. I went in blind and dropped into a hole somebody sawed in the floor. Bottom of the hole was rigged up with these open cans of gasoline. Rigged up so when I moved around they spilled. I thought I was a dead man. I can still hear the ripping. Know how a flammable liquid fire sounds? Sure you don't want a hit?" He hoisted the Jack Daniel's and sloshed the liquid around in the bottle. Fontana shook his head. Kite poured himself another drink, sipped, and went glassy-eyed waiting for it to hit his bloodstream.

"Steve saved my bacon. He stood up there and took a beating just holding a good fog pattern on me. He was the only thing that saved me. Finally some other units got in there and they flooded the place. I'm tellin' you, I was scared."

Fontana crossed his legs, fiddled with the hem of his jeans, and said, "I see you got burned."

"Ears, back of my neck, and up both wrists." He pulled his sleeves up and displayed forearms creased with scar tissue, the evidence adding to the alchemy of his story. "Not bad really. Considering what it could have been. I'll be back to work in another couple'a shifts."

"So how'd he get suspended? Zajac."

Kite smiled a mirthless smile. "I'm still trying to figure that one out. Sometimes a chief'll have a skull session after a fire—ya know, critiquing it so we can all see what we could have done better. Chief Crews gave one right then and there. Said it was the sloppiest piece of work he'd ever seen. Ever. I haven't been to that many fires, but I didn't think so. Neither did anybody else. Anyway, Zajac kinda took issue with the chief. Said the chief was fulla shit. Said he was a crook, too. That's when Crews flat out suspended him. Called Zajac a two-twenty.

"So Zajac just walked off. He turned his back on Crews and started walking up this deserted street about six on a Sunday morning. Crews yelled. Yelled so hard I thought he was going to burst a blood vessel. A couple minutes later the aid unit took me up to the hospital and we stopped and picked up Zajac, took him back to Twenty-sixes so he could get his truck."

"What'd he say?"

"Zajac? Nothin'. But you could tell gettin' suspended really hit him. None of us in the aid car said a word."

"Catch the guy torched the house?"

"Nobody ever did."

"Zajac ever talk to you about that first fire? The one last spring?"

"It was one of those things I guess neither one of us wanted to bring up."

Fontana stood. "Thanks for your time. You think of something else that might be pertinent, give me a call in Staircase at the sheriff's office "

"Sure."

"And good luck with the burns."

"They ain't much."

Despite Kite's earlier protest that the house was a mess, Fontana noted it was spotless.

Issaquah. Ten years before it had been a whistle-stop on the way to the Cascades, and now you could walk for miles on rooftops. The builders were massing for one final assault at the summit, paving, clear-cutting, slapping up house after house—inebriated Monopoly players who didn't know when to quit. Fontana didn't know what to say about it. After all, people had to have a place to live. Maybe he should have moved to Australia.

Wending up through the dark wooded hills on I-90, he spotted a pair of headlights pacing him. He exited the freeway at Staircase and headed north the half mile to town. He pushed the cigarette lighter in. The headlights were still there.

Bouncing over the railroad tracks on the outskirts of town, he hooked a right, pushed his headlight button to Off, hooked another right, then shot behind Quiggly's Pharmacy, did a doughnut in the parking lot, and emerged on Main Street again.

He found himself on the rear bumper of a gray Mustang.

One occupant.

Male.

The Mustang was cruising at five miles an hour, the driver swiveling his head from side to side as if trying to pick up a hooker on the Strip. Except there were no prostitutes in Staircase.

Mac flipped the headlights on, tromped the high-beam button, and blinded the driver with his brights.

Lurching around in front of the Mustang, he cut the Ford off. He killed the engine, vaulted out of the GMC, sprinted to the driver's door, and yanked it open. Instinct drugged him at times like this, and it was one reason he'd balked at pinning on another badge. He didn't trust instinct.

The Mustang's driver gripped a revolver in his right hand. He nearly tumbled out, hadn't been expecting this.

When he'd regained his balance, the driver pointed the gun at Fontana's brisket and unwrapped a steely grin.

17

Squirrel with a Cigar

SUCKING NIGHT AIR, the man's mouth gaped. His eyes were flat and cold. He didn't bother to wait for Fontana's pitch. The gun in his fist didn't waver a millimeter. His voice was a doleful monotone.

"Want somethin', buddy?"

"You've been following me," Fontana said, making certain the badge on his jacket was visible, wondering whether it was a shield or a target.

"Like hell."

"You followed me, all right. Clear from town."

"What you talkin' about? You nuts?"

Fontana held the surprise behind his back, having lit the stick's fuse against the glowing cigarette lighter inside the GMC. He figured if he was wrong about this Dugan he could snuff it between two spit-slicked fingers.

A smoke-generating device, it was a spare from the trunkful they lit off when drilling the Staircase volunteers. Toss it into a vacant house and watch it pollute like a 211 in a tire factory. Resembled a sawed-off stick of dynamite in its red casing. It sizzled a bitter whistling noise just before the heavy smoke blotted out hell and heaven and everything in between.

Fontana brought it around in front of himself and casually lobbed it into the backseat of the Mustang. A hundred thousand cubic feet of the filthiest smoke imaginable.

"What's that?" The fuse was still whistling.

"You're aiming a gun at my navel."

"What was that?" The driver half twisted in his seat.

"A squirrel with a cigar."

"You threw somethin' . . ." His voice refused to accept inflections just as a waxed surface refused paint.

There was a poof, and the smoke began rolling out of the backseat and engulfed the man's head. Even Fontana's position at the half-open door became untenable.

"Police," Mac said, bruskly slamming the door on the man as he tried to spill out of the ramshackle Ford.

The door frame thunked the man's skull. Mac slammed it again on his hand. The jolt of pain didn't elicit a sound from the man. Barking inside the GMC, the dog was pirouetting in circles.

The door business took less than four seconds. Fontana had learned the hard way that the faster you moved in these situations, the better.

"Next time you point a gun at me, the barrel had better be hot before I see it."

Fontana winged the door open again and a blast of chemical smoke whooshed out. He sliced the heel of his right hand at the man's throat. The driver let out a rattle and jackknifed facedown onto the steering column. The horn blatted. The pistol clunked to the floor of the car.

Imprisoning the driver's thumb in his fist, Fontana cranked his arm behind his back, pulled him out of the car, manhandled him to the front and away from the smoke, then slammed his face against the hood. Black billows continued to puff from the open door.

Only a few people were on the small-town main street,

and nobody but a trio of kids on bikes paid attention to the skit. Wrenching the man's arm behind his back, Fontana said, "Answers, Dugan. Fast."

"I want a lawyer," the man gasped. Splashes of red sluiced onto the hood. "I want a lawyer."

"And I want a fairy godmother with big tits."

"You can't do this."

"Watch carefully." Fontana tangled his fingers in a skein of greasy hair and dribbled the man's face on the hood.

"Okay, okay, okay," he said, his voice remarkably flat and unruffled. There had been something empty in his stonelike eyes all along, as if his face had been injected with a massive dose of Novocain. "Dead from the neck up" was hackneyed slang, but in this case reasonably accurate.

"I thought you was this asshole owed me money. Punk looks just like you owes me a couple'a grand. I thought you was him. That's all."

"You on dope?"

"Never use it."

"What is the guy's name? Owes you money."

"Watson. Jerome Watson. Looks just like you. Spittin' image. I swear."

"And I raise buttercups for my grandma."

"Don't you believe nothin'?"

"This guy also wearing a badge?"

"Hell, Jerome's loco. He could be wearin' anything. I was going to follow you home and find out for sure. Then I was going to get a lawyer. I swear."

"You pulled a gun on me."

"Son of a bitch. You gonna stop twisting before you break somethin', or what?"

"Keep talking."

"Jerome. I swear. The gun? I was only layin' it on the seat so you couldn't accuse me of keeping a concealed weapon. Sucker ain't even loaded."

"Call a lawyer, my eye. You're sweating like a flea trying to pass a marble."

"Okay. I was gonna get my money back tonight. Scare the shit out of him and take it. So what? You ain't Jerome. What do you care?"

Frisking him one-handed, Fontana pulled a series of items from his pockets: a flattened wallet, a pair of sunglasses, a bag of marijuana, some unmarked pills, and a smudged sheaf of dog-eared pornographic pictures. He flipped the wallet open, dropping papers, cards, money, and flotsam onto the street. "Jesus, man. That's my shit."

"It doesn't have legs. Don't worry about it."

Still valid, the driver's license had been issued by the Washington State Patrol. The name was Maxwell Pontius Draper. The winky-eyed photo fit the prisoner. He resided in north Seattle and was forty years old, same as Fontana.

In the wallet Fontana found a business card for Dexter Fuel Service, addressed off Airport Way South in Seattle. Draper's name was engraved on it in blue script.

"You know, pal," Draper hissed, "you got a real problem. You ain't carryin'. Noticed that in Seattle. No piece on ya."

"Dick's Drive-In. Went through the lot twice, then parked on the street. You should have that fine vehicle of yours taken in for a ring job. Some of us need to breathe this air."

"You should talk, you and your cigar-smoking squirrels. You picked me up there? Not bad. Mosta you cops got memories about as long as your doodles."

"I'm not mosta you cops."

"You got a real problem all the same, fella."

"Explain it to me."

Bruised and bleeding, brow lumped, Draper was spread-eagled, left arm folded unnaturally behind his back almost to the nape of his neck. He was helpless and in pain, yet his voice remained flat as a zombie's.

114

"Answer me this, little buddy. Tell me. You ain't got a gun. I'm a head taller, an easy thirty pounds huskier. You ain't got cuffs or I'd be in 'em by now. How you going to let me go without gettin' your head stove in? Still got that gun spotted in the car? Ten to one you can't get to it before I stomp you."

"Thought you said it wasn't loaded."

"Maybe I lied. Why don't you go see?"

Mac let go of Draper's arm.

Before Draper could rub the circulation back into it, Mac booted him in the crotch.

Grunting loudly, Draper collapsed onto the hood, then slowly oozed into a heap. Wrapping himself around as much clean air as he could, Fontana stepped past Draper's crumpled form and picked up the gun from inside the Mustang. A High Standard .22 Magnum. Nine shots. It was a single-action cowboy type. He flipped the loading gate open and worked the cylinder. Loaded.

Draper rolled over onto his face, propped himself on hands and knees, and ejected a gob of foamy spittle onto the ground. His disheveled hair was greasy and thin. Fontana watched him slowly pick up the items from his wallet, the porno, then watched him chin himself on the side of the fender, pulling himself to his feet.

"You ain't like no cop I been around."

"Lot of people tell me that."

"Where you from? Not here."

"Back East."

Looking him up and down, Draper averted his pale eyes, growled, and spat again. "They all like you back there?"

"Every man jack. Don't like being followed. Not by anybody. Don't like having guns pulled. And I don't believe this yarn about some guy named Jerome Watson owing you money." He shoved Draper's chest, propelling him toward

115

the GMC. When they got there he made him lie facedown in the street. Draper obliged reluctantly.

Fontana switched on the radio and called the dispatcher, had her patch him to County. He explained his problem, had them run a check. Draper's name came back clean. No wants. No warrants.

"Get up. Confiscating your driver's license and gun. You check out, I'll mail 'em to you. Don't check out, you'll be hearing from me."

"You just checked me."

"Not hardly."

"My car's on fire. I can't go anywhere."

"It's just smoke. It'll clear."

"I might come back to this oil slick of a town sometime," Draper said, staggering. Thick spirals of black smoke rose over the facade of Tintale's Hardware and Sundries. "Yeah, I'll be back."

Coughing, Draper slid into the seat, squinted through the windshield, turned the engine over and reversed to the center of the street, then drove away slowly, trailing plumes of smoke. He was driving one-handed. His door wasn't closed completely. Fontana had broken his hand.

"Should have confiscated that damn Mustang," Fontana muttered to himself. "Nuisance without a ring job."

He studied the driver's license. Max Draper. Six foot five inches. A hundred eighty-five pounds. Skinny. He went over the man's features one by one, imprinting them in his memory. He might need to describe him. Might see him in five years in a supermarket. He wanted to recall it all, down to the length of his grit-blackened fingernails. Brown hair that looked as if it'd been tacked down by a rainstorm. Pale, almost colorless, eyes that belonged on an albino, emotionless, floating in that gaunt, hollow-cheeked, acne-scarred face. Thick, lowering brows three shades darker than his hair Novocain face.

Had their roles been reversed, Fontana wouldn't have fared as well as Draper, wouldn't have walked off with a broken hand, lumped skull, and a car full of smoke. Max Draper had the air of a man who'd dished out plenty of punishment.

Fontana wouldn't have walked off at all.

18

Iron Men and Wooden Ladders

MAC'S RENTED TWO-BEDROOM home was situated on the river in a greenbelt on the north side of the town. After he parked the GMC under the trees, Fontana freed the German shepherd. "Growl at Brendan and you're a throw rug for the workshop."

But the dog, remaining docile as a fresh lobotomy, let Brendan crawl all over him.

"We keeping him, Mac?" Brendan leaped into his father's arms. Fontana noticed his arm muscles were still twitching from his encounter with Draper. "Keeping him, Mac? Mac?"

"For tonight."

Veiled by the screen door, Mrs. Gilliam doted on boy and father. Brendan bounded around the corner of the house after the dog.

"Don't let him pee on your leg, Brendan."

"Mac," chided Mrs. Gilliam, her words cloaked in a faded brogue. "You shouldn't talk to the boy like that."

Mary Gilliam's unkempt hair and buffed-dumpling cheeks shone in the doorway. As usual, her arms were weighted down with back issues of *True Detective* and *Modern Crimes*. In her early seventies, her ambition in life was to become a published pulp scribbler. She studied prospective markets diligently, pored over grisly murder stories and perverse love triangles, ooed and ahhed over rape-murders and shallow graves. She'd left a manuscript at his place once. A howler. It was titled *The Mad Mailman of Mississippi and the Missing Madam.*

"It's all around town," she said. "You being sheriff and finding that fireman up by the mountain."

"Figured it would be."

The dog and the boy raced back around the house, merrily circling each other.

"Mayor Mo swung past this forenoon blaspheming because you refuse to install a phone. Electric can opener, power mower, TV, dishwasher. A man needs those things. No car. It doesn't hardly seem civilized. Mo told me you were to be at a special town council meeting tonight at eight. Something about confirming you as interim sheriff. There's going to be a debate."

"I'm not much on debates."

"She seemed adamant about you attending. I'd be happy to fix you some victuals and watch Brendan a while longer."

"You go home now."

Clutching the baby-sitting money and her magazines, she followed the skittery beam of a flashlight and foraged through the darkened yard toward her house a hundred yards downriver. The path through the pines was only just wider than she was. "Mary Gilliam," Mac yelled. "You weren't so damn sexy I'd marry you."

"Proposal accepted."

"Don't think my ticker could stand up to it."

"Live dangerous, why don't you?"

Inside, Mac and Brendan scrounged around the kitchen for scraps to feed the dog. "Nice day at school?" Fontana asked.

"Mrs. Gilliam says you're the new sheriff." Brendan had his mother's wet-button eyes, and they shone when he was excited.

"For a day or two."

"You going to have a gun, Mac? Can I shoot it? And that's our new dog? Freddy said he was a police dog. He speaks German."

"Haven't heard any German yet."

"I like him."

"I'd have ditched him tonight, but I wasn't up to dancing around the mulberry bush with our mayor."

Brendan fed the German shepherd a bowl of cold spaghetti, slid him a dish of water, and watched him bed down for the night on the porch. Mac made sure the boy washed afterward. In Brendan's bedroom they spent half an hour reading stories before Mac tucked him in and kissed him. "I love you, Brendan."

"Love you too, Mac."

Fontana was a lot less complacent about himself than he had been that morning, particularly after the way he'd treated Draper. He found the whole business irksome, unsportsmanlike, and a bit piggish. What made it even worse was that he wore it like a handmade suit. He hadn't handled the interview with April any better.

In the East he'd headed up an outfit so hard-nosed and foulmouthed, "Fuck you" was a euphemism, and grinding some Dugan's face into the street was done without a thought. He had been brilliant at ferreting out what he needed to know; and a murderous mentality, the implication of violence, had been a small but prized tool in his arsenal. The trouble was he liked it.

After Linda had the accident, things changed. She had never been in favor of his policing activities, had continually urged him to transfer back into the company and ride an engine. Life had a way of unraveling before you could figure out what it was all about.

Linda's crash happened during the trial.

Then the vacation to the Evergreen State to visit relatives

and the decision to move to Staircase. Dump the old life. Recant and revamp.

No more blindsiding suspects.

No more eighteen-hour days.

And now Steven Paul Zajac.

Paranoid? Haunted by fires past? Dead children? He wished he hadn't seen any of it, that he'd never met Mayor Mo. Life wasn't fair.

He slid an LP of Johann Strauss waltzes down the spindle of the stereo and stretched out on his bed. Next to the pillow lay a copy of *The Searchers* by Alan LeMay, which he was reading for the second time in as many years.

It was good to be home.

It was good to know his boy was asleep in the neighboring room. Good to hear the quiet shushing of the river outside his window, to inhale the mountain breeze whimpering through the room from the cracked open window. Tomorrow, if his mule-headed conscience allowed, perhaps he'd cancel this business. Let the mayor take back that silly badge and overblown coat. He would get rid of the dog, too. Benumbed by Strauss melodies, he drifted off.

The bell hit.

He'd only been in a few years.

It was his first shift driving at night. A hasty glimpse of his watch as he scrambled into his bunkers told him it was five till three. The dim lighting in the station blinked on automatically with the alerter. Rain hammered the roof, then, a minute later, thrummed the ceiling of the cab, beat on the hood. He could barely see through the laboring windshield wipers. The old Macks took brute force to steer. Regular drivers grew Popeye forearms. Iron men and wooden ladders. Nowadays, the men were wooden, the ladders aluminum.

They skidded through the first corner. Fortunately there wasn't anything on the streets except an occasional gypsy cab.

They skated on oily pavement through their second corner. The captain sitting beside him muttered.

It was a car/pole accident they'd been dispatched to, actually a pickup truck into a massive utility pole. They couldn't quite puzzle out how it had happened. No witnesses. Must have been the rain.

Snakes of steam fizzed from the grille.

The windshield was cracked in the calligraphy of death. A lone occupant slouched behind the wheel.

The factory had installed a steel rim around the sun visor. On impact the visor must have dropped down just as the man's head whipped forward. Chopped him clean off across the tops of the eyes.

The piece of head was laying there beside him on the seat like something he was hauling home from the market. Firefighters joked about everything. Later one joked in a falsetto, "By the way, dear, bring home half a skull, would you? For the stew."

They waited an hour in the driving rain, the engine's headlights illumining the corpse silhouette. Curlicues of steam rose out of the silhouette's flat skull. Fontana would turn away, then mesmerized, look again, hating himself for it.

By the time the coroner showed, it had been indelibly imprinted into his memory. He kept thinking it was his brother. His brother had died a year earlier driving the same model truck.

It became a dream, the repeated dream almost identical to the incident. But this night's dream had its own frills.

The other firefighters had busied themselves somewhere and the decapitated man in the truck didn't budge. Wearing full dingy yellow bunkers, she jog-trotted up to the sideboard of the Mack, stepped up, and rapped on his window. He rolled the window down and sheets of rain spilled into his lap. "Come with me," she beckoned in an unctuous laudanum voice. "Come with me."

Unbuttoning the heavy steel clasps of the bunking coat,

she stepped down off the sideboard. Beneath, she was naked. She turned and glided to a nearby building.

"Come with me."

The others were gone. He had time. Inside the building he found her huddled on a mattress under the bunking clothes. Humidity from the rain-spattered material ebbed upward. Not even the red hair was visible above the turnout clothes. She had hidden herself completely.

He shrugged off his dull red suspenders, squirmed out of the sweatshirt he wore at night, and dropped his bunking pants, exposing himself. He stepped forward, dropped to the mattress on his knees. Slowly, he pulled the bunking coat off the body.

The redhead was gone.

It was his brother, his skull cleaved, headless from the eyes up.

He grasped for Mac.

He awoke in a tangle of wet sheets, unsure whether he'd made any noise. Shivering, he repositioned himself in the bed and tried to calm his nerves.

It had taken years after that alarm for the decapitated drunk to stop plaguing his nights. Gradually, other horrors superseded the episode. And now, here it was again, sired by the day's events.

The naked woman had never been in the dream before, but he recognized her. No two ways about it.

Mac squandered the rest of the night musing over Zajac's murder. He had a million theories, and not one carried him even a step beyond the facts. Except that Max Draper should have been handcuffed and pitched into a cell. His first major mistake.

In the morning Mac and Brendan got into the GMC.

"I might be a bit late again," Mac said, after they'd driven to the sheriff's office behind the fire station.

"Do ya have to?"

"Afraid so. Mrs. Gilliam'll be around. I've talked to her."

Later, Fontana was comfortably ensconced in the padded rolling chair at the sheriff's desk waiting for a county cop to return his calls when Maureen Costigan's Porsche came to a halt on the street in front. She wore a long skirt, creamy blouse, and sweater. She'd molded and sprayed her hair into something vaguely modern.

Without knocking, she opened the door and marched into the office. She straddled the inside mat and dismembered Mac with a look. Her face was flushed.

"Where the hell were you last night?"

"Looking good, Mo."

"You look like hell. We had a meeting. You were supposed to be there. Goddammit, if you'd only be civilized like the rest of us you could go far in this world, Mac. If you followed some rules once in a while you could be sheriff, work your way up, get another job in a big city somewhere."

"Had a job in a big city somewhere."

"We buzzed your beeper all night."

"I'll bet that was fun. Might as well pick up the dog as long as you're here."

"You want to be sheriff so bad, he's yours. I have Freud, my chow. I don't need that beast running around scaring the crap out of her. Maybe I'm going to give up this mayor business. It isn't worth it."

"I'm expecting a call, Mo. Sit down. I've got mush or cornflakes in the beanery. Coffee, too. The dog took cornflakes."

"Damn you, Mac. He eats Hill's Science Diet."

She sat down across from him, sat so hard she shook. She glanced down at the newspaper on his desk. *"New York Times?* I wondered how you got your news. You are not going to be the sheriff. I want you to give up this silly business."

"Don't see as you have much say at this point. Studied the civil service rules, Mo. And so did you or you wouldn't have convened that phony meeting last night. Didn't have a quorum. Mrs. Petty is out of state. Sundergast's mother died and he's in Ellensburg trying to overturn the will."

"I heard a nasty rumor you set fire to some poor man's car on Main Street last night."

"Termites in the upholstery. Thought it might flush them."

"You did it? Good Lord. I heard you dragged him out of his car, set fire to it, and pulled a gun on the man. Some witnesses even said you beat him. You do know about the Constitution?"

"Settle down, Mo. You're hopping around like a tick on a tambourine."

"You are fired, Mac. F-i-r-e-d."

He displayed his front teeth. "Kiss off." Mo Costigan stood up, bumping over her chair with a clatter. "You insolent—"

"Don't get so riled. I'm going to settle this one little matter and then the badge is yours. Then you can appoint Claude for all I care." Claude Pettigrew was the town space case, of times observed directing traffic between the railroad tracks and the library. "It's not as if you're mayor of someplace big or I'm stealing the sheriff's job from someplace important—Tacoma, for instance."

"That supposed to be funny?"

He shrugged.

When she stepped through the thigh-high office barricade, he could hear the material of her skirt rasping against the grain of the wood.

"When I appointed you I had no idea you would behave like this." She moved on him, grasping the edge of his desk, lifting angrily. It was lighter than she thought. What she did, she lifted the desk and dumped a carton of milk, a couple of half-full cereal bowls, and a cube of margarine into his lap, along with several slabs of newspaper. He rescued the financial section. "Shit," she said. "Now look what I've done. You make me so mad." Even so, capsizing the desk seemed to settle her down enough so she could walk out without spitting on the floor.

"Have a nice day, Mo." Outside, the Porsche's radials shrieked. Her temper was almost as bad as his. He had only just straightened up after her when County phoned.

"Fontana."

"Charles Dummelow here. Still intent on being sheriff?"

"Just had the mayor's confirmation ceremony."

"I understand from your phone message you had a run-in with somebody named Max Draper last evening. What happened?"

Fontana told him, keeping it short, sweetening it, weeding out the gun, the blood, and the smoke bomb.

Dummelow said, "You at the office?"

"Yep."

"Be there in thirty minutes."

19

Ms. Grimm

"WE'VE BEEN WATCHING that Draper bird for years," Charles Dummelow said. "He's a known arsonist. And he's into some other rackets besides torching warehouses. Runs around with a gang. He's done some real hard time in Leavenworth."

"He's been sent up for arson?"

"As a kid. Never got any adult convictions. Eggs to helicopters, that's how he earns a living."

"Thought he worked for a fuel oil company."

"Don't let that fool you."

"Got any known confederates?"

"People you want to talk to are the county fire investigators. Maybe Seattle's team. So what did you dig up yesterday, Mac?"

Fontana kept it brief, making certain theory didn't eclipse fact. Fond of stroking his mustache on either side with thumb and forefinger, Dummelow had a habit of standing so as to make his paunch more noticeable. His red hair was thick and disheveled, and his corrugated face made him appear older than he was. His voice was resonant as a bass fiddle. The day before he had worn a wrinkled black raincoat over a sports jacket and a tacky tie that had yellow tigers printed on it. He wore the same outfit today, same tigers. The raincoat had been ironed, or more likely, he'd gone to a restaurant and absentmindedly walked off with somebody else's.

When Fontana finished, he asked Dummelow about the autopsy on Zajac. "Getting it today around noon. They generally perform them at Harborview in the morning. Tell you the truth, Fontana, I think you're out in left field. Maybe Zajac was investigating this fire. Maybe not. Maybe his girlfriend'll have something to say we want to hear. I doubt it. We found a pillowcase full of grass in his house. We're following the drug angle. He was dealing. Had to be. Lost his job. Looking for some quick cash. Got in with the wrong boys. Somebody rough decided to make an example of him. It happens."

"Grass isn't a big-ticket item anymore," Mac said. "People grow it in their planters. He was dealing, you'd have found something else. You called back East on me, didn't you?"

"What makes you say that?"

What made Mac think it was the chummy manner in which Dummelow had been treating him. It was the way cops treated you when they knew you were one of the fraternity. Mac said nothing.

"The mayor got all over my back yesterday afternoon," Dummelow admitted. "She said you had some skeletons in your closet. I decided to check it out firsthand. I got the skinny from your old department, then I got the rest of the skinny from some friends back there. You were good. Good enough they used to loan you out. I ain't never been loaned out. You had some sort of instinct comes along about once in a blue moon. I've seen 'em before. Seems like they're born to the work. Don't know. Get a guy, turns into the greatest violinist in the world, Isaac Stern or somebody . . . what if his folks were pipe fitters and he never got to pick up a fiddle?

"Maybe the Ruskies have the right idea. Line up all the little kids and give them aptitude tests, then channel them. Me, I 'spose if I had it to do over again I'd end up a schoolteacher, maybe an auto mechanic. What I'm trying to say is, you solved that Marrietta case in Milwaukee. They specialed you in and you cleaned it up. They think a lot of you in that town."

"Luck."

"I don't believe that. And neither do they back there. They told me they offered you a job when you quit yours."

"Twelve other people worked on the case."

"I heard somebody was torching a bum about once a week. Dousing him with flammable liquid and sparking him off. They had a couple of statements from poor old de-horns in the burn ward who didn't die right away. From the routes and the locations you figured out it had to be a bus driver. Even figured out which one. You have a gift. You've got my cooperation if I've got yours." Dummelow extended a hand pimpled across the knuckles in warts.

"Deal," said Mac, grasping his hand. "What about physical evidence up there at the cabin?"

"We got enough to keep the Goodwill busy for a year. But nothing meaningful. So far no bloodstains in the house. Several hundred miscellaneous fingerprints, but you know how that goes. They're no good unless we've got somebody to match them to. And even that only proves somebody was in the house, not that they were in the house the night he died and not that they killed him. The knife in his back was clean. One last thing, though. As a matter of course, we checked out Zajac's record. It stood to reason he wasn't going to still be in the fire department if he'd done anything serious. They give them the heave-ho after a felony conviction."

"And?"

"He got himself booked a couple of months ago—June—in Latitude 47, a restaurant on Lake Union. Took a swing at some guy. Not just any guy, either. Got a pencil?"

"Shoot."

"Name was Neil Attwood."

"Wait a minute."

"That's right. Of Attwood Towers fame. No big production. Zajac waltzed in, tossed down a few drinks, initiated a rumpus at Attwood's table, then took a poke at him. I can't tell from the reports if it was personal, or if Zajac was pie-eyed and just happened to pick on the wrong millionaire. The bodyguard threw him over a hip through a window. Gave him about twenty stitches in his ass. It went to court, but at the last minute Attwood dropped the charges. There you are."

"Attwood as rich as he seems?" Fontana asked.

"Scuttlebutt has it he's worth around three, three hundred and fifty mil, and going for broke. My brother-in-law's a contractor, keeps careful track. Attwood's his hero. Fairly young guy, too, Attwood is."

"Any idea where he'd be on a morning like this?"

"I think he's got a suite in the new towers. But I wouldn't waste my time. This drug angle looks like the thing. We've been getting some real stinkers out in this neck of the woods. Last May a pair of teenagers got their throats cut over a black-tar deal that went sour. Mother came home and found 'em that way. A hell of a deal."

"There was that autopsy report. I'm wondering how Zajac got his hands on it."

"I couldn't tell you. See the Browning automatic rifles in the bedroom? Eighteen-carat gold on a blued background. Beautiful work. Like to get me one before I retire." Dummelow fingered his mustache. "That mayor sweet on you?"

"She is, I'd hate to see her change her mind."

When Fontana walked Dummelow outside, Dummelow knotted up his face. "Jesus, Bounty's dog again?"

"Likes to hang around. I musta stepped in something."

The detective chuckled. "Well, I'm going out to the cabin again to take another look. Here's a key. Use this if you go. Don't remove anything without telling me."

"Thanks."

Alone, Fontana tossed Draper's gun into a drawer. He slid Draper's driver's license into a shirt pocket, then used the phone to track down Neil Attwood at the Towers. The

Teflon-coated voice on the switchboard at the other end wouldn't plug him through.

Outside when he tried to pull out of the parking spot, the scrofulous dog blocked the Carryall. He inched the truck forward, but the dog refused to move. Fontana shut the engine off, got out. The dog only looked at him, twisting his head. "You need a psychiatrist, you know that, Booger?" They stared at each other, Mac seething, the dog, head bowed, ears flat back, the picture of dejected humiliation.

"Damn it all to hell," said Mac, jerking the door open. Head lowered, the dog scampered past him into the truck. "Hurry up before I change my mind. And quit looking at me like that."

From a distance, the Attwood Towers were impressive. Closer, the noise and the dust and the sheer magnitude of the project were overpowering. Four towers, ninety-six stories apiece, the southwestern one completed, the others looking like gaunt skeletons. Today one could see only twenty stories before the smog took over.

Mac idled at a light a block away and stared up at the whiteness. The sounds of machinery and of men working came to him.

The single completed tower in the Attwood Towers project sported thirty-foot ceilings on the first floor and an open escalator crawling with men and women dressed to the nines. Glass-windowed shops fronted a lobby the size of a hanger. A Christian bookstore. Plant shop. Lingerie boutique.

A small radio station broadcasting booth.

A real estate office dripping with huge blue and gold velvet banners proclaiming office space for lease. A trio of sharpies in three-piece suits collectively wearing enough cologne to bring down small birds patrolled the corridor outside the real estate office.

Bypassing Attwood Realty, Mac found a building index alongside a glassed-in scale model of the towers project.

Attwood's business offices took up all of the seventy-eighth floor.

The receptionist squinted at him from a pair of slitted green eyes and pushed a blue-veined hand at the switchboard.

"Ms. Grimm? There's a policeman here to see Neil."

"I need to talk to Attwood himself."

"Ms. Grimm will see to you," said the woman at the switchboard, her smile deflecting his objections. "She'll be out in just a few seconds. I'm sure she can help."

It took her five minutes to show. She was black, big, and taller than Mac. She wore a gray business suit, white cravat caressing her throat. Harvard Business School. It was written all over her. She was gorgeous. Her hair was short, combed back. Her makeup was subdued. She had a model's cheekbones, the buxom body of an Iowa farm girl, and a brassy confidence.

"How can I help you?"

Fontana told her.

"I'm afraid Neil is booked for weeks in advance. Today he has meetings with the planning committee, the mayor, and a news network. He's been on a long-distance conference call to the Near East all morning."

"All I want is three, four minutes. This doesn't even concern Attwood, just peripherally. My victim took a poke at him in a restaurant a while back."

"That doesn't sound as if it would take too long. Let me see what I can do. I thought it was something else at first. Yes, of course. Follow me, please." She was civil, polite, and patronizing.

Something had registered behind the woman's eyes when he'd mentioned the restaurant, surprise perhaps. He trolled along behind her, following her through plush corridors that could have belonged to any major corporation in the world. They found Attwood's office halfway down the second corridor on the right. A male secretary with a hoarse voice asked what the problem was, then knocked tentatively. He came out a few seconds later. "You have five minutes," he said.

It was a large corner room with high windows facing north and east, original oils on the walls, including one of Jackie Onassis, a brace of personally autographed celebrity photos on another. An ancient four-foot-high bejeweled hookah sat on a pedestal under glass. The rest of the room was taken up with about half an acre of desk. Today the windows looked out on the milky guts of a cloud, though it was paler up here, as if the sun might soon slice through.

Attwood sat in a plush high-backed chair, legs crossed. He was less than impressive. Turned so that only a snippet of his face showed, he manipulated a calculator in his lap.

"I take it you're Sheriff Fontana. From Staircase? How nice to see you." When the door closed behind Fontana, Attwood said, "A female bodyguard disarms the opposition in a way you wouldn't believe until you've seen it."

"She's your bodyguard?"

"And she does very nicely, I might add." The room went silent, and Attwood measured Fontana. Attwood wore a suit that looked as comfortable as the cat's pajamas. He stepped around the desk and extended a hand. "Neil Attwood. Dahlia's saved my life more than once. Very strange circumstances. She doesn't care for my repeating them, so I won't. When you lead a high-profile life, as I do, you meet the occasional kook."

"In Latitude 47 last June? A guy named Steve Zajac? Big? Bushy mustache? Dark hair?"

Attwood moved to the windows and waved his hand. A trough of sunlight was beginning to bare another dim tower opposite. When the whiteout cleared completely he'd be able to see to the far-off windows of April Sumner's apartment on Capitol Hill. The muffled rat-a-tat-tat of a rivet gun breached their aerie.

"You're not awed by this?" Attwood asked, as if reading his mind.

"Not as impressive as what I've got, but impressive."

Attwood chuckled and considered Fontana. "Someday I'd like to see what you've got."

"Anytime."

Attwood guffawed.

20

Trebuchet

IT WAS NEIL ATTWOOD'S PINCHED, raspy voice that most stunned Mac. That and the fact that he looked like a nebbish.

Chinless, his face had a solid brow and good hairline. He had formless cheeks, slight jowls, and a lower lip that slid off into an Adam's apple the size of an egg. His watercolor-blue eyes were sincere as a deacon's and, unexpectedly, just as steady. He was Fontana's height, yet sedentary living and rich food had marooned a pot belly at his belt line that didn't match the rest of his bean-pole physique. A scrawny goatee had been carefully cultivated to simulate a small helping of chin, but it hadn't worked.

What Fontana couldn't figure was, how a man who looked so inconsequential, who wasn't any older than he was, could have attained all this hoopla.

Drive? Brilliance? Luck? It had to be a unique fusion of all three, with a smidgeon of some other qualities Fontana couldn't fathom.

"I like your style, Sheriff Fontana. Let me get this straight. You want to ask me some questions about a man name of—?"

"Zajac. Steven Paul Zajac. Latitude 47. You were there

last June. Some sort of commotion. Somebody got pitched through a window? Any of this jog your memory?"

Nibbling the inside of his cheek, Attwood sized up Fontana one more time, turned to the window, and said, "Seattle is going to be to the country what San Francisco is to California. Beautiful city. Truly beautiful."

"You like stacking people up?" Fontana asked, smiling.

Startled at this unexpected attitude, Attwood cocked his head around, left his body facing the window like a park pigeon. "What are you getting at?"

"Seems to me the role of a building like this is to squash as many people into as little acreage as possible. Stack them on top of each other like peas in a straw. If we thought about it, maybe we'd be working at just the opposite. Give people some room to breathe."

"Somebody's going to do it, and make money while they're at it. Might as well be me. That way I can at least do it right." Scratching his beard with one finger, Attwood said, "Enough of this. About this fight in the restaurant in June? This guy came over and said something. Don't remember what. Yeah. He was very drunk. Then he started trying to pick a scuffle with me. Fortunately it was a business dinner and Dahlia was there."

"She handled it?"

Attwood looked defensive. "A guy might handle crap like that himself. I used to. But I used to work on my own cars, too. She bungled it, actually, got him hurt worse than she had to. It was all very messy. One of the perks of living in the big city."

"Do you know who that was who came to your table?"

"Not really."

"Steven Paul Zajac. You might have read about him in this morning's *Journal-American*. We found his body yesterday. Zajac came to your table."

"You're kidding?"

"Ever see him before that night at the restaurant?"

"Never. You're kidding? When I read it in the paper I never dreamed . . ."

"How about after? Ever see him after?"

He shook his head solemnly. The tone of the exchange had altered irrevocably. Neil Attwood appeared a bit shocked in the way somebody who's seen everything appears a bit shocked. Only a bit.

"I meet literally hundreds of people every day, Sheriff Fontana. Generally, I make a greater impression on them than they make on me. I didn't recognize him at the time. And I don't recall ever seeing him again. I assumed he was a crank."

"What did he say?"

Attwood sank into his padded armchair, rotated, grew distracted. Finally he turned, smiled pleasantly, and said, "I actually wish I could remember. I'd like to be of help. He was drunk. And then he was swinging and Dahlia stood up and it was all over in about six seconds. We had to switch tables."

"She's that good?"

"I've heard somebody who knows say hand-to-hand she's probably the most dangerous woman in North America."

"What about the rest of the world?"

He grinned. "There's always Margaret Thatcher."

"Mind if I talk to her on my way out?"

"Of course not."

"Tell me something. Why drop the charges on Zajac?"

"I figured he was drunk. Sheriff, I've been thinking. Like all of us, Zajac's life must have had a lot of threads. What made you follow this particular thread to me just a day after his death?"

"Outside of some monkeyshines in the fire department, it's the only trouble he's been in. That I know of. Things like that usually have some meaning."

"This one didn't."

"Yeah."

Dahlia remembered only that her lower lumbar region

137

had given her trouble for weeks after dropping Zajac. Their conversation was short and brief. For some reason she remained glum and slack-faced. He noticed heavy calluses on her knuckles. She spent a good part of her day in a dojo.

Sequestered in the truck, he mulled over the last two days. The wild card in this whole thing was Max Draper.

It was no coincidence that Draper, a known arsonist, had been shadowing him. Yet it didn't make sense. Unless Zajac had actually found the arsonist responsible for the fire, and that arsonist was Draper.

But that left a million loose ends. What possible reason could Draper have had to follow him? What were the crisp hundred-dollar bills doing in the cabin? And why the torture? Even so, it didn't stand to reason that Draper would show himself. But then, Draper hadn't meant to show himself, hadn't meant to get spotted and bushwhacked.

It all reminded Fontana of something else.

The night before, he'd read Brendan a book about castles in the Middle Ages. In the text they'd come upon a description of a trebuchet, or catapult, a huge contraption designed to sling rocks and other appurtenances over the walls of a besieged castle. Sometimes dead horses were lobbed over the walls with the intention of spreading disease. Mac had a vivid mental picture of a dead horse careering through the air, arching high over the walls of a castle, thumping in the dirt. A thing like that would boggle. Disease or no, it would be unnerving enough to distract the defenders from their task. He wasn't so certain Draper wasn't the dead horse in this investigation, flung from some unseen trebuchet, that somebody hadn't lobbed him over the parapet just to unnerve Mac.

He drove to Airport Way just west of Interstate 5 to look at the stables.

21

A Straightened-Out Kind of Guy

THE BOYS AT Dexter Fuel Service gave new meaning to the word *greaseballs*. Plunk Dogpatch under a leaky oil derrick and you'd come up with a fair approximation of the premises, enclosed inside a cyclone fence, presided over by a wooden sign whose ocher paint had been abraded by Seattle's damp weather.

Three grungy tank trucks in various states of disrepair were parked or abandoned in the lot. The office was a rusted turquoise house trailer teetering on stacks of concrete blocks.

He found Draper inside with two other men watching a small black-and-white television: *The Price Is Right*. There was only one chair, and the two others lounged against a wall in oil-stained dark green coveralls with "Dexter Fuel" imprinted on smudged chest patches. Draper's left hand was in a cast. The shadows under his eyes were darker than they should have been. His upper lip was swollen. His legs were propped on the TV table, clumps of mud from his boots laying like rabbit pellets beyond his feet.

"Morning, Max."

"You."

"Thought you might be needing this." Fontana removed Draper's driver's license from his shirt pocket.

A typewriter. Some order books. A girly calendar on the wall complete with obscene pencil jottings. The cramped office smelled of fuel oil and coffee and BO.

"Lay it on the counter." Draper's voice was flattened by the same lack of inflection Mac had noticed the night before. His facial muscles seemed incapable of contracting. In daylight, under the trailer's fluorescents, he looked paler, meaner.

"This where you work?"

"What does it look like?"

"Heard you did a little moonlighting with a wad of newspapers and a match."

"Boys, this is the asshole I was telling you about."

There was a general rustling, shifting of feet, and then things were as they were. Drop a rock in an ant nest, you get the same commotion. He should have known these Dugans weren't just co-workers. Confederates was more like it. They had the same lazy look about them, the same insolent eyes. None of them had done as much time in the slammer as they should have, or as much as they would. Suddenly the trailer seemed crowded. Mac was glad he had a gun out of sight in his waistband.

"I'm trying to figure how you got onto me yesterday, Max."

"Yeah, well just keep figuring."

"Thought maybe somebody I visited might have made a phone call. Seems like a lot of luck if you'd just picked me up on the street by accident."

"Where's my goddamn gun? How about my goddamn gun?"

"In Staircase."

"Thought you said you was mailing it back when I checked out?"

"You ain't checked out."

"So what's to check?"

The two men standing were younger than Draper. One was large, short-haired, barrel-chested with a face so fat his cheeks almost pinched shut his bright-blue eyes. He was busting out of the dark-green fuel service jacket. He might have just been drummed out of the Marines. If so, he had been a cook.

The other was slight, smaller than Fontana, the tidiest of the three, and about as cute as a snake in a boot. He looked like he could be Draper's kid brother, except that his face had a trace of animation: a sneer. Fontana wasn't unaware of the double-barrel shotgun standing in the corner behind him, made sure he kept himself between it and them.

The fat one put his weight on his elbows on the counter, the curve of his broad back partially obscuring the line of sight between Fontana and Draper. The kid brother leaned against the wall over a baseboard heater, bouncing his buttocks against his palms.

"I know about you, Max. Might not have put it all together yet, but I will."

Without looking away from the set: "What do you know?"

"You torched a place last spring in South Park. Zajac was at the fire."

"Who?"

"You know who. You're tied into it, and I think I know how."

Draper scratched a knee, spit a mouthful of pulped sunflower seeds he'd been storing in his cheek into a wastepaper basket, clunked his booted feet to the floor of the trailer, and slowly stood up. "You don't know shit."

"By the time you figure out what I know, it'll be too late."

Sauntering around the outside of the counter past his heavyset friend, Draper came within a pace of Mac, who made sure he was balanced, ready for action. The other two were behind, not looking dangerous, just behind. Draper's cast extended to just below his elbow. The graffiti artists had been quick and vulgar.

"Just what do you know?"

"You're somebody's gofer. That's what you are. People like you always end up taking the rap. Somebody tells you to jump and you ask how high. They say shit and you say where's my hat. You set fire to that place. Zajac had the goods on you. Was he trying blackmail? Okay, maybe that's not it. But he had the goods and you people didn't ditch all of it. I got the rest."

"You're full of it," said Draper.

"You better hope so."

"Cops are always comin' around here tryin' to pin bullshit beefs on me. I used matches when I was a juvey, but I ain't since. I got a regular job. I'm a straightened-out kinda guy. And I told you last night. That was purely accidental. I know nothin' about anybody named Zokalski or whatever the fuck you called him. You're just like all the other cops I ever known."

"These your co-workers?"

"The ugly one up against the wall's my kid brother. The big guy is Charlie. His pop owns this outfit."

Afterward Fontana had to admire the way Draper worked it.

He turned to the door to open it, then turned back, swinging his cast wildly across the distance between them, clubbing the side of Fontana's head.

He saw it coming, but before he could move it seemed like somebody upended the trailer and he found himself on the floor on the other side of the capsized counter. He reached behind his belt for the pistol, caught a fuzzy glimpse of somebody playing with the double-barrel shotgun.

"You crazy, Max? He's a cop. A cop!"

"Look out! The cop's got a gun!"

There was a deafening roar. Something kicked Mac in the ribs simultaneously with the roar. The voices got louder.

Another roar and Fontana heard a load from the shotgun thud into the wall behind him. He'd only been hit once. The second shot missed. His ears were singing, a bat scream in one, a roar of ocean-in-seashell in the other. He was facing a corner on his hands and knees and the trailer was still spinning, but he figured if he could whip his revolver out, he could stop this carnage.

Another explosion.

His whole body leaped to the side, slammed into the wall. Laughter. Shuffling. "You see that? Looked like a puppet on strings."

"Gawd, Max, what the hell's wrong with you? In my daddy's office? He's gonna have a cow."

"The asshole knows. I gotta boff him."

"He don't know nothin'. He was bluffing."

"He knows."

"Leave him be. Let's get the hell out of here."

"Leave him, hell. He's finished. It's him or me."

"Not here, you don't. Not in my daddy's trailer."

"Too late, lard ass. Don't worry about it. You saw him drive that old battle wagon up. Ain't nobody with him."

Snick. Snick.

The shotgun was loaded again.

Knowing he'd been hit by the blasts, Fontana had tried to play dead. He couldn't tell how badly he'd been wounded, but his side felt as if ribs had been extracted. Then he thought better of playing possum and groped in the mess for his pistol. He didn't have a plan. You were always sunk when you didn't have a plan.

"Look at that sucker. He don't know his ass from an empty tin can."

They laughed and he knew he was moving like a drunk trying to crawl across a trampoline. More laughter. Two of them. The third remained silent. Mac struggled to his knees and reached around behind his back.

The waistband was snug against his back, the pistol gone.

The next explosion slammed Fontana into the wall and folded him double. He retched, dry heaves, and slowly sat up. Another blast hit him high in the sternum and threw him into a heap. He couldn't breathe. So this is it, he thought. This is the day I go. These Dugans. What were they waiting for? Why not finish it?

22

Mass Hysteria in a One-Man Grave

THERE WAS A REASON they hadn't killed him.

Rubber bullets.

He was merely broken and bruised.

Draper was raking him with rubber bullets of the sort fired by riot police. At twenty or thirty yards, the missiles were immobilizing. He couldn't guess what damage they would wreak at this range, whether they were giving him greenstick fractures or what.

"Stop it, Maxy. Quit playin' around, man."

"Go get that tarp from Ben's truck."

The door opened and closed. A gust of foggy air wafted in and licked Fontana's sweaty neck, wormed down the back of his sweater.

The gun went off.

It kicked Fontana in the stomach, twirled him off the knee and foot he'd staggered to, and smashed him into the wall. The trailer's windows rattled like castanets. A second jolt smacked him square in the forehead. He couldn't see, thought his neck might be broken.

"Christ, Draper. How many shells you got? That last gizmo bounced. Almost put my eye out." The fat one was grousing. Charlie.

"We'll just bag him in that tarp and that'll be the end of it."

"Christ, he's still breathin'."

"I said, that'll be the end of it." Footsteps. Sour beer breath wafting into Fontana's face. "Well, looky here. Handcuffs."

The bullet that cracked him in the sternum had impaired the action of his lungs. He was having a hard time moving his arms, too, wondered if a collarbone was shattered. Rough hands gutted his pockets, relieved him of his wallet, handcuffs, money. He couldn't break out of a fierce, blinding squint.

"Can you believe this cheap bastard? Forty-two dollars? You want his gun, Rafe?"

More cool air. The door had opened and closed again. Little brother was back. So he had Maxwell P. Draper, Rafe Draper, and Charlie Whatsisname. Always the dick. Toting up facts. The part of him that could still think things were funny thought it was funny.

"Hell no, I don't want his gun. I don't wanna have anything to do with this bullshit. Maxy, you're gonna make sure we all end up pullin' time in Walla Walla in a four-by-eight."

"Think positive. You're implicated. You should be more than happy to police up the loose ends."

"His truck's right out there in the lot in broad daylight. When he turns up missing, some old windbag stuffed to the max with Pepto-Bismol is going to fink on us."

"We'll move it."

"You seen that thing inside?"

"I ain't never had any trouble with a dog."

From his right eye Fontana saw three sets of blurry legs and boots. They were growing off the wall. And then they tilted at a forty–five-degree angle. His arms had a jagged, broken feel to them, as if they'd gone to sleep and been run over by a truck.

"Yeah, where the hell you gonna put him?" It was Charlie. The brothers' voices had the same timbre, though Charlie sounded like a scared fat woman in a kissing booth waiting for her first customer.

"Put him? I'm thinking about number four."

"Like hell."

"Why not?"

"Cause'a my dad, that's why not."

"Think about it. We don't know nothin' about this. Somebody dumps a body on the property. So what? What do we know about it? And your dad ain't gonna find out. When was the last time anybody used number four?"

"I don't like this."

"Just what the doctor ordered."

Grasping Fontana by the shoulders and legs, they wrapped a heavy, moldy canvas tarp around him. He tried to struggle but nothing happened.

His second major mistake of the investigation, letting Draper get the drop on him.

His last mistake.

Outside he could hear the faraway rumbly sounds of the dog barking. Booger was going crazy. He'd left him locked in the GMC; there wasn't much he could do from there. They were carrying Mac slung between two of them, his limp body hammocking the canvas. They dropped the load and the impact woke him out of his trance. He heard a heavy metal lid squeaking. Rough, fumbling hands groped the canvas.

Rafe said, "He's still alive. He's moving in there. Don't you think you oughta—?"

"What? This bunghole doesn't deserve nothin'."

"But Christ, Maxy. My dad finds him in there and he'll call the cops, sure."

"Don't even think about it."

They were unwrapping, freeing him, and the cool fog was airing his sweaty body. Three sets of hands. They handcuffed him. He looked up at them, trying to decide what to do. Some

147

strength was coming back. Enough to jab a pair of stiff digits into somebody's eyes. He poked at Rafe's face.

"Shit! Christ!"

Now only two remained. He might have a chance. He'd taken on two before. He kicked at a nearby pair of legs.

He saw it coming but didn't bother to duck. Or couldn't. The plaster cast came across his temple again. He was lying across the mouth of a garbage can—no, it was a tank. They were stuffing his torso into a tank and he wasn't doing a thing to stop them.

And his legs were inside already, dangling, and he was frantically holding on to the lip of the cylindrical hole and they were kicking at his fingers. He looked down past his shoulder and saw only blackness, then particles of grit smote the surface, dimpled it. An underground storage tank! Filled almost to the top with fuel oil. One foot was already in.

Then he went down splashing, managed to keep only the top of his head and a piece of the back of his neck dry.

Everything else was instantly soaked.

Freezing.

He hadn't thought oil could be this cold. The liquid permeated his clothing, shoes, underwear, seeping instantly through his pants into his crotch. His loafers filled, oozed off, popped up near his face. Draper was topside gaping down the chute. Charlie's head appeared in the opening a hundred and eighty degrees from Draper's.

Treading his legs to ride the surface, he stared up at a three-foot circular opening. He'd skinned himself on the way down. The perpendicular chute had oil coating the sides, sticky and half dry. He'd never be able to scale it.

Draper said, "Haven't had so much fun since Aunt Sara got stinko and fell in the grain silo. How you doin' down there, Sheriff?"

Judging by the slow, sinuous action of the waves on the surface, the tank was enormous. Fontana could see eight or ten feet in all directions, and he hadn't glimpsed a wall, just the surface of the oil, which was quite pretty.

"God, he looks like a skull on a platter," said Charlie. "You sure you wanna do this, Maxy? That's a bad way to croak a guy."

Draper leaned in and said, "Now, Sheriff, don't be hacking your lettuce down there."

Charlie said, "You sure we can get away with this?"

"How's it feel to know you're a dead man, Sheriff? I calculate you can swim around in there a couple of hours before the fumes snuff you. Probably come green as a seasick cat first. Ever try to tread water and puke at the same time? Wish I could stick around and take pictures for the old album, but I got a truck here I gotta ditch. Hey, what year is this thing, in case I wanna sell it? Got me a new pup for the kid, too. Think I'll call him Fink. No, maybe I'll name him after you. Bubbles."

"Draper?" Fontana strained to keep the shudders out of his voice.

"Yeahbuddyboy."

"The county cops know all about this."

"You trying to say something, buddy boy?"

"They know I'm here. They'll find me and you'll get your neck stretched. Leave me a rope and scram. Worst you can get in that event is aggravated assault. The way it stands, you're all going up on murder one. All of you." He wanted to say more, but his lungs didn't have enough air to say more.

Charlie and Draper looked at each other.

Draper reached for the lid, lifted it, slammed it shut.

Afterward, he could hear them fiddling with the hardware topside. A padlock. It was like hearing somebody nail the lid on your own coffin.

The darkness.

It was so black he reflexively reached up to feel the base of the maw fifteen inches above his head, holding it for a moment to make sure it was still there. He couldn't see his hands. Couldn't tell if his eyes were open or closed.

Listening for footsteps in the ground above, he heard only a dull purling, coming like a far-off buzz of a fly on the windowsill in the next room. The freeway. Perhaps the Burlington Northern tracks.

Oil had permeated every pore below his neck, splotched his hair, gooped his left cheek. It filled his lungs with the stench, but against his skin it was slick and womblike. It was the cold that disturbed him. Hypothermia, he knew, rendered a dull, painless trip into the next world. It wouldn't take hours. Forty-five minutes was more like it.

His corpse would bob along the surface for months, mummified in an oily batter, until somebody opened the hatch.

He thought about Brendan.

At school now, he'd be coming home this afternoon and Mary Gilliam would be there with her milk and cookies. And they'd wait for Mac. And wait.

He'd become another missing person, a number in a lengthening list of numbers. Dummelow would grill Draper and Draper would profess ignorance in his steely deadpan and Dummelow would know he was lying but wouldn't be able to do a thing.

Mary would baby-sit Brendan all night, and tomorrow morning she wouldn't know where to go. Although he'd never done it before, she'd surmise he was out on a bender and wait until the next afternoon to report him missing. Poor Brendan. It was bad enough he had to lose his mother when he was four and a half. Now this.

It took several tries, but he dug the keys out and got one cuff off, then the other. He pocketed the keys; didn't know why. He felt like a man on death row nursing his last meal, then setting his reading glasses on a shelf so he wouldn't break them. Why bother?

Inexplicably, as soon as he dropped the handcuffs he

began to think of all the times he'd almost bought it. When he was ten he'd done a back flip off the diving board at his friend Randy's pool. The richest people they knew. He was alone in the pool, a hot July day, the others lunching inside. He flubbed the dive, and as he dropped into the water in a lazy spiral he felt the tip of the diving board brush the back of his head. Another inch and it would have knocked him cold. He would never have seen eleven.

In college one night he was speeding recklessly on his motorcycle on a tollway exit, applying the brakes as quickly as he could, ninety-five, ninety, eighty-five, and a curve was coming up, and above the curve was an overpass, and at the bad side of the curve stood a concrete pillar six feet in diameter. He was heading straight for it, and it wasn't going to move for him or God or anybody. Seventy-five, seventy. He couldn't turn the handlebars, the gyroscopic motion of the wheels forcing him into a straight line. At the last second he pulled it out, escaping by inches.

He sold the motorcycle to a man in the National Guard, who killed his girlfriend in a wreck six months later.

Two weeks into the company.

One of his first fires outside of training. The house was puffing yellowish smoke from the eaves. The hose lines filled out and stiffened. Fontana cleared the air out the brass Rockwood nozzle, then braced himself to kick in the front door.

A firefighter jogged up behind him and knocked him down.

One blow.

Knocked him to the ground. And then the door, which Mac had battered open just then, blew off its hinges with a low woofing sound, jetted across the yard.

He would have been cut in half.

It was a back draft, a condition where the fire in the house has burned all the available oxygen and the atmosphere has become a collection of super heated gases awaiting the

151

reintroduction of O_2. When the oxygen came, so did the explosion. They found the doorknob spindle imbedded six inches into a maple, the door itself buried in the side of a panel truck.

The firefighter said only, "Gotta watch those puffers, kid."

Looking back on it, it seemed almost as if half his life had been one close call after another. Yet each one had been spaced out by years of relative security and boredom.

Then he thought about Brendan. About Linda. She had died in a car wreck. Lingering two weeks in intensive care, she had regained consciousness a handful of times, talking to him, to Brendan, who wept at the grim sight of the tubes and needles and lines and machines, and who didn't recognize her, didn't want to believe it was his mommy. And to make it all worse for Mac, the guilt ate at him because he'd been sleeping with Frieda. On a lark.

He was facing the one thing everybody faced alone. He laid his head back, floated on the surface, motionless, the only movement in the tank the imperceptible trickle as the tears divided the chill on his cheeks and dribbled into the number two fuel oil.

23

Quiet as a Cockroach in a Coffin

HE WAS DRIFTING in and out of consciousness, half comatose, three quarters dead. He didn't know how much time had elapsed or how many moods he'd allowed to embrace him, terrorize him, and then parole him into the numbness.

The light hit him first, blinding, made him feel as if his eyeballs had been sunburned, his brain fricasseed.

He was bobbing directly under the lid to the underground tank, didn't have a clue what was happening, in fact had been dreaming about the woman in the bunking clothes, a bizarre continuation of the slinky succubus dream from last night. The redhead. Could that have been last night?

An ominous feeling swept over him, as if things could actually get worse, as if Draper and company had come back to push him under with sticks. His inclination was to roll over and do a crawl stroke out of there. Except what he'd do would be to roll over and aspirate a lungful of oil. And then he'd be floating on his face instead of his back.

Then he heard the woofing.

Booger.

The animal was barking down the maw, the cavern acting as a megaphone.

He'd seen hypothermic patients so paralyzed they could

153

not be resuscitated. Conscious. Alive. Yet their body core temperature had plummeted beyond the point of no return. They stared at you and did not answer when you spoke to them, and sometimes they would bellyache and snivel, always in an unintelligible deaf-mute squawk.

Then came the artificial lights, a string of them dangling down the hole, and a man slipped into the oil with him, hissing at the discomfort. It took only minutes, working in the soup, to slide a safety belt around his torso.

Firefighters.

Brothers.

He was too enfeebled to do anything but watch and he was too numbed to do that well. What he wanted was to lie down and die. Preferably next to the stove with the cat.

The firefighter who'd dunked himself hunched on a bench seat near the foot of the stretcher and rode to Harborview with him, shivering, webbed in oil-stained white blankets. They scraped a patch clean on Mac's right arm and stuck an IV into him, injecting warm ringers into his bloodstream. They had oxygen on him, but he kept gasping.

He didn't pay much attention to the rest of it. Nurses and doctors stripped him. Exclaiming over the mess, they wiped their hands on towels, unintentionally smeared daubs of crude on their brows. They used scissors to cut him naked.

They were trying to decide whether to intubate and flush out his insides with warm liquid. It was a relatively new technique: warm the poor bastards from the inside out. He would just as soon forgo that, and he suddenly had enough chattering energy to spit out the thermometer and give them an opinion. He'd seen lavage before and it wasn't pleasant, having your stomach pumped over and over. "Screw that," he said angrily. But he was angry at himself, not them.

Three and a half hours later a pair of Seattle cops took his statement and drove him to Staircase. One cop chauffeured him and the dog in a Seattle police cruiser, another drove the GMC.

The SPD had issued a bulletin on the Draper brothers, Rafe and Maxwell, and also on Charlie. Dexter turned out to be his last name. His pop owned the fuel yard. Dexter Fuel.

It seemed the dog had attacked the trio, had broken a hole in the side window of the GMC with his snout, leaped out, and torn into them. An anonymous CB'er driving on the freeway reported a guard dog was mauling a man. Homing in on the faded ocher sign on Airport Way, the cops dispatched Animal Control and a Seattle canine unit from home, as they didn't work during the day. The dog cop lived on Mars Avenue at the south end of Beacon Hill overlooking Boeing Field and got there before you could say boo.

He was the one who recognized Satan.

Typically, dog handlers knew most of the other handlers and dogs in the area. The German shepherd had scratched and sniffed at the fuel tank until the dog cop got suspicious and pried the lid off.

On the trip to Staircase another cop filled Mac in.

Her name was Meadows. Her head was about the size and shape of a cantaloupe and was balanced on a pipe stem neck. She had impossibly tiny wrists. She kept glancing over at him, petting his leg.

"Me and my partner must have just missed them. We'll make the collar. I bet we have at least one of them downtown inside twenty-four hours. You just relax. Gosh, it's beautiful up in these foothills. The trees all turning. I wouldn't feel like talking either, I were you. Is that heat high enough? Doctor Radley said we couldn't have it too high. Want more to drink? There's a thermos right there. Warm juice. Yeah, they beat feet."

"Near as we can figure it, your dog broke through the side window and cut himself up a little. Might need stitches. Then he must have ripped into them good. Blood from here to China. They had to have hurt him to get away. They musta hit him with something big. There's tire marks all over the place. Maybe with a car. I'd call that a dog and a half."

"I call him Satan," said Mac. "Mister Satan."

She prattled on, but Fontana was having a difficult time hearing. Pea-size doses of fuel oil clogged his ears. Meadows told him she was going to school part-time to win a law degree.

When he asked her if she knew the difference between a run-over lawyer on the freeway and a run-over snake on the freeway, she rolled her eyes and patted his knee under the borrowed hospital greens and said she'd heard them all. The snake had skid marks in front of it. The lawyer didn't.

When Brendan came home, Mac ruffled his hair and gave him a squeeze, then spent the afternoon making small talk with the boy, piddling around by the river, charting the prowess of a spider as it engineered a fly trap between two rocks. Mac needed to decriminalize his thoughts.

"We keeping Booger?"

"Sure are. I misjudged him badly. Got Lassie beat all to hell."

"Don't say 'hell', Mac."

"Sorry. We get back to the house I'm going to give him my favorite slippers for a snack."

Brendan laughed and said, as he habitually did, "You're funny."

It was only fate that had kept him alive. The doctors had told him another fifteen minutes and he would have been unrecoverable. The wildest luck.

Satan.

Goddamn dog broke clean through a window to save his butt. Astonishing. Beautiful. Never in his wildest daydreams had he ever thought he would owe his life to a dog.

The next morning after Brendan walked to school, Mac took the river trail. It was cool, brisk, with a high cloud cover the newscasters on the radio cautioned might spatter snow onto the higher elevations. Neither he nor the dog was walking normally, the dog favoring his right hind leg, Mac favoring his left thigh. He had never been angrier.

Yet revenge would only befuddle the issues. He needed answers. Had Max Draper killed Zajac because he found out Zajac could prove he set fire to an apartment house where two children died? There had to be more. The money. The investigation, autopsy report, the botched crucifixion. It was all ugly enough to make a hangman weep. There had to be more. And how had whoever attacked Zajac mesmerized him into dropping his guard?

April was lying through her teeth. She had to be.

Maybe he hadn't realized it before, but after yesterday, after meeting Draper and considering the plot, the subplots, he knew it now.

The graveled river trail was flat and easy, employed by plodding housewives to burn off fat, joggers to toughen up their hearts, and at the right time of the year by fishermen toting creels and six-packs. The path paralleled the river. Two miles farther upriver one could cross over the rapids on the abandoned railroad bridge and, eventually, beating through the brush, find Zajac's cabin.

Mount Gadd loomed over him, a slab of the river churning white below, then fifty yards of smooth slate-colored rocks, birches, willows, wild apple, and alder coloring the blank spaces in the afternoon: yellows, burgundies, oranges, shades of tan. Leaf-peepers drove hundreds of miles to spend the afternoon in these woods.

24
Canis Familiaris

FONTANA GAVE SATAN ORDERS but he didn't know what he was doing. He tried "Search," and after a couple of tries it seemed to do the trick. The dog began looping around Zajac's cabin, scuffing his nose along the ground. The dog inspected every brush, rock, and mole runway within two hundred yards of the house.

It took an hour and twelve minutes.

The weatherworn briefcase had been cached in the crawl space under an oil-stained kitchen wash basin. Zajac had taken great pains to hide it. "Good dog," Mac said, patting the dog's neck after they'd both scuttled out from under the house, the dog pawing his snout and sneezing at cobwebs, Mac flicking a spider off his trousers.

Squatting on the stoop of the house, Fontana riffled through the briefcase. Papers. He was disappointed, though he didn't know why. No drugs. No bricks of hundred-dollar bills. Just Xerox copies, handwritten notes, and signed affidavits. He found another copy of Kim Sung's autopsy report and stapled to it a brilliant glossy color photograph of the two fire victims.

When he had stuffed all the materials back into the briefcase, he used the key Dummelow had provided, went inside Zajac's house, and began a grid-by-grid search.

Ninety minutes later nothing of note had surfaced. The cops had confiscated all the weapons and ammunition. In the bedroom in a hidey-hole in the wall he found a small amount of hashish the police had overlooked. He left it.

When a van pulled up outside and parked between Zajac's Bronco and the cabin, he recognized the driver through the living-room window, retreated to the back bedroom, ducked, and threw an arm around the dog's neck. "Hush, Satan."

The van's driver made a production out of rapping at the door, cupping hands to the window, shouting halloo, tapping a key at alternate windowpanes. When he got to the locked back door, he wiggled the knob. A moment later it boomed open, propelled by a boot. He bypassed the bedroom and made a beeline for the living room.

As Mac walked down the hallway behind him, the intruder was windmilling through Zajac's possessions, scattering objects, papers, and books helter-skelter.

"You lose something?" Startled, the intruder jumped three inches, then wheeled, faced Fontana brazenly, and forked his fingers into the pockets of his ratty jeans. "Or do you spend all your afternoons breaking and entering at random?"

"Huh?"

Motioning with his revolver, Mac said, "You know the routine. Up against the wall. And don't try any funny business."

"Sheeeit. Who do you think I am?"

"I don't know. Whatever, I didn't think you were a housebreaker."

"I've got an excuse."

"You know what they say about excuses. They're like assholes. Everybody's got one, and they're all shitty."

Mac frisked the man, came up with a ring of keys and, surprisingly, a pistol in his left boot, a .38-caliber blued automatic, a Llama model VIII. Mac spun him around, looked down at Satan. "Guard." The dog lowered his head and emitted a low growl. "I wouldn't try anything, Don."

"Hell, I wasn't planning to." Reinholt slouched onto the sofa, pried a pack of cigarettes out of his shirt pocket, and lit one. He wore a plaid shirt, a gray jacket, jeans, and work boots. Out of uniform he looked younger, unmasked, and somehow naked as a clown without his makeup. He draped himself in a pall of bluish-white smoke.

Without any reason, Reinholt stubbed the cigarette out in his palm, glanced around for a repository for the butt, and finally lifted the flap and poked the broken thing into his shirt pocket. Mac noticed tears beading up in his gray eyes.

"Damn. You didn't tell me Steve was dead. You knew, didn't you? You must have found him, what, the day before?"

"Few hours before. It rattled me, too. My apologies. Now. What are you doing here?"

Reinholt had been avoiding Mac's eyes, not wanting to draw attention to his circumstance. Public expressions of grief were an anathema to firefighters. It was considered bad form to grieve publicly. Reinholt blinked and tipped his pasty face at the cracked ceiling.

"Me and Steve were best buddies."

"This better be good."

"You'll love it," Reinholt said bitterly. "A couple years back, when his marriage had busted up and he was going crazy, we got smashed in a Belltown tavern, Steve and me. I mean smashed. We picked up some woman. Steve was the kind of guy, if he wanted, could pick up a beauty queen in any alley in town. I think that's why his girlfriend was jealous. But this was no dazzler. We're on the floating bridge driving over to a friend's vacant apartment in Kirkland with her and I'm drivin' and she's sitting between us guzzling a bottle of MacNaughton's and I've got my hand down her skirt and Steve's got his hand down her shirt and we all know a good time is going to be had by all.

"Suddenly she says, 'Hold it right there, fellas. What do

you think you're dealing with here? I'm a lady. One of you . . . one of you . . . take your hand out of there.' " Reinholt laughed, but it was a worn-out Chevy of a laugh, low on octane.

"So what does this escapade have to do with coming here?"

"We drove her to my friend's empty apartment in Kirkland. It was the only time Steve ever did anything like that. That I know of. He was still crazy over his wife leaving. Afterward this woman wrote some letters to Steve. I was mentioned. The long and the short of it is, I thought they might be laying around. The letters. They weren't something I need Nancy finding out about."

"Nancy?"

"The wife. She's part Indian and she'd come at me with a tomahawk. So I played around—that ain't no reason for my life to cave in around my ankles. Steve said he destroyed them a long time ago, but I hadda be sure."

"Why didn't you call and ask me?"

"I thought this would be less embarrassing."

"Is it?"

Reinholt bobbled his eyebrows without enthusiasm.

"So why the weapon?" Fontana asked.

"I carry a gun most everywhere. 'Sides, Steve ran into some trouble. Thought I might run into the a-holes who done Steve."

"Yeah, well, I got the jump on you. Chances are they would have, too. You wouldn't be thinking of tracking down whoever dusted Zajac?"

Slouched on the sofa, Don shot him a canny look. "I was, I sure wouldn't tell the law about it."

They regarded each other for a moment. Reinholt peeled off his wire-rimmed glasses and buffed them on a scrap of his flannel shirt. The house was in disarray, partially from the police search, partially from Reinholt's frenzy.

"I don't think I believe you, Don."

"Fuck you."

"Maybe I should run you in. Let you stew in a cell for a while. How'd you like that?"

"How'd you think I'd like it?"

They locked eyes. Reinholt, under other circumstances, would be a formidable opponent, yet the camaraderie Mac had felt the other day was still there.

"Okay. Do me a favor, don't run me in. I was looking for those letters, but I was also after something I thought Steve might have hid up here. Soon as I got inside, I realized how dumb that was. Anything here, the cops would have lifted. What'd you guys take?"

"Serious business. You crossed a police line. Breaking and entering. I put two fingers in my mouth and whistle, I could have every cop in the county standing on your toes asking questions."

Reinholt sized the smile again. "Typical cop. Answer a question with a question. What were you doing here? Laying for me?"

"The same thing you were, except I'm not doing it illegally. Been here almost three hours. I'd probably have been here until dark. Your chances of running into me were outstanding."

"Shit."

"So what were you actually looking for?"

"Things. The letters. His girlfriend's name. She took a shot at him once. Didn't tell you that, did I? Yeah, she was a little brain dead. Took a shot at him one night when they were having a fight at Greenlake."

"So you thought she might be implicated in his death?"

"Damn right."

"What were you planning for her?"

"A chat."

"Tell me about the gunfire."

"You mean, was she serious? Steve mighta been shook up a little. It was hard to tell with him. You know, all that stuff with the chief's putting the thumbscrews to him? It was hard to tell with that, too. If I hadn't worked alongside him so many years I don't think I would have known he was bothered by any of it. He came in one day and just casually mentioned she'd taken a shot at him. None of us knew her, you gotta remember. When I asked for details he said they had some sort of spat. I never did figure out if she'd fired the gun at random, or if she'd actually been trying to pot him. Don't know if Steve knew."

"You're sure Zajac left this woman? Not vice versa?"

"He talked about it for weeks before he dumped her."

"Fretted that much, he must have liked her. You sure you don't have any idea who she was?"

"Steve and I were both opposed to women in the department. They watered down the standards to get them in, and what's worse, everybody in the department knows it. From the mayor on down. Nobody's got the balls to admit it. Right now Seattle's got more women in uniform than any city in the goddamn country. Me and Steve used to shoot our mouths off about that. Around the time he took up with this new gal, he stopped shooting his off."

"What are you driving at?"

"A goddamn women's libber. He was living with one of them. Gawd, that Steve. I loved him. I remember this time we'd gone to a ball game somewhere and we'd all had a few beers and we were driving on I-5 right smack through town. All of a sudden somebody spots this chief behind us, Chief Walden, who's retired now. The assistant chief then. Had a lot of clout. Liked to mess with people. Somebody says, hey guys, here comes Walden, let's all moon him. We're giggling like kids now and we all pull our pants down and get ready. He slides up alongside in the next lane and we count to three and everybody's ready, but the only guy gullible enough to actually moon him is Zajac. Everybody else just laughs. We all knew he was the only one'd fall for it.

"Somebody says, hey Steve, he recognized you. No he

don't, says Steve. But Steve's worried. Yeah, he recognized you. He did, we saw it in his eyes. Anyways, we get Steve so goldanged flustered he can't sleep that night, thinking Walden seen him. We convinced him he better trot his ass down to Walden's office and confess before Walden fires his ass. We even offer to go down with him, lend moral support. So we're up there on the fourth floor, all of us, and Steve, hat in hand, in his high-water blacks, goes in to see Walden. We figure Steve's got about as much chance as an orange under a Sherman tank. We're all outside trying to keep from laughing.

"He goes in there and starts telling Walden he's sorry, that he was the one on the freeway the other night. Halfway through his spiel it becomes clear even to Steve that Walden didn't know what the hell he was saying. Walden hadn't seen a thing on the freeway. Walden hadn't even been on the freeway, just some guy looked like him. So here's Steve confessing and all of a sudden Walden is getting very interested and now Steve can't think of how to squirm out of this, so he tells the truth. When he came out, we were all laughing so hard we were on the floor."

"Was he mad?"

"For a day or two he was."

"Think I would have liked him."

"Hell, yes, you woulda." They ruminated on that for a few moments. "The name Neil Attwood come up yet?" Reinholt asked.

"What's Attwood got to do with any of this?"

"Steve got into a row with Attwood one night. I was looking for something up here with Attwood's name on it."

"Thought you were looking for letters."

"That, too."

"And something with his girlfriend's name on it."

"Attwood's name rang a bell, Sheriff. I could see it in your face."

"What did Zajac say about him?"

"Nothing, really," said Reinholt. "But he figures into this somehow, don't he?"

"Only in what you've already said. Zajac got into it with him one night. I talked to Attwood. He doesn't appear to have had any ties to Zajac. By the way, you know a woman named April Sumner?"

"Never heard of her."

For some reason, Mac had a hard time believing that.

25
Old Fires

NOTHING WAS HAPPENING. By Friday night, despite all his highway time, Fontana felt stymied. After conferring with the King County medical examiner, Dummelow advised Mac that Steven Paul Zajac had not died directly from the knife blade, or the torture, but had, in fact, cheated death for several hours.

Mac was incredulous. "You're saying somebody left him like that? Tied to the log with a knife in his back and he was still alive?"

"Piss you off?"

Thinking about it made Mac want to knock down a wall. "A little."

According to Dummelow, the three men who had put Fontana in the oil tank had managed to elude the SPD's tentacles.

Having Xeroxed the materials in Zajac's briefcase, Fontana surrendered the originals to County but could not get the steadfast Dummelow to concede they were related to Zajac's death. To Dummelow it was a drug deal gone sour. Period.

The material in the briefcase had been a potpourri. Bills from and canceled checks to a detective agency in California.

A score of letters from the agency detailed their findings in regard to a company named the Hildreth Building Corporation. There were papers indicating the company, operating under various pseudonyms, had jacked up the price of the Eldorado Arms over the past three years by buying and reselling it to themselves.

The only item missing was an owner, some living person to pin the scam to.

The California detective agency had come up blank. So had Zajac. Most of the corporation officers' names were rip-offs. Phony titles. Bogus addresses.

Renaldo Pardew was the sole legitimate name in the crew. The information Steve Zajac had collected on him was sketchy.

In 1969 Renaldo Pardew had contracted cancer; had died in Bellevue in 1971. Yet he had been signing corporation papers and deeds of trust as late as March 1986. The only person they had found who might benefit from the fire at the Eldorado Arms was a dead man.

Convinced of illicit hobnobbing between city fire department inspectors and business owners, Zajac had engaged in a breezy correspondence with the Olympia city building department, and even swiped copies of Seattle Fire Department Form 6s.

Widely touted as employing one of the most comprehensive inspection schedules in the country, Seattle also bragged of a corruption-free program. At least it had until now.

Annually, Seattle inspectors combed each building open to the public, searched out fire code violations, safety hazards, Uniform Building Code infractions. Lieutenants and firefighters riding the rigs performed the majority of the inspections, maintaining contact with their dispatcher through portable radios. When they received an alarm, they would dash into the street, doff what inspection clothing they could leap into bunkers, hop the rig, and be off. When an inspection cropped up that required special knowledge of hazardous materials or presented particularly awkward problems, somebody from the fire marshal's office assisted.

The SFD was considered untainted. No whiff of scandal. Nary a smell of collusion.

In the bottom of the briefcase, Fontana found a rough deposition, crudely typed and signed in an indecipherable cat scratch.

Elmira Erlandson, recently widowed, was willing to swear her husband had once given five thousand dollars to an unnamed Seattle Fire inspector so their auto parts business could escape thirty-five thousand dollars worth of revamping. The inspector had promised nobody would bother them again. She had seen the SFD man, but didn't recall his name, nor would she necessarily recognize him if she saw him again.

In the margins of the deposition Zajac had scribbled in black ink: "Mrs. Erlandson's skimpy description fits Chief C to a tee."

Whether C was Crews was anybody's guess. Fontana leafed through the department phone directory. Three chiefs bore names beginning with C: Crews, Crutchfield, and Correa.

Typically, arson for cash involved a scheme wherein a party would buy a worthless piece of property and resell it to a confederate for considerably more money than it was worth. They would repeat the process, jacking up the price over a period of months, years, while taking particular pains to keep the insurance premiums paid up.

A businessman might purchase an apartment building for a hundred grand, resell it six months later with only superficial improvements for three hundred grand, then again nine months later for three quarters of a million. All the sales were to confederates, and generally no money changed hands; they did it all on paper. Finally, somebody burned it to the ground and the owner collected seven hundred and fifty thousand on a rundown tenement worth less than a hundred. It happened all the time.

It happened at the Eldorado Arms and, as a result, two children who should have been skipping rope and watching cartoons were dead. And now Steve Zajac was decked out on a gurney at Harborview.

On a whim, Mac phoned Station Six's Lieutenant Grady at his home and inquired about bad blood between Zajac and Reinholt. Wishy-washy as ever, Grady explained that Zajac and Reinholt had quarreled. Zajac had hinted he might spill something that would get Don fired.

"I thought Zajac was the one in danger of getting fired."

"Steve said he could get Don booted ass over teakettle right to the unemployment line. I swear he did. This important? Hey, I got a question for you. The paper said Steve was killed with a knife, but there's a rumor going around work that it was a machete. Or a power saw. We was wonderin' . . ."

"You ever get a clue as to what Steve was holding over Reinholt?"

"None of us could figure it."

The day after his frolic in the fuel oil, Fontana visited Issaquah again and went over Bill Kite's story. He obtained the locations of the two fires: the one in the spring where they'd lost the children, and the one that had precipitated Zajac's dismissal. The two sites were only a couple of miles apart.

The night of the first fire, Kite explained, Zajac had roughed up the dispatcher, then teetered between duking it out with Chief Crews and resigning. That same night Kite had come within a cat's whisker of quitting the department. He hadn't told anybody, but Zajac, sensing something was out of whack, had taken him aside.

"You're thinking about quitting, aren't you?" he had asked. When Kite looked perplexed, Zajac had continued,

" 'Cause I was thinking about it myself. Hard to go through something like this and *not* think about it. I mean, you start wondering, how many more times can you walk in on a couple dead kids?"

Consoling, battling the deep melancholy that was smothering them both, he had given Kite a low-key pep talk. It was the only thing that kept Bill Kite from resigning. And now, after hearing on the television that Zajac had been murdered, Kite was in shock.

"I hardly knew the guy," said Bill softly, "just worked with him a few times. Yet he probably did more for me than any other man in the department. Know what I mean?"

"Sure."

Driving to Seattle, Mac found the location of the Eldorado Arms a quarter mile off Des Moines Way South. It had been bulldozed into the mud. Somebody with a finger on the quick buck and an eye for kitsch had slapped up a set of fiberboard condos, then slopped on enough gaudy lime-green to last at least into next month. He asked neighbors about the fire last spring but nobody knew anything. The second fire had been set in a two-story vacant house at the end of a graveled road overlooking the Duwamish River.

Attempting to visualize the fire and its aftermath, Fontana spent twenty minutes touring the charred house, getting his pants grungy, mucking up his shoes. It had been a hot one. Deep black alligator ripples marred the remaining walls. Arson. The night of the fire they had smelled kerosene fumes.

Acting as lieutenant on Engine 26, Zajac had warned the crew as they drove to the location.

"He was good," Kite had said. "Only a firefighter, but he was acting lieutenant that night and he was good. As good or better than any officer I've worked for. He always kept calm. It's contagious when the officer keeps calm. Laid out the instructions. Made the driver go past the house so we could see three sides of the building. Gave a danged good report to the other incoming units. Somehow he cottoned to that arson deal before any of us. Then Crews showed up and ripped him a new asshole."

Inside the house, Mac saw where the floor had been sawed away, where topless kerosene cans had been set up to tumble into the flames as unwitting firefighters knocked out their frail props. Back East they filled balloons with gasoline and dangled them on strings. In a fire, the balloons would burst open over the firefighter's heads, dousing them.

Booby traps.

Nasty business.

One year in Toledo a pair of firefighters caught a man setting a booby trap and pitched him headfirst out a twelve-story window. The newspapers and community leaders had decried it. Everybody in the department back there said it was too bad.

Too damn bad.

26
Queer Duck at the Bedouin

FRIDAY NIGHT Mac duded himself up for the Bedouin.

The local dance and booze joint, the Bedouin was a barn of a building, incorporating a twenty-four-hour-a-day restaurant and two bars, one ritzy, one the scene of a recent knifing. Situated on the old highway, the Bedouin, oddly enough, sported an alpine motif, including brightly colored shutters and scrollwork. Except for a fresh coat of chocolate-brown paint, it looked like a Swiss chalet gone to pot.

On any Friday night it would be ricked hip to hip with truck drivers, loggers, sawmill workers, lawyers, and businessmen who commuted from the boondocks into Seattle—all on the prowl. From time to time the junior-college crowd made an appearance. The Bedouin also held an inexplicable attraction for a certain category of slumming single women from Seattle, a phenomenon Mac had never quite understood. Two hundred people might turn out for a social whirl of darts, drinks, and rowdy palaver. This night Mac craved relaxation, slow dancing, a beer or two, and chitchat with any volunteers who might show up.

He'd already quaffed a Rainier and was dancing in the push of couples with Mrs. Kilpatrick, a svelte woman of substantial endowments who drenched him in a soft Georgia accent and steeped him in a cloud of perfume. Local gossips said Mrs. Kilpatrick was considerably worse than a coquette, but he'd never bothered to test the high-water marks of her flirting.

When the number ended, Mac excused himself and plowed his way to the main foyer where the air was cool.

"April."

She turned, fixed him with watery eyes, and said only, "Oh," as if dumbfounded.

"What are you doing here?"

"I . . . I've been looking for you," she said, glancing around uncertainly as a boisterous group entered and jostled her. "Your baby-sitter, Mrs. Gilliam, said I would find you here."

"I'm glad you came"

"You said anytime. I've been feeling a little blue and you said anytime." She chewed on her lower lip.

"You look marvelous, April. Smashing. I called you a few times but you weren't home. I would have tried harder but I wasn't sure you'd talk to me."

He slipped her coat off and they grabbed a table in the back. A Neil Sedaka ballad boomed out of the jukebox. He asked her to dance, and once on the floor, she melted against him.

"How have you been?" he asked.

"Considering it all, okay. I've been thinking about some of the things we said."

"And?"

"I don't know. I've just been thinking. I've been doing a lot of thinking. You dance well. You and your wife dance a lot?"

"Linda passed away a couple of years ago. Didn't dance, though. Just something we never did."

"I thought you had a wife. I saw your kid."

"Yeah, well, she died."

"I'm sorry."

"I know you won't believe this, but I think I know some of what you're going through. What I wanted to tell you was that it gets better. It gets a little better every time you wake up, and then finally one day you realize you're living a life again."

A segment of the male population of the Bedouin was having a hard time taking their eyes off April. She was more feminine and attractive than he had ever seen her, downright slinky, in contrast to her mood.

She said, "I can't think of anything else. All day. It's the only thing in my head. I've even thought about going to a doctor and getting a prescription or something. Just anything to knock me out. It's all I think about. Steve and me. And the trouble is, we weren't even living together anymore. I know we were going to get back together. Steve denied it, but he knew it, too. I know he did. It's like unfinished business."

"You're doing better than you think, April. I was comatose for weeks."

"You?"

"Flat on my back. I couldn't talk to anybody. If it hadn't been for the boy . . . I don't know what would have happened. You're dressed. You're here. And you're lovely."

"Thanks. I've been talking to friends and things. It doesn't help."

"It's nice to know they're there, but they don't know what to say."

"That's it exactly. I had a different feeling about you, though. Even after we quarreled, I just had the feeling you really empathized. You told me about this place that first day. Is it all right that I came? Do you have a date or anything?"

"I do now."

"Thanks."

"Don't thank me. I'm the envy of the town."

As they shuffled in the crush of couples, Mac mentally reviewed the case, replayed his aborted lust from the day in her apartment.

If Reinholt was right about her, she was in the throes of

some unknown neurosis, had deluded herself into thinking she had moved out on Zajac, instead of vice versa. She'd asked Mac to look around the cabin, then had run out on him. According to Reinholt, she'd fired shots at her lover. There was a possibility he was dancing with a killer. An ironic thought, he mused, because she was certainly dancing with one.

"You make it to work the other night?" he asked.

"Oddly enough, yeah, I did. But I was sleepwalking. In fact, I was sleepwalking until I came in here. In a purple haze. A lot of things got clear when I came in here."

"Like what?"

"Things."

"Where do you work?"

She hesitated, perhaps deciding how involved she wanted to get with him. Something spurred her. "An insurance company. Computers and printouts and claims. All very dull."

"Dullness has its advocates."

Fontana felt a tap on his shoulder: Mo Costigan, in jangly cowboy boots with spangles on them. She wore a fringed shirt and jeans so tight they could tattoo stitch marks onto her soul.

"May I cut in?" she asked.

"What do you have in mind, Mo? You wanna dance with me or her?"

"You. Don't be silly."

"Excuse me, April."

When April had gone to the table, Mo said, "With all these women, you're in hog heaven."

"What's the matter with you, Mo?"

"You're still calling yourself sheriff, aren't you? Sheriff?"

"Zajac's killer is still running around loose."

"So?"

"Might be in this very room, Mo."

The notion paralyzed her so that he could feel her ribs

175

against him. Finally, she exhaled. "Might be running loose ten years from now, too. You'll probably never find him."

"Won't be the first time I've been skunked."

"So then what are you going to do? The full city council convenes next Wednesday. I can revoke that badge if I want."

"Do what you have to."

She thought about that. "I've been considering the other day. When I got so crabby and said you couldn't be sheriff. And I spilled that stuff off your desk. And I shouldn't have brought up that other thing—about back East?"

"That."

"Mac?"

"Ummm?"

"It's really starting to bother me." They danced silently for a stanza. "You did kill somebody, didn't you?"

"This is not for public consumption."

"Sure, Mac."

"I mean it. Between you and me."

"On my word of honor."

"I arrested a woman for burning one of her kids with a match. She was deranged. We knew that. When they got on her nerves, she would touch one of them with her cigarette lighter, maybe sit them on the stove. She got counseling, did some time, and they took her kids away from her. 'Bout four years later I ran into her again."

"Uhhhh. Mac, I don't want to hear this. Sicksicksick." Mo tried to wriggle out of his grasp but Fontana wouldn't release her. After a moment, she quit wrestling, loosened her grip, and moved with him to the music. "Okay."

"You wanted to know. You're going to hear this. She went to jail, but when she got out, she was eight months pregnant from a guard or visitor or something. So she was released on parole and got her kids back somehow and the baby on the way. I got Children's Protective on her case and followed up on it for a while, then lost track. This wasn't a simple thing. She'd disfigured the one I jailed her on. Permanently disfigured the little tyke. That doesn't even take into consideration the mental scars."

Mo spoke hesitantly. "Was she . . . you know . . . black?"

"What are you?"

"Me?" Mo pulled back to look up at his face, trying to see whether he was serious. "Me? I'm three-quarters Hungarian."

"Strange coincidence. She was Hungarian. Anyway, one night I'm working on something completely different and we're in this seedy—"

"Hungarian? Very funny."

"You want to hear this or not?"

"But you—"

"Mo, let's do everybody a favor and leave race out of it. Some street cops and whatnot can look at people and get a pretty good idea of what they're dealing with. Blacks, whites, green, polka dots. They get so they can read people. It's called street smarts and it comes from years of making mistakes, from getting flimflammed and having your fingers chewed up in doors. You've been down on Kingsley ever since I've been here. You want to get down on somebody in this one-horse fire department, you get down on Lieutenant Allan. He's about half the fireman Kingsley is."

"Kingsley's done very poorly on his tests. Allan's been exemplary. And I haven't been down on Kingsley. I've had complaints, things I have to follow up on."

"Right. So I'm in this seedy apartment building—"

"What do you mean by that? You are the goddamndest man I've ever met."

"Forget it. I'm in this apartment building doing an interview, and when I get done talking to this old geezer he asks me if I can look into this situation downstairs with this woman and her kids. And all this time I've been talking to him I hear this squalling, but I think nothing of it because you always hear squalling in those places. So he tells me there's a lady downstairs everybody thinks hurts her kids, though the kids won't talk, not even to the other kids in the building.

They don't act natural. Tells me she's got five of them, all under six years of age. Tells me her name. Whitehead. Hell, I know the lady. I arrested her.

"I sprint down there, my partner running after me hollering about warrants and judges, but before he can stop me I smash her door in. My partner tells me to be careful but it's too late because there's Lilly Whitehead dandling a baby over a candle, two other kids cowering in a corner. She tried to push the kid away like she wasn't doing anything, but I saw it. She's got a boyfriend in baggy Jockey shorts, drugged out of his gourd on a dirty mattress. I kick her in the butt and take the screaming baby and give it to my partner. My partner testified in court that I hit her six times, but I would have sworn it was sixty."

"I'm glad you hit her."

"Don't be. I killed her."

Mo didn't have a rejoinder for that.

"I went off my rocker. I dunno. Maybe it was only six times. The adrenaline made my hair grow an inch. She dropped on the floor with a broken neck. Her boyfriend woke out of his stupor and started blubbering about calling the police on us. I stuffed his head through the wall. Later on he sued. Said I knocked out his teeth and gave him a complex so he couldn't hold down a job. Claimed the anxiety over my attack turned him into a junkie."

"And they cleared you on the lady's death? They must have. You're here."

"It was complicated. My partner quit on me, said my temper had been out of control too long. I don't know. Maybe he was right. Living in the big city was only part of it."

"Is that why you don't own a TV?"

"Yeah, Mo. That's why I don't have a TV. Where was I? So we went through this rigamarole in court. My side dragged in the burned baby, then showed some pictures of the other kids. Sure, I killed her. But the jury acquitted me. Maybe

178

what they did wasn't ethical, but they aquitted me. They said she might have been trying to burn me. That I was defending myself and the baby. The department was horrified. Instead of ending up in the clink like I thought, I was put back to work. They didn't like it. I was on the captain's list. So they promoted me and gave me a ton of paperwork. My wife died during the trial. It was an emotional time."

"And here you are?"

"And here I are."

"Would you consider being sheriff full-time? Would you ever consider that again?"

"Never considered it in the first place, Mo. You have a habit of putting words into my mouth. First, you want to fire me and then you want me full-time. Make up your mind."

When the woman tapped Mo on the shoulder, Mo cocked her head around and let out an audible gasp. It was Neil Attwood's security manager, Dahlia Grimm, bodyguard, karate expert. Fontana was as shocked as Mo.

As she walked away, Mo bumbled into a dancing couple, patted their shoulders, and apologized. She was sure a queer duck, thought Fontana, yet he couldn't help liking her.

Dahlia said, "We may as well dance while we talk. It seems to be the thing to do."

"Don't mind if I do," said Mac, grinning. "How'd you find me, anyway?"

"Stopped by your office," Dahlia said. "Some volunteer fireman or something said you'd be down here."

Dahlia was the most businesslike of his dance partners, holding him the way a lady dance instructor might hold a fourteen-year-old boy. There were few blacks in town, but she was the only one in the Bedouin just then. She wore a persimmon skirt along with a matching jacket. Her heavy muscular thighs bounced against his. She smelled sweeter than any of the women he'd danced with that night. He watched shafts of light glance off her smooth, high-boned cheeks. Johnny Mathis sang about a woman named Sunny.

"I'm surprised to see you," said Mac. "I really am. I know how busy you people are. Attwood send you?"

"In a manner of speaking, he did. I've been trying to get out here all week but we've been so jammed up. Fourteen-hour days. You wouldn't believe what those towers have done to us. I was on my way to eastern Washington for a conference this weekend and took a chance you'd be around. I've been watching. You're pretty popular."

"I guess."

27

Whistlestops and Whoremongers

MAC AND DAHLIA GRIMM danced through that number and deep into the next, a fast-paced tune by Phil Collins that cleared the floor of all but the hardy.

"Actually, Neil and I each decided on our own that we should do something," she shouted over the music. "Neil really feels rather bad about your dead man. He gets like that sometimes. So here I am. On my own time yet, if you can dig it."

The tune ended and a slow one began. The floor grew cluttered. Soft as a baby blanket, her black hair caressed his cheek. Dahlia said, "When I called the cops to check you out they said you almost got killed a couple of days ago. It sounded a little weird, what they said."

"It was a lot weird."

Mo Costigan was back, her fist pecking at Dahlia's shoulder.

Fontana winked. "Right back," he said, taking Mo into his arms and swooping her off near a cluster of college-age dancers in hiking togs. "What the hell are you doing, Mo?" What she was doing was squeezing closer than she had all evening. When she finally unglued herself, his chest would have a pair of clammy sweat stains the size of silver dollars.

"That business about race?" said Mo, her voice shaky. "You have a black girlfriend, don't you?"

"What if I did?" he said.

Her tone was scathing. "Mac? If you're going to be sheriff you're going to write reports. Monday I want every detail of your investigation on my desk."

"Don't write reports, Mo. I don't write reports and don't go to meetings."

"You went to that housing meeting."

"To complain. I like complaining."

"What are you trying to say? That you only do things you like?"

"That's the arrangement I've made with myself."

"You can't live your life like that."

"Watch me."

"What am I going to do with you?" she asked.

"Let's think about that."

It was obvious Mo had concocted some sort of blueprint for this evening and events had thwarted it. When the number ended she left without a word. He found Dahlia and asked her to dance again. She craned her head back and peered at him from eyes opaque as ink. Mac said, "How'd you get mixed up with Neil Attwood, anyway?"

"Around the Attwood Corporation I'm famous for my temper. I'm working on it, but sometimes I blow off like a can of beer on a hot day. Attwood calls me his ebony tiger. Got out of junior college and I didn't see any recruiters from Paine Webber or Shearson American Express bustin' my door down, so I enlisted in the army. They needed women martial-arts instructors. I found I had a talent for it."

"That how Neil found you? In the army?"

"That was later. I was in eight years, then I got out and worked in construction for a while. They were giving black women jobs like crazy to keep from giving 'em to black men. One day I got into it with somebody, some big sloppy dude hanging Sheetrock. He thought he could take advantage of me because I'm a woman. I knocked him cold. A week later Neil asked me to come up. He checked me out. Had me show my stuff and gave me a three-month trial as his bodyguard. I've never touched another hammer. I've been auditing law and business classes at night." Pride poisoned her voice.

"You been thinking about what I asked you the other day?"

"About Zajac? He kinda weaved over to our table and started lipping off. I think he said, 'So you got people watching me? I've got your number, Attwood . . .' Something like that. Know what I think? He was addled. He needed a sweater with no armholes."

"That all you remember?"

"That's it."

The song ended and somebody punched a quarter into the jukebox, selected a rendition of "Light My Fire" by the Doors. Most of the couples left the floor. Standing soldier-straight, Dahlia tugged at the hem of her jacket, peered down, and lined it up neatly. "Neil wants you to know, anything we can do, he'll do. In fact"—she looked doubtful—"he claimed he'd free me up for a couple of weeks if you need an assistant. Somebody to run errands. We've got a lot of contacts in town. We might be able to smooth your investigation along. Of course, you're sheriff and everything, but we might be able to help."

"I'll get back to you."

"Fine. Well, I've got a long drive. I have to be in Yakima by eight in the morning. Remember, we'd like to help. Neil's got a social conscience, whether people want to attribute one to him or not." She brushed his hand with her fingertips as she moved away. Burnished in a deep shade of fuchsia, her nails were long and flawless. "We can make things easier."

"Sure."

Guessing by the array of paper napkins branded by wet shot glasses, April had drained at least two martinis, was paddling a swizzle stick in a third.

"Regular Lothario, aren't you?" she asked.

"It was business."

"About Steve?"

"Peripherally, yeah."

"Those two bitches know something about Steve? Sorry." She swung her head over her drink and smiled. "Did I call them bitches? I apologize. I've been thinking about him all week. Steve. A love like that comes about only once in a lifetime. Know what I mean?"

"I think I do."

"Think? What? Haven't you ever loved anyone? I feel sorry for you. Wanna dance?" She was hammered.

They slid out of the booth and made their way to the floor. Mac started to sweat right away. He hadn't danced with this many interesting women in one night in a long while. "You mind clearing up a few loose ends, April? As long as we've got some time."

"Ummm," she said, pressing her cheek against his chest, dancing as if she were on a twelve-hour furlough from a women's prison.

"You said you knew Don Reinholt, Steve's best friend at work."

"So?"

"He doesn't know you. Not your name, what you look like, nothing."

Her voice came softly, and he had to strain to hear above nearby talkers, the unbridled laughter, and the jukebox. "Steve spoke of him. I saw him when I visited the station."

"Reinholt claims you never visited the station."

She readjusted her plump cheek on his damp shirt. "I did. I think it was before Steve and I were an item. Maybe that's why he doesn't remember."

"Why would Steve want to keep you a secret?"

"I have no idea."

"There's more, April. Steve's investigation. You said he

was following Chief Crews around. What about Neil Attwood?"

"Who?"

"Seems Steve got into a row with Attwood last June."

"I didn't know anything about that."

"You sure?"

"Certainly."

They danced for another hour, danced until they were limp with it, perspiring against each other. They drifted under the multicolored lights, purples, pinks, oranges. Shortly before midnight, sobered somewhat, April whispered, "Mac, it's getting late."

"It is. Let's go somewhere, April."

"Somewhere?"

"Where we can be alone."

She pulled back and stared at him for a moment. Her cat-gray eyes appeared yellowish under the dim lighting. Part of him was saying this was not a good idea.

"Okay," she said.

Outside, the air was sharp and humid. The chill bit through his shirt. A fog was descending on the town. High and thin now, it would blanket Staircase by sunrise. To the northeast, a sliver of moon shone, creating a halo around Mount Gadd. A wispy cloud hugged the face of the mountain.

Avoiding each other's eyes, they walked three blocks on the quiet streets. Her hard high heels made hollow, drumbeat sounds in the stillness. A diesel-truck motor coughed to life a block away.

He took her to the sheriff's office.

On the narrow, squeaky bunk in the jail cell they made love. She was quiet and voracious, wrapped up in herself, eyes shut. Her muscular, tawny, sweaty body seemed remarkably tiny under him.

It worked—her artlessness was appealing in its own way. Afterward, when he judged that she had fallen asleep, he pushed himself up and made a move for his clothing. She slid two strong arms around his waist and tugged him back. His hard stomach smacked hers.

"Where do you think you're going?"

"Thought you were sawing logs."

She grew quiet and very still. "Mac, you have a talent for intimacy. Maybe I said that wrong. I don't mean for making love."

"Thanks."

"Now I know I'm saying it wrong. It's the way you talk to people. So soft and personal, like you and them are the only ones in the room. Mac, I hardly know anything about you."

He rammed his fists into the thin mattress above her shoulders, planted them on either side of her head, pushing himself off her. "You want to know about me?"

"Every detail."

"Me? I'm the kind of guy who works in a job and lets it consume his every moment for eighteen years and then one day quits in a snit. Gives the boss five minutes' warning and walks out the door with his coffee mug."

April reached up and cradled his face in her hands, hands callused by weight bars. She drew him down for a kiss, and tried to read his eyes. "I can't quite figure you."

The light in the room came from a conglomeration of moonlight and neon. It washed her in shades of sepia; her mussed red hair stood out. He watched her frowning lips, thin and drawn.

She said, "I like weight lifting and the high you get after a good workout. I like handsome men and my job and fast cars. I like riding bareback. I like sunbathing in the raw. I like Stevie Wonder and Lionel Richie and I like cats. But I don't own a cat. Is that funny?" Tilting her head to one side, she kissed the ropy veins on his forearm. "Maybe I'll get some clothes and move them in tomorrow. You have a lot of room? It looked like kind of a small house."

"My house?"

"I was wondering if I should put the TV in storage."

"April, what are you talking about?"

"Moving in, of course. What did you think?"

"April, I'm sorry, but you're not moving in."

The confusion in her face evoked pity. Suddenly he felt as though he were about to be drawn into an argument with a retarded person. He wished this conversation wasn't taking place, much less in a jail cell on a bunk with the both of them wrapped up like snakes. But it didn't seem to bother her. Not a whit. Not the conversation. Not the look on his face. Not the rebuff. She reached down between them and took him into her hand.

"Sure. Okay. I won't move in. It was a thought." It seemed as if nothing of moment had been proposed, nothing of moment had been nixed.

Before he could sort it out they were making love again. Gone was the futzing. As if she'd flipped a switch, she became an enchantress with the dexterity of a high-priced call girl.

When they finished, she nodded off. He marked time for a few minutes, letting the sweat in the small of his back dry, then uncoupled and climbed off the bunk. He pulled a blanket over her, took his clothes into the sheriff's office, and dressed.

Move in? She had wanted to move in? Where had she gotten a notion like that? After one hour in a jail cell? She thought they were both taking it for granted.

He fished her car keys out of her handbag and slowly worked the knob on the outside door. Satan joined him outside. On the walk over, he'd spotted her yellow Corvette parked in the vacant lot of the bank. He jogged over, unlocked her car, sat in the passenger seat, and rifled the glove box. Searching the storage space in the rear, he pawed through a travel bag in the backseat. Nothing of consequence.

He found the shoes under the passenger seat.

Nike running shoes.

Studying the tread of the right one, he unfolded a piece of

paper from his hip pocket and held it up. It was a Xerox of a footprint, the print they'd found in the hardened mud at Zajac's cabin Tuesday.

It took him only a few seconds to decide the shoe in his left hand had made the print in his right. She'd been up there sometime either at the time of or shortly after the rain, but that was no secret. She'd admitted as much. At least he knew the print didn't belong to someone else. He wondered whether the footprint had been made the night of the murder. Matching it didn't settle a thing. Searching her car had not only been a waste, it made him feel like a heel.

28

High, Wide, and Handsome

FONTANA WAS STILL PLUMBING April's 'vette for secrets when the single aid-car door on the fire station rolled up, tinny panels clanking.

The aid car headed up Alice Street, red lights soiling the facades of nearby buildings in spatters of light that reminded Mac of bloodstains. The two volunteers sleeping over tonight, wise to the duty, didn't bother to butcher the town's tranquillity with the siren.

It was Dempsey, a kid just out of school, and Mackelroy, a male nurse, who worked at St. Joseph's in Tacoma and who slept in the station a couple of nights a week to tap into the twenty-five bucks a shift.

When the aid car parked in front of the Bedouin, Mac ran the four blocks to see what the trouble was. The jukebox hadn't been squelched. A man named Truck Anderson who was about half the size of a Ford Escort in suspenders had imbibed four or five too many, grown dizzy, then kissed the floor with his head.

Kneeling, Mackelroy squeezed the bulb on the blood pressure cuff and listened to the Velcro make its tearing sound, while Dempsey waved a clipboard and tried to piece together the mechanism of injury from the shouted comments of onlookers. Young Dempsey had secured his First Responder's card only a month earlier.

Fontana made a knuckle out of his middle finger, and scrubbed it back and forth across Truck Anderson's sternum. It was a trick for reviving patients, stung yet caused no damage. Anderson came round slowly, bawling, "Cut that shit. You wanna me rearrange your face? Cut that shit."

Mac left them to it.

Outside the Bedouin, a small chow raced at Mac's foot, tore into his pants. He'd never seen the dog before, had no idea where it'd come from. No warning. Just barking and then tearing his pants. He kicked at the feisty mutt, but it didn't back off.

Satan got up from his resting spot near the aid wagon, pushed his nose under the caramel-colored dog, and shoveled him three feet to the side. The surprised chow came marauding around in a large circle, yapping at Satan and alternately at Mac.

When the pugnacious dog got close, it nipped Mac's leg again.

Before he could act, Satan had the smaller dog by the neck and was shaking. Mac yelled but it was too late. The chow looked like a rag doll in a Mixmaster. Satan released the animal in mid-shake and the small body whirred onto the sidewalk. Mac inspected his leg to see if it was bleeding, then went over to nurse the chow. It was dead.

"Geez almighty. Nice work, Satan," said Mac. "I thought you were just an aircraft carrier for fleas, but it turns out you're a hit dog. What's the matter with you? Dummy." Mac raised a hand as if to swat his rump, but didn't. Satan flattened his ears and hugged the ground.

"You better lay low."

Mac had just deposited the chow into a nearby dumpster when Mo Costigan came out behind the boys with Truck Anderson, handing out orders like handbills at a carnival. Everyone was doing his best to ignore her. "Mac?" she said, startled. Several times in the past they had exchanged harsh words about her interference in the department.

"Evenin'."

"Mac. You're alone. Or are you?"

"Not exactly."

She looked disappointed. "Oh. Anyway"—she glanced around—"have you seen Freud?"

"Who's that?"

"My dog."

"Oh, Christ."

"Where is she?"

"You named a female dog Freud?"

"Yeah, where is she?"

"I wish I could tell you, Mo."

"You haven't seen her?"

"Mo . . . look. No, I haven't seen her."

In the dark cell April had quartered the blanket, squaring it with the bunk mattress. Outside, her 'vette was missing. He wondered how she'd done it. He still had the keys.

In a hazy patina of moonlight and descending mist, he walked home.

Saturday morning the town was socked in. Fog. Mac spent a couple of relaxed hours with Brendan and the Legos, constructing jets, crab pots from outer space, piecing together blockheaded aliens in blues, yellows, and whites, bricking up elaborate castles. They played crazy eights for an hour, and Mac found himself not listening to what the boy was saying. He hated that. It was part of why they were in Staircase. So he would have time to listen.

At nine-thirty, hunchbacked from the cold walk, Mary Gilliam bustled through the back door toting a bag of tatting. Under her arm she had wedged a paperback book about a serial killer who collected body parts in his freezer.

"Are we getting any closer to solving the murder?" she asked.

"It's a little like looking for the light switch in a pitch-dark room, Mary. You only know you're closer when you've got it."

"People are a wee bit frightened, Mac. Mrs. Kilpatrick bought a shotgun and told Bert he could move back in."

"Didn't know they were on the skids," said Mac, trying to recall how the Kilpatricks had treated each other last night.

"If you jail this killer, you'll be the town hero."

"If I don't?"

"Don't worry, Mac. You'll solve it and I'll write the goldangdest article you ever saw."

After bussing Brendan on the cheek, Mac drove the GMC to the sheriff's office. Earlier in the week he'd scraped out the shards of glass from the window Satan had broken, then inserted an identical sliding pane from a junkyard in Issaquah.

He spent an hour dithering over next month's volunteer roster for night and weekend duty, perusing the fire and aid reports from last week, all the while thinking about Steven Zajac's murder. He made a phone call. Saturday morning or no, Charles Dummelow was at work.

"Got anything on the Draper boys?"

"Not a whisper," said Dummelow.

"Charles, were there any witnesses to this incident last June between Zajac and Neil Attwood's bodyguard? Somebody besides Attwood and the bodyguard?"

"Hang on a sec. Got a copy of the report right here. Lemme see." Rustlings marred the connection and then he was back. "Here it is. Was a woman with Zajac. Saw the whole thing. Apparently was quite confused."

"Name?"

"Falwell."

Mac sighed. "That burns a couple of theories."

"Sorry to hear that. Yeah, Falwell, April."

"Say that again."

"April Falwell. Mean anything to you?"

"She the only witness mentioned?"

"Only one I got listed. Why? You think she might be this other April I spoke to? The bodybuilder?"

"I'll look into it."

"Do that."

When he'd hung up Fontana grabbed the slim mouse-colored SFD telephone directory he'd pilfered from Station Six. Falwell. It rang a bell. He thumbed through the book page by page, beginning at the back in the Seventh Battalion. He didn't run it to ground until he'd scanned "Fire Investigation." Seattle staffed its fire investigation unit with eight investigators and two Seattle cops, and he had paid a bit more attention to their names than he might have, since it had been his specialty.

Theodora A. Falwell was listed as an inspector in the fire investigation section. The only woman. And a woman named Falwell, April, had been with Zajac that night at Latitude 47.

April Smith, April Sumner, and Theodora A. Falwell were all one woman, they had to be—his recent cellmate and would-be roommate. Remembering the chopped-up shifts they worked, he dialed Seattle's fire investigation section on their business line, requesting Inspector Falwell.

"Unless we have a fire, she'll be back directly after lunch," said a sleepy-sounding man. "She's got an appointment here at one o'clock."

"Thanks."

"Can I tell her who called?"

"Better not."

Mac got Fred Crews's number from the department phone directory, a Mercer Island listing.

He dialed, asked a woman with a bassoon voice whether Fred was there, then hung up when she went to fetch him— surprise was what he had in mind. There was no point in warning a witness that you were coming to ask thorny questions, no point in letting him rehearse evasions.

In Staircase the fog had risen, but the closer to town he got, the lower, thicker it remained. Traffic came in dribs and drabs, all with headlights piercing the whiteness. They had been working on the I-90 traverse on Mercer Island for a couple of years, readying lanes for the third floating bridge across Lake Washington. Making room for more inmates. Lots on the Eastside were selling as fast as roads could be bulldozed into them.

When he finally swung south and forged through to East Mercer Way, he found it a tortuous two-lane road snaking along the east side of Mercer Island.

He steered the bulky GMC down a windy, gravel road under a canopy of bare trees that resembled something from a Stephen King movie. The road was carpeted in wet leaves, descended in a deep gulch. Three houses shared the road. All three had beach access.

At the last lot a wrought-iron sign announced FRED AND MARTY CREWS. A monstrous beige home, it sported a white picket fence, dock, and cabin cruiser. A chain saw screamed at the rear of the house.

Confining the dog to the Carryall, Mac followed a macadam driveway around the back. The yard had been landscaped by experts, decked out in Texan overkill and Canadian greens. Firs. Spruces. Rhodies. It was all young and woodsy, and only a few of the plants were taller than Fontana.

There was half an acre of landscaped backyard. The foreground was open, consisted of a lawn that was more of a field. It ran down to a dock and a cabin cruiser large enough for a lower and upper wheelhouse. Forty feet long, it would gobble more fuel in an hour than it took to heat his house for a month. The far side of the yard was taken up by an arboretum. A logger had jockeyed his rig in and off-loaded a stack of twenty- and thirty-foot logs on the property.

Two men were chain-sawing the logs into chunks stubby enough to split with a maul. One of the men was Crews.

The temperature was in the low forties, yet the chief wore a V-neck T-shirt and a baggy pair of outdated suit pants, boots, nothing else except a gold-plated Longines that should have been on a tray under lights. Standing with his back to Mac, the other man was tall and hulking, wore a plaid work shirt and jeans.

When Crews spotted Fontana he set his chain saw down, choked it until it sputtered and died. Unless Mac could goad the old man into saying something rash, this would probably be a wasted trip.

Glowering at Mac, Crews stiffened and planted a fist on either hip. He looked furious, but Mac noticed it had taken fifteen or twenty seconds of concentrated thought to crank himself up to it. Fontana suspected Crews was, in reality, a shy man. Most of the time he kept his shyness cloaked beneath a cape of indifference.

"What are you doing here?"

"Came to talk with you about Steve Zajac."

"I know he's dead. You might have had the courtesy to announce that fact the other day. I've just worked a twenty-four-hour shift and I'm not up to your shenanigans."

The man in the plaid shirt cocked around, chain saw handle butted against his hip. Sam Ring, the aide. He nodded a solemn greeting, then shut the motor off with a black-nailed thumb.

"Mr. Crews, I have reason to believe Zajac's death had something to do with his suspension and with the events leading up to his suspension."

The "mister" hadn't gone unnoticed. Fred Crews was a man who'd devoted his life to jousting for a title, and it rankled him when somebody stripped it away. Mac had known a fire officer in the East whose kids were under orders to call him "Chief" and whose stuttering wife addressed him as "sir." He wondered if Crews was that whacked out.

"We telephoned your township or city or whatever," announced Sam Ring, mopping BB's of sweat off his broad brow. "Staircase. Little outhouse of a town. The mayor was a woman, said you ain't even the goddamn real sheriff. Just a temp."

Crews said, "I was informed you have no real authority."

"What made you think Zajac was two-twenty?" Mac could see by the look in the old man's eye that he'd appealed to Crews's vanity. Crews prided himself on being an infallible judge of men, morals, and malfeasance.

"Zajac had been slipping for quite a while. Some people just aren't able to cope with the job."

"That's not what I hear from his co-workers."

Ring spat. "Everybody's got friends. That doesn't mean he could put out a fire in a toilet."

"He may have had his moments," admitted Crews, sitting heavily on a new stump. Following his lead, Ring monitored a nearby log for pitch deposits, then gambled the seat of his pants on it. He had the look of somebody who saw a queue and had to stand in it.

"Look, just want a few minutes of your time. There's a murderer running around loose and you might know something that could help the cops pinch him."

Using a thumb and forefinger, Crews flicked wood chips off his trousers, the saggy muscles of his arm wobbling. He sucked his gut in. He found Fontana distasteful, yet was beginning to acknowledge the inevitability of the interview. "Five minutes."

"What's your recollection of the incident last spring?"

"Zajac went out of his head. I advised him to talk to the department chaplain. He wouldn't listen. He went to a fire and it was too hot for him or some such thing and he tried to blame his troubles on the dispatchers. Did you know he went to the FAC and started a fistfight? Nobody there would admit it, but I know it happened. Astonishing. Then he came up to Tens and confronted me. I'm not used to insubordination."

"Rubber-room city," said Ring. "Zajac was a moron."

As a matter of habit, Crews spoke so softly that you had to strain to hear him. The tactic was one of control, and he never relinquished it, not even in his own backyard in a breeze that blew half his words away. Fontana moved closer, stood in a pile of yellow-white wood shavings, and inhaled their fresh scent. The yard overlooked the narrow East Channel. Several marinas were on the opposite shore, and the wooded slopes a quarter mile across the glassy lake water were peppered with houses. A cruiser chugged up the channel under the one-dimensional gray sky.

"Nice place," said Mac.

"We think so."

"Been here long?"

"Twenty-two years. Designed and framed the house myself. Added on to it over the years. Just redid the back."

"Nice."

"Sheriff Fontana, I won't mince words. The fire last spring on Des Moines Way wasn't the city's jurisdiction. It was a county fire. It just so happened that there were some injuries. Zajac was an excitable sort and it bothered him. If you know anything about this, you know he wasn't supposed to be anywhere near that area. He had been told to do night hotels on Beacon Hill. He had been gallivanting all over the city with a department car and department gas on department time."

"Cut the bull," said Mac.

"What?"

"Who are you trying to kid? You think somebody got a sliver in their pinky? Two kids died in that fire! I've got the pictures out in the truck if you'd care to see them."

Crews's Adam's apple pistoned up and down his neck, but aside from that nothing and nobody moved for almost a minute. Mac was glad the man didn't have a gun handy. Ring was still as a sparrow in a cat's mouth.

"There are casualties in this line of work," Crews said finally. "It's the nature of the beast. Doctors. Cops. We can't be taking it personally. It's a lesson we all have to learn. We stay calm. We do not lose our temper."

"All I know is you're the one who blocked city units from responding. You said no and two kids ended up critters. You were in the alarm office when Zajac radioed for help. Had you said yes, those two kids might have survived. Zajac blamed it on you, and I don't see any reason to reverse that call."

Irritation knurled Crews's tones. "You've spoken to department members about this?"

"And others."

"I don't have anything to say to you."

"Sure you do. Tell me why you wouldn't send units. Tell me that and we'll all be fat and happy."

"Why I wouldn't send units?"

"You've had time to think about it by now."

"You're in no position to be second-guessing me. Neither was Zajac. I'm a chief."

"Who *is* in a position to second-guess you?"

Crews thought about that for a moment as if it were a legitimate philosophical question of some weight. Finally, he said, "Nobody."

Fontana clapped an open palm to his forehead. "I can't believe I heard that. Nobody? You're the ultimate authority? What about God? You believe in a God?" The reaction put a look of uncertainty, almost of dismay, on Crews's saturnine face. "What did Zajac accuse you of after the fire?"

"Incompetence," said Ring. Fred Crews angled a look at his protégé calculated to check any further outbursts. It did.

"That was it, basically," admitted Crews.

"Nothing else?"

"I said that was it!"

"And what occurred between the time of that fire and the alarm a couple of weeks ago when Zajac was suspended?"

"Between Zajac and me? The normal department business." From the sharp look Ring gave his boots, Fontana knew there had been more.

"I heard he was following you around. You know anything about that?"

"How'd you find that out?"

"I'm an investigator."

Crews mulled it over for a moment, trying to decide how much to cop to. "We went on a cruise up past Orcas, anchored for three days, entertained family friends. We got back late on a Thursday. Marty said she didn't recall leaving all the shades in the back up like that. They were expensive shades, had them custom-sized. See, when they're down . . . We can't prove it was him that broke in. But Marty and I are almost certain it was. He was a man on the ragged edge. He hadn't gotten himself killed, I wouldn't have been too awfully surprised to hear he committed suicide."

"Anything missing from the house?"

"That's what clued Marty and me. Burglars remove property. Nothing was taken. Our books and papers had been sorted through. I'd seen him behind me in traffic a couple of times, too. I never let on."

"You ever confront Zajac with your suspicions?"

"He came out here, oh, about five weeks ago, maybe two weeks before I suspended him. He came to the house and asked Marty a bunch of sarcastic questions. When I entered the room he got even more sarcastic. Sass was all he had on his mind. You remind me of him. I wouldn't be surprised if he was on drugs. Marijuana, crack. He accused me of all sorts of wild things."

"Such as?"

"I'm not going to dignify them by repeating it."

Fontana had left his jacket in the car, was in jeans and a brightly striped orange-and-white rugby shirt; consequently the breeze was beginning to rob his fingers of feeling. He jammed them into his pockets.

"How about if I speculate?" said Fontana. "You worked in the fire marshal's office. You were in charge of inspections. Zajac thought you were taking a personal interest in some of the files, that you were giving variances to people who paid you under the table. Tell me when I start getting warm."

"How on earth . . . ?"

"Whoever killed Zajac destroyed his records, but he kept

a second set hidden under the house. I know they weren't complete, but they were enough to give me the general idea. Over the past couple of days it's taken me a lot of reading and a number of phone calls, but I think I'm getting the gist of it. I think if I were to turn some of the materials in my possession over to a prosecutor with a nose for dirt, he might be able to charge you with something."

"Poppycock."

Ring chimed in. "Not the chief."

Despite his plea of innocence, the color drained out of Crews's olive-complected face and the jowls sagged. Fontana said, "Tell me about that last fire, the one where you canned Zajac."

Eager to scuttle the ship of conspiracy, Crews said, "He was out of line. He fought the fire from the outside. We don't do that here. We go to the seat and extinguish it. It's quicker, more efficient, and it saves property and lives. When I questioned him about it, Zajac not only offered no explanation, but he went . . . all I can say is he went ape. Began ranting."

" 'At's right," said Ring. "He did. I thought maybe he got a snootful of chemicals in the fire or something and they'd affected his brain. That's how out of it he was. He kept accusing the chief of siccing people on him, underworld bad guys and people to beat him up and break into his house. And all this after he'd already broken into the chief's place. And all the chief was asking was why did he fight the fire the way he did. They got it out all right, but their hydrant hookup was ass backwards."

Crews continued. "I wanted to know basically why, as the first-in officer, he'd directed everyone to stay outside. Now, later, it became apparent that it was an arson fire, that it had been booby-trapped. Young Bill Kite was burned a bit when he disobeyed orders and went in. The way I understand it, he mistakenly thought he heard somebody inside. Traps don't happen much in Seattle, so how did he know? How did Zajac know?"

"You suspect him of starting the fire himself?"

"We never considered it. The alarm came in at five-thirty in the morning. He'd been on duty at Twenty-sixes almost twenty-two hours by that time."

"So how did Zajac know this was going to happen?"

"Zajac was paranoid. He thought people were following him. All day. Every day. He thought people were out to get him. He was lucky at this fire. Somebody *was* out to get a Seattle firefighter, but it was coincidence, pure and simple."

"You prove that?"

"Don't have to prove it. I know it."

Fontana was growing sick of the patter. He'd needled a bit already, but this old bull's hide required sharper instruments.

29
More Dead Horses from the Sky

"WANT TO KNOW SOMETHING, Fred?" Mac ruptured the boot-packed surface of the bright pine chips with the heel of his running shoe. "You're the most arrogant man I've ever met."

The three of them waited as the insult dried. Color flooded Crews's fleshy face. The flaccid muscles in his arms knotted up like washrags screwed tight from opposite ends.

"I happen to believe Zajac was on to something," Mac said. "And it was something involving you. He was murdered for it."

"If this is slander I have a witness."

"At a fire Steve gets upset because a couple of children die. You deny complicity. He rags you for it and you decide to ride him out of the department."

"That's simply not true."

"At another fire he gets a hunch that saves somebody's life and you tell him his hydrant connection was fouled up. Must be a kick to look at life through a one-way glass. *Your* mistakes don't count, but *his* stink. For a guy who worked around a bunch of firemen, you've got a funny attitude. Nobody you know ever uses apologies, Band-Aids, or Bondo?"

"I want you to remove yourself from my property."

Despite his earlier feigned candor, Crews had been hampering, stalling, sidetracking. When he rose, Ring's knees cracked. A gritty look disordered his flat-gray eyes. A head taller than Fontana, fifty pounds heavier, he was more than eager to dish out grief. Part of Fontana wanted to see him try, but then, he didn't need to meet T. A. Falwell with a torn shirt and a bloody lip, either.

"Last spring you made a mistake that resulted in two dead kids."

"You have bad information."

"When Zajac called you on it, you decided to make his life hell. You put so much pressure on him that when you jumped him about this latest fire he came out of the gate bucking. Drummed him out of the department. He saved Bill Kite's life. You should be pinning a medal on him, not cutting him down from behind."

"Do I have to call the Mercer Island police?"

"Power has a lot of uses, Fred."

"Sam . . ."

Stepping forward grimly, Ring physically blocked Crews from further verbal onslaught. Crews had visibly deflated during the tirade, and for a few seconds Fontana thought his blustering had worked.

"By the way," said Mac, firing a last salvo. "You know somebody named Elmira Erlandson? Or her late husband?" He couldn't tell if he'd scored. Crews's face had jelled a while back. "You do, you better grab the discount special to Tahiti."

Ring gestured with his head.

"It's okay. I'm running out of insults."

He walked to his truck, keeping Ring, who was trailing him, well inside his peripheral vision. He wasn't about to get coldcocked twice in one week.

Thick arms folded across his chest, knees locked, Ring posted himself ten feet from the truck, sneered, and looked at Mac through tortoiseshell glasses thick enough to deflect hail, pebbles, and flying squirrels. His lenses seemed to glimmer with amusement. "You know it, don't you? Got yourself into a heap of hot water talking to the chief like that."

Mac gave him a mischievous smile. "Was having so much fun I couldn't stop."

"You better just bend over and kiss your ass good-bye, 'cause your career is finished."

"Give me a break."

"Freddy's got political connections all across the state. I wouldn't be surprised if he yanked that dingleberry job of yours right out from under your ass."

Fontana's horselaugh rolled across the yard for longer than seemed sane. At the rear of the house a chain saw quibbled with a pine log. "When I got into the service back East I had an old-timer take me under his wing. He said, 'Mac, don't piss into the wind, spend real silver coins, or argue with a chief.' It was good advice. For the time. It'd be good advice for you. But I'm not in your silly-ass fire department, and he can't touch me."

"Freddy got into a rumpus with a state patrolman on a rescue response on I-5. That patrolman's driving a cab now."

"What's in this for you? You're out here ripping up timber for firewood and what?"

Frown lines lacerated Ring's doughy face. "Whatdaya mean?"

"I mean, did you cut lumber with the last chief you worked for? Paint his house? Wash his poodle? What?"

"You're full of it. Freddy and I've been—"

"I bet you've got your name written on the soles of your shoes."

"Huh?"

"Your name. Write it on the soles of your shoes. The way you follow him around, he's liable to stop real sudden and you'll get jammed up his ass. They'll have to read your shoes to see who's up there."

Ring said, "Just bend over and . . ."

"Yeah, I know."

It was too early to intercept Theodora A. Falwell, so Fontana found a QFC on Mercer Island, bought both Seattle papers, and perused them in the front seat of the GMC. The dog panted over his shoulder. There was something comforting, almost maternal, in the animal's devotion, and he felt an unexpected pang of guilt over what had happened to Mo Costigan's dog.

The region was aghast over a spy scandal at Boeing. The Seahawks had a big one the next day in the Kingdome. Nobody mentioned the Zajac murder case.

In Seattle on Jackson Street, he located a parking place and hoofed it to Tens. In the watch office he BS'ed with two firemen for forty minutes.

The clock read thirteen hundred when Mac drifted out of the watch office and made his way through the murky corridors of the concrete monolith.

Marshal Five's office was one level up in an alcove at the back of Ten's apparatus floor. A catwalk stretched from the second-floor stairway across to a windowless office that was long and L-shaped, the bottom of the L hidden from the entrance. A narrow aisle led through the clutter of desks against either wall. The whole kit and caboodle was about as cheery as a mouse hole.

Near the rear of the room around the corner on the invisible side of the L, he heard two women talking. Glancing up from a typewriter, a chubby man with a frog in his throat greeted Mac solemnly. "Yes?"

"Looking for Theodora Falwell."

"You a friend?"

Mac nodded. Wanting to be dead wrong, he knew by the disembodied sound of her voice that she was around the corner.

A well-dressed black woman held down the guest slot at the first desk beyond the corner, legs crossed, bony knees dimpling her skirt like big arrowheads. April sat across from her.

He felt like a clodhopper. She'd been a member of the Seattle Fire Department all along, and it made him wonder what else she'd lied about. He should have been investigating the jilted lover from the beginning.

Clad in jeans and a simple rose and tan print blouse, she wore a gun on her hip and a frown on her lips. Her face was pale and puffy. She'd been up late screwing his brains out, knowing all the while she had to work in the morning. When she saw him, her eyes widened and grew empty. Her face suddenly took on a jittery animation. Fontana catapulted her keys onto the desk. "See you got home all right."

"I'm conducting an interview just now," April said. "If you would—"

"But I won't."

"You're being rude."

"You lied to me," Mac said.

"And you to me. I saw you last night searching my car. I couldn't believe it."

"You were a suspect. You still are."

The rat-a-tat typing at the other end of the room ceased. "So I suppose you want the whole story?" said April.

"It's overdue."

"You're right." She seemed to collapse. "I should have told you about this that first day. I don't know why I didn't."

April got out of her chair, walked around the desk, rose on tiptoes, and kissed him. Perplexed, he didn't contribute to the sham. The black woman glanced uncertainly from Fontana to April and then down at her arrowhead knees.

"Mrs. McGrath," said April, avoiding Mac's eyes, "I'm really sorry. I know you made time in a very busy schedule to meet me here today, but this is unavoidable. Can I persuade you to make this next week?"

"Like I have a choice?" the black woman asked, pushing her chair back.

"I'm so sorry."

"Not as sorry as I am."

After she'd gone, April dropped into her swivel chair; her red hair was loose and wild, rippling past her shoulders. Jaw muscles flexed in her chubby cheeks. Mac sat on the desk in front of her. The male inspector came around the corner and gawked. "It's all right," April assured him sheepishly, rocking her chair back in tiny, quick arcs.

"We get anything, I'll be across the street," said the male inspector.

"Sure."

They were alone, only the sizzle and hiss of a department scanner skating across the tension. Mac said, "Smith. Sumner. Falwell. You've got more aliases than a social disease."

"Let me explain."

"I'm dying to hear it."

She tried to scoot her chair back and distance herself from him, but the empty desk behind blocked the move.

"I'm the third female investigator. The other two didn't work out. You don't know how glad I am to have this job, this spot in life. I came into the department as Sumner. I was married. We weren't living together or anything, me and Scott. When I got divorced, I decided to change it back to Falwell."

"Falwell at work. Sumner at home. You kept your married name off-shift."

"I meant to change it, but there were so many forms and things that it just got to be a pain. The department change was easy and I never bothered to retract it. Somehow, it let me keep my lives separate."

"And Smith?"

"You know Smith was bogus. I thought I could go up there and ask you to look for Steve and you'd find him with some woman and I'd never see you again. And he'd be all right."

"Except that he wasn't all right."

"Yeah."

"Why didn't you tell me you were in the department?"

"I was scared. Christ, I'm still scared." She stood and tried to embrace him. "Hold me? Just for a minute?"

"Forget it, darlin'. We've been doing too much holding and not enough coming clean. I was happy to see you up there last night, April. But you're right. I searched your car. We've been treating each other like rented mules. Did you investigate the fire where the two kids died?"

"It's complicated. Reinholt," she said. "Reinholt didn't know about me because I used to work at Station Six. Steve didn't want him to know."

"Except your name was April Sumner when you worked at Sixes, correct?"

"That was another reason I didn't mind changing it back to my maiden name. I got kind of a bad rep as a boot. I was real plump. All my life I was. Like one sixty-five, one seventy when I came in. I got up to one ninety at one time. But I was strong. Heck, I was stronger than a lot of the men. One of the other women in the department got me into bodybuilding. It was a secret, me and Steve. He was never in favor of women in the department. Neither was Reinholt. He didn't like blacks, either. Called them lazies."

"If he didn't like blacks in the department, why did he talk Bill Kite into staying?"

"Did he? It sounds like Steve. He was against certain groups, but if he knew you, even for a few minutes, he became your friend, no matter what. It was the same thing with me. He was always giving me encouragement. Me. Not the other women. He hated the thought of women in the department, but somehow I was an exception.

"We didn't get together until after I'd left Sixes, but he didn't want the others to know. They would have razzed him bad, and he wasn't good at verbal sparring. I didn't much care for it, but I strung along. That was one of the things about Steve I admired. Always Mr. Nice Guy.

"At first, in Staircase, that first day, I just suspected something really wrong had happened. I was sick about it. And so scared. Then, when I found out—when you came to my place and I found out Steve had died and you were bound and determined to investigate—I got even scareder."

"What were you afraid of?"

"How much do you know?"

"No, April. That's not where we are. The question on the table is, what have you been hiding? Zajac and you were investigating together, weren't you?"

She nodded "The original information about the fire at the Eldorado Arms, he got that from Guerciotti in county fire investigations. Guerciotti told him it was a guy named Max Draper. You know about him? Draper?"

"He and two others tried to kill me Wednesday."

"They shot at you?"

"It was a lot more fun than that. I'll tell you about it someday."

Her eyes held him hostage. She yawned, plugged her mouth with her fist, and exhaled loudly. Finally, she said, "Phooey."

"My sentiments precisely."

"They couldn't prove Draper did it but it was his MO," said April. "Guerciotti is a pretty sharp dude. He went to a nearby 7-Eleven and went through all their surveillance photos looking for known arsonists. He discovered Draper had been in the store two hours before the fire. About twenty minutes after it started he bought a six-pack of Oly in the same store. Maybe to celebrate, I don't know really what would drive a cretin like him. When they questioned him he turned up a bruised girlfriend in Mountlake Terrace who vouched for him. Everybody was sure he beat her up and made her his alibi."

"I found papers at Steve's," said Mac. "They sold the Arms until they boosted the price up and then they had

Draper light it. HBC. The Hildreth Building Corporation and about three other corporations were all tied into it. And the only name common to all of them was Renaldo Pardew."

"You *have* been digging."

"And there was some SFD dirt, too."

She shivered. "You've done too much, Mac."

"Or not enough."

Her posture wilted. For a moment he thought she was going to try more grappling. She'd seen too many movies, believed in the magic kiss. "Come on. It's in the basement."

"What?"

"Where we store our records. I have to show you something. You'll find out anyway, I might as well show you."

In the basement of Tens one large low-ceilinged room was reserved for underground parking for station members. There was a print shop. And a locked storeroom. In the dimness April used a key, flipped a switch, and escorted him into a room ricked high with cardboard boxes.

She moved to the far side of the room, selected a carton, and began rummaging. Presently, she handed him a file folder.

"What's this?"

"Read."

"You people keep your files down here? Back East we had it all on computer."

"Read."

It was an arrest report from 1973 on Maxwell Draper. The SFD had convicted him of torching his girlfriend's apartment. Nobody had been hurt. He had been sentenced to three years; suspended. The surprise was on the front. He had been a firefighter at the time, assigned to Marshal Five. F. Crews.

Chief Crews had arrested Max Draper in 1973.

"Steve talked me into looking this up. Steve was . . . after that fire where the kids died, he was beside himself. I've never seen a man take anything so hard. It was like they were *his* kids. Susan, his ex-wife, moved to Montana to be with her folks and ended up marrying Steve's best friend from when he was in high school, if you can believe that. It devastated him, losing her and the two boys in one fell swoop. Then he started getting all these harebrained ideas about this Arms deal. Like, what if Crews had been in the alarm office at that moment on purpose—what if Crews had known the Arms was going to be torched and he wanted to be in the FAC just in case? It sounded crazy.

"I thought if Steve wanted to run around on his free time investigating, maybe it would be good for him. Maybe he'd burn out and then he could forget it. But he didn't. He got more and more involved, until I urged him to see a psychotherapist. He'd be up bouncing around the house all night. Never slept. Then he asked me to check through our records for anything on Draper. And I blundered on this. And he got an affidavit from some woman. She claimed somebody in the fire department accepted money from her late husband to let a bunch of violations slip by. A lot of money."

"Elmira Erlandson."

"You know?"

"Some. Go on."

"That's about all. When I found out Crews might actually be involved, I got too scared to continue. I fought like hell to get this job, and I'm not about to give it up because somebody else is playing fast and loose with the city ethics policy. You know what they say about the messenger—he's always the one who gets his head lopped off. Steve and I fought about it." She traced her tongue across her lips. "It was part of the reason I asked him to move out."

"April, I'm tired of letting this slip by. Steve left you. He moved out in the middle of the night."

"No, I . . ."

"Reinholt told me. Steve talked to him before he did it."

Her voice shriveled. "You knew all along? I guess you think I'm a—"

"You're prideful. Aren't we all? What did Steve make of this link between Draper and Chief Crews?"

"He thought sure Crews had something to do with hiring Draper to burn down the Arms. He wracked his brain trying to find some sort of connection on paper between Crews and the Arms. He thought maybe Crews owned it. But all he had were suspicions and a habit of getting into it with chiefs. I told you he beat the bejesus out of some poor slob in a car one night, thought he was following us?"

"You think he would resort to blackmail?"

"Blackmail? Why on earth—?"

"I found a couple of hundred-dollar bills in his house. I had the feeling they had fallen from a brick of bills."

Acting confused, she shook her head. She was seated on the concrete floor. He was kneeling on it, the file between them, not another soul in the basement. "I never even considered blackmail," she said. "Although, he was strapped for cash. He had child support and he took it seriously. And his kids moved to Montana so he spent gobs of money flying back and forth."

"You considered something. Didn't you, April? You have a theory."

"The department was invited to put a couple of members on a city advisory board to oversee the building and designing of the Attwood Towers," she said. "Chief Crews is on that committee."

"So there it is. Flimsy, but there it is. Crews knows Draper. Crews knows Attwood."

"The committee meets with him a couple of times a week."

"So we have reasons why Zajac might have been following Attwood. I don't know if the reasons stand up under scrutiny, but we have reasons."

"It scares me," said April. "I didn't want anybody to know I knew. Can't you see?"

"April, there's nothing to—"

"Don't tell me not to be frightened. You said yourself Draper tried to kill you last week. And you're a man. Just think what he'd do to me. I carry a gun but I'm scared. Steve carried a gun and look what happened to him."

"Do you know who killed Steve, April?"

"I don't know. I wasn't there. But it had to be Max Draper."

He couldn't tell if she was faking. Bad as her acting was, she'd fooled him before. Fright? Or complicity? "April, do me a favor."

"Yeah?"

"Tell me about when you took a shot at Zajac."

She gave Mac a withering look, then redeemed her nonchalance so quickly he almost laughed.

"Which time?"

30

See You at the Big One

"How many times were there?"

"A trip to British Columbia with me was all we needed. Just him and me. Give him a chance to clear his mind. He didn't want to listen. Don't you think a man has a certain obligation at least to listen? I mean, when he's not listening and you're making sense he deserves what he gets. I think so."

A startling amount of vehemence had hatched in her voice. Zajac had taken a knife in the back and still hadn't cashed in her forgiveness.

"So you took a potshot at him?"

"Only twice. Once, he made me so mad." She pinked up. "So mad I just got my service pistol and put one in the wall. He might have thought I was shooting at him. I don't know."

"Were you?"

"I don't know."

"Where did you shoot, exactly?"

"In the wall. I said."

"And where was he standing in relation to this wall?"

"Under the table, I guess. That's where he dove when I started firing."

"You said 'put one in the wall.'"

"Yeah, well, I guess I put them all there. A couple came close. Okay, okay, don't even ask. Six inches, maybe. But I didn't hit him. We made love afterward."

"What about the other time?"

"What other time?"

"Don't diddle me, April."

"The night I found out he was living in Staircase I went up there. Hey, look. I had a few vodka tonics, okay? I shouldn't have and I was driving and everything, but I had a few drinks. It screwed me up. My mother was an alcoholic. Did I tell you that? It really screwed me up. I guess we never get over our mothers. And here I am in the fire department. Did I tell you I'm scared of heights? I almost didn't get in. We had to climb up an aerial ladder for the entrance test. Seventy feet, I think it was. I was shaking like a leaf. I wet my pants a little too, but luckily nobody saw it. That's how scared I was."

Fontana sighed. "You went up to Staircase and did what, April?"

"He wouldn't let me in. It was cold and I thought maybe he had a woman in there, so I put a couple through the door."

"That work better than a doorbell? Maybe I should hang a loaded gun outside. That way I'll never miss another box of Girl Scout cookies or a UPS man."

"I guess the noise sobered me up. I turned around and went home." She uttered one more sentence as if it were a perfectly normal thing to say. "I don't think he really had a woman in there, anyway."

They were quiet for a while. She was still dunning Zajac for past debts.

Fontana paged through the report. Standard stuff. In 1973 Draper was twenty-two years old, out of work, given to rages, and earning a passable living doing burglaries and selling the loot at swap meets. He avenged himself on a girlfriend by hurling a lighted pop bottle of gasoline through a window.

The girlfriend managed to flee out a rear window in her underclothes, but the house sustained twenty grand in damages. Crews made the case.

A fidgety April intruded on his thoughts. "You don't know how glad I was to get into this department. You can't know. I mean, up until eight, nine years ago it was unheard of for a woman to get in." Bitterness raised and quickened her voice. "Then I found out I was terrified of heights and had to hide it all through drill school. How does a girl find out she's scared of heights, anyway? It's not fair. I didn't know. It was something boys would know automatically. They owed me because it wasn't fair. They should have given me a special course in heights. Instead, I faked it. I could have been killed and it would have been their fault. Then I got out in the company and Reinholt was a beast. Even Lieutenant Grady. They thought I shouldn't be in. They said I wasn't strong enough. Shit. I was stronger than Grady."

"Of course you were."

"They made fat jokes behind my back. Only Steve was never part of it. He never talked about anybody behind their back. It wasn't in his nature. The guys on the ladder were neutral, but Steve, he tried to honestly help me. I loved him for that." She inhaled deeply, and the breath stuttered on its way down. Emotion freighted her eyes with teardrops.

"I always admired those tall firemen in their blacks," she continued. "Every woman in town loved them. Of course, when you look at them, a lot of the men are fat, too. Then the night of our graduation ceremony we had a party and I was in my blacks, and I looked in the mirror and I looked like a butterball turkey in a Safeway freezer. I was just so porked out. I broke down and cried. But I am a firefighter. I am."

"April, darlin'. Let's get on with business. You were at Latitude 47 with Steve. What happened?"

"Some black woman whacked the stuffing out of him. Sort of looked like the woman you were dancing with last night. But then, he was pretty well under the influence. She finally threw him through this big picture window. She moved like lightning, or I would have stepped in and tried to rescue him."

"You knew it was Attwood?"

"Neil Attwood. That's somebody else Steve had a fixation on. He found out something really strange. This guy Renaldo Pardew who signed all the documents for the various companies involved in the Arms deal? Before he died he lived in Bellevue."

"Doesn't seem particularly strange."

"He lived next door to Neil Attwood's stepmother."

"And?"

"That was it. That was the connection. Don't you see? Crews and Attwood knew each other from the committee. And Attwood is connected to Renaldo Pardew. And Pardew— dead or not—ran the company that stood to profit when Draper set fire to the Arms. I mean, the whole thing is a snake eating its own tail."

"He found no stronger link between all these people?"

"Not that I know of. He tailed Max Draper. Tailed Attwood. Crews. He spent months tracking the paperwork and hiring detectives, until he ran low on money. Getting migraines all the while."

"Crews told me he thought Steve had broken into his house," Mac said. "Know anything about that?"

"I knew after the fact. He didn't tell me what he found, if anything, and I didn't ask. I didn't want to know. Not after I saw this file. That's part of what broke us up. I know it was. It was all Steve's fault. If he just could have settled down. You know . . . okay . . . he did leave me. But I told him to. I did tell him to and I told him it was his fault."

"You don't know how much more he found out, do you?"

April fingered a page of the document from the box, pretending to read. "After he got suspended he wouldn't talk to me. I called him but he was so snippy. Vanity, I suppose. I mean, he was out of the department in disgrace and I was still in. And I was a woman. Suddenly, it mattered. You know what I mean? He could be such a lovable, klutzy goof. Do you know what he did when he broke into Crews's place? He brought his own lunch and forgot to police the mess. He wiped his prints off everything and then accidentally left an empty box of extra-crispy with coleslaw on their kitchen table."

Fontana said, "My feeling is he might have told somebody what he suspected them of."

Somewhere upstairs a huge metal door clanged open. A vehicle left the barn. They could hear the trilling of a faraway siren. The aid car.

Out of the blue, she said, "A rumor's been circulating around the department for years that somebody walked in on a woman firefighter and some man screwing in the basement of Thirty-twos. Supposedly, they were going at it on top of a pool table. I hate this department. I hate these rumors. I hate them. Ever notice how the woman's name is always mentioned? The man's never is. Men are sluts, too."

"Fire departments are like that," said Mac. "Firemen are the worst gossips on earth."

When they'd tidied the files and gone upstairs, April said, "See you at the big one."

"Sure, April."

He divided the rest of the afternoon between the county fire inspector's office and the Seattle Public Library. Guerciotti wasn't in, but his supervisor confirmed what Fontana already knew about the Arms fire. They'd been in touch with Seattle concerning the second fire in South Park. Seattle didn't have a suspect. County thought it was Draper again but had no hard evidence.

The library was a waste of time. He wasn't able to dig up anything on the HBC, on Neil Attwood, or on Pardew. The original newspaper reports of the two fires were sketchy.

Nightfall blotted out the foothills surrounding Staircase.

Mary Gilliam, in a stretched-out leisure suit, was baking meat loaf and potatoes. "I had no idea when you'd be home," she said. "I prepared enough for the Royal Marines. Just you relax and I'll finish up."

"Mary, I can't let you do that."

"You will or I'll never sit for you again."

He took a shower, dried his hair, dressed, and got tackled by Brendan on the living-room rug. Satan sat in a corner and watched them roughhouse until dinner.

Hoping Mac would fill her in on the case, Mary lingered until after Brendan's bedtime. Rosebud lips, a twinkle in her frosty blue eyes, she waited until he'd finished telling her what he'd learned that day, then said, "Sounds to me like the crux of the situation is Draper. You find him and make him talk, you'll have something."

"That's two big if's, Mary. Finding him. Then making him talk. And the last one is the most improbable. He's not much on chitchat."

"Perhaps one of his pals will sing in exchange for a lighter sentence."

"What I'd really like to know is who sicced Draper on me that first day. Figure I have three suspects: Crews, Reinholt, and April."

"Why would Reinholt call Draper? Or April Falwell, for that matter?"

"To stir up trouble, throw me off the track. If April murdered Steve . . ."

"I was suspicious of her from the first. I think she did it. If you weren't twitterpated you'd see that."

"If she did, she could have phoned Draper and told him I was at her place, that I was asking questions, that I was hot on his trail. She had time enough alone to make a clandestine call. She knew all about Draper. Jilted lovers have done worse. And Don Reinholt's as cagey as a three-legged fox. I don't know for sure what Zajac had that Don didn't want the world to see. Claimed they were compromising letters, but it might have been worse. He might have alerted Draper for the same reason."

"That's weak," said Mary, sipping tea. "How did he know about Draper?"

"Zajac had been investigating this for a long time. He might tell his best friend. Trouble is, I like the guy. Reinholt reminds me of somebody I knew back East, somebody who died of lung cancer about six months back."

"A lot of firemen go that way?"

"From eating smoke. So . . . There were only three people who knew I was in town and could have sicced Draper on me. Crews is the most likely. It's just that I can't believe he would have guessed I was going to Sixes after he told me not to. He's too vain to think I'd flout his authority like that."

"April showed up last night looking for you," said Mary. "Dressed to kill. You didn't get back till late, Mac. Real late. Know what I think? I think she's got your noggin in a tizzy. I think she got fed up with Zajac and went up there and tied him to the tree, thumped him until she was weak from it, then planted a knife in his back. Leaving him like that . . . A woman's touch: She figured she'd put the knife in his back. When it didn't work, she didn't have the stomach to do it again."

"I don't see how she could have tied him."

"Oh, Mac, Mac, Mac. Use your imagination. She hit him from behind in the cabin, then dragged him out there. She's a weight lifter, isn't she? She killed him in a fit of jealousy and then left evidence around to make you think it had something to do with this conspiracy business. Only it didn't. When she was done she burned most of that file he was keeping so's to throw you off the track. She put just enough under the sofa to taunt you. Think about it. Who was the one wanted you to go up there in the first place?"

They kicked Mary's theory around for a few moments.

Mahler spilled softly from the stereo in the living room. Mary nibbled a cookie she'd baked that afternoon and said, "Is that an owl I hear out there? We had owls when my husband was alive."

"Mary, I'll walk you home."

Satan tried to come but Mac said, "Guard," and left the dog on sentry duty at the door. In the moonlight on his way back down the hundred yards of path to his own property, he stopped.

"Mac?"

Leaning his elbows on the sill of his propped-open window, Brendan watched him. Mac walked over to the house. "Thought you were asleep."

"I've been thinking about the dead man."

Mac ran his fingers through Brendan's mop of hair, watching the individual strands shiver in the moonlight. They gazed up at Mount Gadd. The base seemed a bow shot away, yet it flowed into a series of wooded foothills, almost humps. Then the river. Then their place. If a person was careful and the river was low, he could ford the stream, hike north, and never spot another soul until he struck Canada.

"Why did they stab him?" Brendan asked.

"Good question. I'm trying to find out."

"Did it hurt?"

"I won't lie. I think so, Brendan."

"Did it hurt when Mom died?"

Mac watched Satan meander around the corner of the house to eyeball him in the dark. "I don't really know. I don't think so."

"I'm never going to kill anybody when I grow up."

"I know you aren't."

"You won't either, will you, Mac?"

Mac kneaded one of Brendan's skinny shoulders. "I hope not, Brendan. I sincerely hope not."

They talked until the boy shivered with the cold, then Mac pushed his window down, went inside, tucked him in,

221

latched the window, and went to bed himself. Brendan loved to rattle on at night, got garrulous as soon as the sun sank. Linda had been that way. He looked so much like her, the same coarse walnut-stain hair, the same fair skin, same cheery oval face. The faint swatch of freckles across the nose.

It was almost three when the beeper on his bedside table went off.

A fire.

Flames showing.

When he padded to the west living-room window in his Jockey shorts, he saw the rosy glow enameling the sky. After the initial units confirmed the location with the dispatcher, Mac squeezed the Send button on his portable RCA and said, "This is Chief Eighteen-ninety. I'll be responding."

"Okay, Chief Eighteen-ninety," replied the woman dispatcher. "Be advised, that's a church fire. Said to be fully involved."

"Eighteen-ninety, okay."

31

Chromosome Damage

MAC PITCHED HIS BUNKING clothes into the Carryall in two separate bundles, fired up the engine, left it at a high idle, then webbed a sleepy and muttering Brendan in a quilt and packed him through the dark yard to Mary Gilliam's.

"Fire?" she asked as she answered the door, hair ratty, most of her teeth basking in a jar somewhere. She glimpsed the glowing skies over his shoulder. "Mary mother of God. The town's a grounder."

"South of town, Mary. Watch him, I'll make an honest woman of you in the morning."

Flickering and winking, the pink-tinged sky was disfigured by black plumes. Sooty, quick-rising firebrands jiggled skyward, like flopped fireworks on the Fourth. This was one of those fires they'd be able to track from a satellite. He listened over the truck radio to the first-in report, to Pete Daugherty, the regular, who frequently slept weekends at the station to earn bonus money.

"Engine 1 on Dovey's Road. We have a fully involved church approximately eighty by two hundred feet. Wood frame. Three stories. Flames from the roof and east end. We're laying a two-and-a-half. Tanker One, give us a supply and don't block the road."

Anybody who heard that knew the Episcopalian Church was burning. It was located half a mile southwest of town on a triangle of wooded property near the old bridge.

In the football field of a parking lot volunteers were laying a five-inch supply line to the Seagrave from the tanker at the head of the lot. Mac got on his portable and asked County for another tanker so they could set up a relay.

Crackling sheets of flame licked at the huge A-frame edifice, at the night sky, at the nearby eighty- and ninety-foot firs. The noise was like thousands of pencils snapping underfoot. As soon as he exited the GMC, Mac could feel the blast-furnace heat on his face and bare arms.

A second diesel pumper roared down the lane, its Jake brake blatting powerfully. Pete would have them take a supply line from Engine 1 and wet down the woods at the far end of the church.

As was the custom, the first-in paid man took charge until someone of higher rank took over. Lanky Pete, the youngest and least experienced paid man in the Staircase FD, orchestrated the operations of Engine 1 and the hordes of eager volunteers.

Until three months before when Mac took up the reins as chief, Mo Costigan had been in the habit of indiscriminately ramrodding the volunteers at large fires. She knew nothing about firefighting but she liked to boss. Mac had put the kibosh on that.

He climbed into his bunkers and circled the church once, one side of his face baking, the other side exposed to the frosty night air.

The fire seemed to have begun at the far end, behind the pulpit, had already progressed through the apex of the steeply pitched roof on the far end, then wormed its way through cedar shakes for half the roof's length. On the far side, geysers of flame were already tasting the lowest fir branches. He buttonholed the officer on the county unit, asked him to stretch a line around the back of the building to douse the trees.

The primary consideration now was to make certain nobody got injured. Mac had witnessed nine men falling through a church roof once. Two of them had burned to death. Another had broken both femurs and bled out.

If they got lucky and didn't dump too much water into this end of the edifice, they might save the downstairs offices. Mac didn't hold out much hope of that. The Staircase department had battled a house fire the year before and dumped so much water they flooded the basement, drowned three canaries.

Tonight he saw several Seattle and Bellevue firefighters volunteering on county lines, knew they were schooled to use as little water as possible. Water damage was almost as embarrassing as a rekindle.

The largest church in the valley, it boasted enough knotty-pine pews to seat four hundred worshipers, plus meeting rooms, offices, a summer-school annex, the works. Add up the furnishings and draperies and the fire load was boggling.

"What the hell are you doing about this?"

Mac looked into Mo Costigan's brown eyes. "Mo, get out of the way."

"You should be up there giving orders."

"How many fires have you seen a chief put out, Mo? Pete's doing a splendid job. I'm here for backup. That's how I run it. You don't like it, bring it up at the next civil service meeting."

"You never show up at the civil service meetings."

County's second and third pumpers roared down the lane three minutes apart and Mac had them lay lines outside the building. They used a cherry picker to dump water on the peak of the roof at the east end, directing it down into the conflagration. The building had already vented itself so he wasn't worrying about chopping holes. When the hose lines began to go limp, what little orange they had blackened out began to return.

Though it carried twenty-two hundred gallons, the new tanker would be sucked dry almost as soon as the pumpers finished their connections. There were three two-and-a-half-inch lines out. Three hundred gallons a minute discharged from a two-and-a-half. Three of them out. Five hundred gallons a minute from the Elkhart on the cherry picker. If everyone squirted at maximum capacity, it wouldn't be nearly enough.

Fontana threw a mask on and guided a group of volunteers to the main entrance of the building, communicating by radio to the tanker driver who'd just left, asking how long the refill would take. "Twenty minutes," somebody reported.

He left Daugherty in charge and directed a small cadre inside the main vestibule of the church with a two-and-a-half. A pair of volunteers had already axed open the main doors and inhaled a snootful of black smoke. Kingsley Pierpont rushed up to the gang around Mac, bypassing a chance to take over from Daugherty.

This end of the church had more smoke than flame. Mac reached low behind his waist and cranked open the ratchety main valve of the Survivair, cinched up the blue rubber and Plexiglas face piece, readjusted his helmet, flipped the regulator at his waist to Pressure, breathed deeply, and took one last gander at the troops in the parking lot. He wanted to be in on this, crawl in under the heat with Kingsley.

Fires this large wooed gapers. A crowd teemed in the lot: concerned neighbors, wives of volunteers, children of volunteers, drinking buddies of volunteers, vacationers who'd been cruising down the highway and been distracted by the crimson sky.

Near the edge of the crowd Mac spotted a small two-door Datsun, late-sixties vintage. Something about the body language of the three men huddled around it stopped his

226

sweeping gaze. They weren't tourists. Oblivious to the fire, they stood beside the winged open doors, conferring.

He slapped the buckles at the sides of his head and dropped the face piece off, thumbing the waist valve from Pressure to Demand so his air wouldn't whoosh out. He needed a clear view. Tasting like an oil roustabout's boot heel, a swirl of smoke gusted out of the church, blotting his quarry. Interlaced in the odors was the unmistakable pungent odor of kerosene. The church had been hit by an arsonist.

Not a disgruntled Baptist, either.

When the skein of smoke notched itself on a blast of cold air and he could see again, Mac recognized the Draper brothers, along with the squinty-eyed Charlie Dexter.

An object that appeared to be a portable radio was clutched in Max Draper's fist.

Except that it wasn't an AM-FM jobbie.

It was a sender.

It had to be.

They didn't see him. Two dozen helmeted figures were running around in bulky, balloonlike bunking suits, and Fontana was just another anonymous yellow doughboy.

Draper turned his back on the crowd.

Mac rushed through the thickets of smoke into the foyer and clamped a hand on Kingsley Pierpont's shoulder. Pierpont, who had the nozzle, was throwing a blast toward the back of the church as volunteers reefed more line through the front doors, coiling it for the assault.

"Booby traps," said Mac.

"You shittin' me, man?"

"Nobody go in. Pull the coils inside the door like you're working your way down the aisle. I want somebody to think you're inside. Hit what you can from here in the doorway. Deal?"

"Gotcha," said Pierpont, turning to the volunteer at his back. "Hear what the chief said?"

Skulking out of the church through a chopped-out side window, boots crunching musically on the sheets of glass, Mac unbuckled the Survivair's waist belt, released tension on the two chest straps, doffed the heavy cylinder, and dropped it into the wet grass.

Charlie Dexter was fifty yards away, had separated himself from the others, and was talking to Mrs. Kilpatrick, who hadn't had time to throw on more than a skimpy Titian-red nylon robe. A pair of headlights somebody had left on in the excitement X-rayed her from behind. Spine to the fire, Charlie stood in front of her, arms folded.

Scrabbling in a rockery, Mac bagged a piece of timber three feet long. As he plodded in a large semicircle toward Charlie and Mrs. Kilpatrick, he found himself accompanied by Mo Costigan. Satan had come out of nowhere, pranced at his heels.

"Mo, this is going to be dangerous."

"What? A fire? I'm out in the lot for godsakes. Shouldn't you be directing troops or something?" She hacked as they passed through a stray ribbon of smoke.

"Mo, I thought I saw a county cop. Go get him and tell him your sheriff is doing some psychological counseling."

"What?"

"Tell him I'm arresting people. We'll need some stretchers."

"Stretchers?" Mac stopped and watched Mo gasp for air, her face sooty. His long-legged strides had been eating up the pavement, and in order to keep pace she had been trotting.

"Mo, get a cop."

"What are you going to do?"

"Keep out of this, Mo."

Fontana turned, slapped his knees, and spoke quickly to the dog. "Wanna find some bad guys? Satan? Bad guys?" The dog whined, wagged his tail, sat up in a begging posture, then did a couple of quick doughnuts, clearly ready.

Lowering the scratched face shield on the white chief's

helmet to make himself harder to recognize, he stumped up to Charlie Dexter's back. The Drapers were twenty yards away and might not even notice in the confusion. Dexter was a whole lot larger than he remembered. He didn't dare warn him. Wielding it like a bat, Mac hefted the piece of lumber. A two-by-four, waterlogged and heavier than normal.

"Mac?"

Mo Costigan's querulous voice alerted Dexter, so that the bulky man jerked aside at the last moment, absorbed the brunt of the blow on his shoulder instead of his skull.

Dexter pivoted, feinted, got clipped, and slipped to the ground.

Still framed by the auto's headlights, Mrs. Kilpatrick gave a sigh of disbelief and sprang back. Another rig came rumbling down the narrow wooded drive to the parking lot and stopped, blocking the line of sight between Mac and the Datsun. The Drapers no longer had a clear line of sight. It was the white fire-buff wagon. In the confusion neither of the Draper brothers had seen Mac coldcock Charlie.

On his hands and knees now, Charlie Dexter peered up at Mac, moved into a three-point stance.

Mrs. Kilpatrick waved her arms, and the glare of the headlights limned her.

"Mac, are you nuts?" shrieked Mo. "That's assault and battery."

Charlie huffed, grunted, and launched himself.

Fontana thwacked Charlie alongside the head.

Before he could flop on the pavement, Fontana swung again, stove in the ribs along Dexter's right flank. When he hit the arm above the elbow it cracked and Mac knew he'd broken it, finally knocked him out when he started to struggle to his knees. Mac didn't have a thought in his head, had no idea what kept him from killing the man.

Mo whispered shrilly, "That was assault and battery before witnesses. You're fired. I'm firing you right now."

After he felt Dexter's pulse, checked both eyes and his

respirations, Mac stood up and wiped droplets of sweat off his brow. Mrs. Kilpatrick, silent until now, said, "He a real-estate agent, or what?"

Mac knelt on hands and knees and peered under the fire-buff unit. He smelled hot cocoa and the gritty-tasting wash of exhaust. He watched the Draper brothers from the shins down as they climbed into the Datsun. Satan, next to Mac's face, peered under the buff truck with him.

A carpet of smoke rolled across the lot watering Mac's eyes, some of it from the fire, some of it diesel wash from the idling fire engines. Red lights from a dozen emergency vehicles strobed the night, turning the wall of dark fir trees around the lot into a huge carnivorous forest. Engines roared. Cops. A county medic unit. A state patrolman.

As Mac climbed into the truck he heard the *poof*, watched a gout of flame the size and shape of a railroad tank car hiss out the side window of the church.

An explosive device.

Draper had set it off.

He could see in light of the fireball that the group he'd left with Kingsley Pierpont was still tucked safely in the foyer. He saw their hose line twitch as they opened the bale on the Wooster nozzle to shield themselves with a heavy fog pattern. If it hadn't been before, it was a grounder now. They would save the foundation and some of the painted parking lines in the lot. Anybody inside on their bellies would have been incinerated.

But then, that had been the idea.

Mac closed the door of the GMC. Satan leaped in beside him through the passenger window, whining. Mo scooted into the passenger seat.

"What the hell are you doing?" Fontana asked.

"You're over the edge, Mac. Stop right where you are and you won't get into any further trouble."

"Sheesh." He handed her the waterlogged two-by-four. "Hold this."

He turned the motor over and slipped the truck into compound low. When he swung the GMC around the front end of the buff wagon and brought the headlights to bear on the Datsun, the two long-faced men in the Datsun suddenly realized the jig was up. One or both of them must have recognized the truck. In that blinding light they surely couldn't see his face. Rafe, the saner of the brothers, was behind the wheel, jammed it into reverse, and backed up toward the mouth of the parking lot. It was slightly uphill. Mac pursued.

Mo screamed, "What on earth do you think you're doing?"

"Patching up chromosome damage."

"What?"

Rafe was wide-eyed, hands frantic at the controls of the small car, head twisting like a rabbit in a hawk's talons. The GMC was bearing down on them, the body of the massive vehicle jerking forward on the soft springs, gaining inexorably. Rafe executed a nice spiral, skidding from reverse to forward in one quick motion, tires screeching. Except that he was too late. The narrow lane was blocked by an incoming tanker.

Mac rammed the side of the Datsun.

Inside the truck, Mo screamed at the top of her lungs and braced both arms on the metal dashboard.

The dog barked.

Mo screamed again.

"Damn road hogs," said Mac. "Somebody oughta run 'em all off the highways."

"Mac, you're crazy," shrieked Mo. "You're a raving lunatic!"

He reversed the truck for another run and torpedoed the Datsun a second time. The two vehicles collided in a roar of shrieking sheet metal and shattering glass.

32

Crooks 'n' Things

SLOUCHED IN THE passenger seat, Maxwell Draper remained stock-still, eyes forward.

Pulling the stick into reverse, Fontana backed up twenty feet, then floored the accelerator until the GMC's rear tires smoked. He packed the small car against a tree. When he disengaged and reversed, the Drapers were snared in an irregular, metallic sphere.

Mouth foamy with spittle, Mo slapped at Mac's wrists, tried desperately to wrest his hands from the wheel. The dog barked. Mac said, "She makes another move, take her arm off at the elbow."

"Satan, don't you dare. After all I've done for you. Satan?"

The growling dog pushed his snout over the seat. Facing backward, the mayor sank into the dash, teeth bared, as were the dog's.

"Mac, this is a loony bin. Think about what you're doing. Think."

"Next time you want a ride, call a cab."

Blue light shuddered through the interior of the GMC as a state car from the other end of the lot pulled alongside Fontana. A patrolman leaned across his empty passenger seat to peer up at him. The last impact had left room enough in the Datsun for a man to breathe, nothing else.

Trouble was, only one man was inside.

Rafe. Bloody, semiconscious.

His brother Max had somehow escaped, and now was dashing up the hillside between the trees. The wash from the GMC's headlights spotlighted his blurred figure. Fontana stretched across the seat, sprang the glove box, removed a pistol, and checked the load. Dropping a box of bullets into his bunking coat pocket, he stepped out of the truck.

"Just a minute, you!" It was the trooper, clumsily disentangling his revolver from his Sam Browne belt.

"Sheriff Fontana from Staircase. Man in the woods is wanted by Seattle. So's this one."

The trooper didn't know what to make of that, failed to decide before Mac vanished.

They were moving up the ridge, Fontana chasing, Draper in the lead. Mac skidded on the slope of a mud bank, stumbled in patches of briars, eventually felt layers of spongy pine needles underfoot. Another hundred yards and Draper would crest the peak.

Satan passed Mac like a bug disappearing into a vacuum cleaner. As the dog raced into the darkness, Fontana heard the first pop. A second pop.

Gunshots.

He glimpsed the match-head muzzle flash from the second one, high and to the right.

Sweating heavily in his bulky bunking pants and coat, Mac tramped over deadfalls and downed branches, overtook the dog, saw a tiny glittery flash from Draper's gun, and simultaneously heard a third shot. So far, all of Draper's bullets had gone astray.

Bracing his right arm against a thick tree trunk, Fontana leveled his pistol, found the sights in the darkness, cocked the serrated hammer with his thumb, and let fly a round.

The .38 bucked in his fist.

Draper did not return the fire.

Mac knelt beside the panting dog. "Stay, big guy. Stay. You've already saved my life once this week. This one's on me."

Alerted by a movement in the pine trees at the top of the rolling hillock, the dog whined and darted forward.

"Satan!"

Fontana ran behind the animal, branching off to the left, working his way back toward the path he guessed Draper would be following. It was the barking that stopped him.

"Careful, Satan, you idiot."

More barking. Closer. Less than twenty yards away now. Fontana cocked the gun and pointed the muzzle at the treetops. When he found them, the dog was on the rim of a small gully, looking down, woofing. Shielding himself behind a tree, Fontana fished his heavy flashlight out of his bunking coat and played the trembly beam into the culvert.

Three quarters of the way down the rocky wash lay a broken bundle. Mac couldn't see a gun but he did see dingy white tennis shoes and a tan windbreaker. He kept the light on the mass for another thirty seconds. The body didn't budge. Both of Draper's hands were clawed open. Neither of them held a weapon.

"Satan, knock it off."

The barking stopped.

The dog licked his chops, sat.

Draper's eyes glinted wetly, face scratched and bloody from his earlier misfortune in the Datsun. Through the trees on the hillside Mac could hear engines, men, sniffed the smoky residue of disaster.

When Fontana stalked close he could see that the bullet he'd loosed almost randomly through the tree trunks had struck Maxwell Draper in the forehead, had punched a cookie-cutter hole he could have covered with a dime.

Any of Draper's bullets could have done the same to him.

The explosion inside the church would have done considerably worse. He stood in the dark and thought about that for a while, thought about other things, let his mind slowly break free from the last few minutes. When he walked down the hillside the fire was nearly under control. The trooper had Rafe Draper in cuffs. Mo had run off.

During the remainder of the early-morning hours they mopped up. The Episcopal Church had been gutted.

The area stank of smoke, burnt wood, charred wallboard, insulation, plastic. The ground was littered with ruined Bibles, collection bags, and fragments of blackened stained-glass window.

Shortly before the King County medical examiner's station wagon arrived to scoop it up, Charlie Dummelow drove out to look over the body—cops could get away with that. A citizen tried it, they'd say he was a ghoul.

In a dismal morning light that made his skin look like pizza dough, Dummelow stood in a raincoat and suit he planned to wear to church later. The paunch riding his skinny belt hadn't gotten any smaller. The eyebrows worked against each other. His thick, reddish hair was neatly combed, looked wet.

"I'd say that's Max Draper."

"Yep," said Mac, his voice hoarse from smoke and yelling. He couldn't recall yelling, but he must have hollered at the dog.

"Did I ever tell you I interrogated him? 'Bout five years ago. Strange duck. In Leavenworth somebody thumped him bad with a hunk of steel pipe. A gang thing. Caved his skull in. Lingered on the point of death for weeks. When he woke up something upstairs had gone haywire. His emotions were skewed. They say he didn't feel nothing. An automaton in a man's body. Made him into the cold-blooded bastard he was. I'm glad you pegged him."

They stood in the gully on either side of the body. Draper lay spine down on a piece of flat gray granite saturated with moss and lichen. The gun lay where it had fallen eight feet from his hand. Nobody had bothered to shut his eyes or cover his face or straighten his twisted jacket or flick the pine needles off his cheek. Nobody would bother.

"Where'd you say you were when you got him?"

"No difference. Sheer-dee luck."

"Was a bizarre character," said Dummelow. "This whole affair was. Zajac. You going into that fuel-oil tank. This fire. Well, you think we got it all wrapped up now?"

"What do you think?"

"These yahoos seemed bound and determined to do you in. I mean, if you're right and they set this fire just to get you . . . makes a body feel they must have had a powerful reason. More than simple revenge because you slapped Draper around."

"What about the drug angle?"

"You don't mind, I'll buy into your arson investigation thingamajig. Zajac was investigating the arson on Des Moines Way. We know that. He got too close. They tortured him to find out what he knew, then tried to ice you when you got too close. Case closed."

"Maybe," said Mac wearily.

"What are you saying?"

"Somebody made a lot of money off that arson. These three were driving a '64 Datsun that looked like it'd carried a basketball team around the world twice."

"Probably stolen."

"How did Draper latch on to me that first day when he tailed me to Staircase? Who told him I was in town?"

Dummelow hunkered down beside Draper, gloated over his dead face, then squinted up at Mac. "He got dentures. You know he had dentures?"

"Nope."

Dummelow levered himself upright and turned away from Fontana. It wasn't until Fontana saw the reedy yellow stream under the tail of his raincoat as it splattered down the face of the granite rock bed and made the rocks steam that the county cop spoke. "It'll be a frosty day in you know where if and when we catch whoever was responsible for all this. Too much goddamned money tied up in it. You know that, Mac? Relax. You did your job. You know as well as I do we never bat a thousand. You got the bastards killed Zajac. You fixed 'em for dropping you into that tank. The other two, I don't know what they'll draw, but this one here bought the bargain-basement death penalty."

"You out all night drinking, or you just pee once a week?" asked Fontana.

Dummelow waited until he had adjusted his goods, turned around and grinned. "My teeth were floating. Gonna stay sheriff?"

"Doubtful."

"We could use someone like you up here. Be nice to have you around."

"Heart's not in it. 'Sides, think I ticked off the mayor."

"Well, this is finished." Dummelow spat and headed out of the gully, talking as he moved, grunting because of the steepness of the ridge. Fontana followed. "Heard you did a number on them other two."

"I got a little carried away."

Later Mac showered and took Brendan to church with Mary Gilliam. Afterward, Brendan spent the afternoon with his buddies, the Roth twins, while Mac snored on the sofa.

Although he'd shampooed his hair, it would reek of char for another day, perhaps two. The smell of smoke lingered on the pillow. He rolled over on the sofa, stared at the ceiling, and thought over that morning's events. The Drapers and Charlie Dexter had gone to a lot of trouble to rig up that exploding church. Sloppy work, any way you looked at it. They would have ended up slaughtering at least two others besides him, possibly more.

So he'd lucked out, killed their plan, broken Charlie's

arm, knocked out Rafe with a truck, and plinked Max between the eyes. That had been the last thing he wanted. To kill someone. Draper might have tattled on his bosses. His brother and friend still might.

Incarcerated in the new King County jail on charges of attempted murder, neither Rafe Draper nor Charlie Dexter said anything to anybody. Their attorney was a snazzy middle-age criminal lawyer some anonymous benefactor had flown in from San Francisco.

Aside from a two-day series the Seattle *Post-Intelligencer* ran on the case—most of which was taken up in gossipy columns about the San Francisco attorney, a reputed womanizer—the local media didn't get excited.

When Mac read the series and realized how cavalierly it was being treated, he couldn't help thinking that somebody, somewhere, was heaving a sigh of relief.

He spent almost half a day with the county fire investigators digging through the ruins of the church. The upshot of it was that yes, it had been arson and no, they couldn't tie any of the physical evidence to Draper, or to anybody. Not now, probably never. Draper had been too foxy for that. If Draper were going to be linked to this fire or to any other fire—the Eldorado Arms, for instance—Fontana would have to do it another way.

Three days running he took Brendan to school, then hiked to the summit of Mount Gadd. One afternoon he got a maul and cleaned out the woodpile, cutting wood for Mary Gilliam, chopping, splitting, and stacking until dark. In Staircase everybody and his mother stoked a wood stove. Only the winds raiding down off the mountains flushed the air clean.

Friday night, long after Brendan had gone to bed, Mo Costigan showed up unannounced on his doorstep, dressed to kill in a black wool coat, a sheeny maroon dress, and high heels. Mac didn't know why, but there was something endearing about her that night, something vulnerable and almost vampish. She hadn't seen or spoken to him since the church fire almost a week earlier.

"Mac?"

"Come in, Mo."

"You know you've got owls out there?"

"Barn owls. Call 'em Destry and Dietrich."

"You don't."

"Sit down. What can I do for you?"

"No, really." She took in his rugby shirt, wrinkled jeans, moccasins. "You look as if you're ready to turn in. I'll just stay a minute."

She glanced nervously around the snug living room.

33

Grampa Scott

"Take off your coat, Mo. Sit down. I was just reading. Glad to have the company."

"Mac, I know we haven't always seen eye to eye. I know that. In fact, we've had some knock-down-drag-outs. I've said some things I'm ashamed of. Mac?"

He shrugged. His smile was crooked. "So who always sees eye to eye?"

"All the same . . . you seem perpetually angry with me."

He moved across the room, took her coat, and strung it up on a wire hanger in the guest closet.

"I gave you a fright the other night," he said. "At the fire."

"For a while there I thought you'd dropped all the bricks in your load. But then I realized what you were doing. I suspected those people in that car had something to do with the arson. I did. I know you didn't think I did but I did. The County cop, Dummelow, tells me you think they were connected to Zajac."

"Anybody tell you the odds against my proving it?"

"I wasn't really that panicked. Really. You patched the truck up real nice. Can't even tell a mania . . . can hardly see the dings."

"Headlights was about all it needed."

He stood awkwardly and recalled the daft sound of her voice early Sunday morning, the ear-splitting skirls. She'd laid low all week like a cat that had been hosed out of the garden.

"Stopped in at the Bedouin tonight," she said. "You weren't there."

"Wasn't up to it tonight."

"Not much going on anyways. Bunch'a Cascade hikers in their REI corduroys. Truck Anderson got wiped out again and hit his head on a chair." She blinked at him, and he realized she blinked more frequently than most people, birdlike, affected. He wondered if she didn't need glasses. "You're generally there on Friday and Saturday nights."

"Like to dance."

"Slow dancing?"

"Any kind, Mo."

He walked across the room, removed a James Taylor album from a rack of albums, put the platter on the turntable, dropped the needle arm onto a track, and closed in. He took her into his arms and they danced.

"Badge is on the mantel. You can take it with you later."

"What if I don't want it?"

"Whatever."

"Did those men you brutalized . . . were they the ones who murdered Zajac?"

"Don't think I brutalized them, Mo. They left me for dead the other day. I did what needed to be done. That's all."

"It still gives me the heebie-jeebies. What we found up there. I even dreamed about it a few nights ago. You know how when a neighbor's mother passes on or a co-worker's spouse dies, how, after a week or two, it's like it didn't even happen. Sure, because to you it doesn't mean that much. One less Christmas card to lick a stamp for. And how if you stop going to all the funerals you end up trying to recall who's dead and who isn't? This was a lot more like it feels when a relative dies. One of those things you'll never forget. And I didn't even know the guy. But when I saw him there and vomited and everything, I felt this . . . kinship. I knew it wasn't something that would go away."

"Me too, Mo. Me too."

"Did *they* kill him?"

"Doubtful, Mo. Real doubtful."

"Why?"

"Part of it's a gut feeling. Part of it has to do with what Dummelow told me about the questioning early Sunday morning. Dummelow thinks these two guys didn't have much to do with Zajac. I trust his instincts. Not anybody you're going to snow."

"Tell me the whole thing."

"Long story."

"Got all night."

"I know," he said.

It was apparent from the way she moved with him that she had all night. As they danced in the shadows, edged away from the union of light and dark, they made the room smaller. Exaggerating the promise of her visit, she danced quietly, moved as close as he was willing to pull her. They danced. And talked.

"Mo. I've been working this over and over in my mind all week, but I never went back to the beginning. I even phoned the detective agency in California, the one Zajac hired to research the corporations. Listen, can you stay here a few minutes? Mary's still up. Saw her lights. I'm going to make a call. Back in a minute."

Clad in a sloppy Chinese robe, Mary Gilliam met him at the door. "Mac? Everything all right?"

"Use your phone?"

"Dump all the modern conveniences, but you end up borrowing them once a week in the middle of the night. Video recorder's over there. Microwave's on the counter. I can mail-order a cordless phone, if you want."

He stepped inside. "Mary, darlin', I had my own phone, we wouldn't be able to meet in the middle of the night."

"Fiddlesticks. You think I don't see the mayor's fancy car over there? Pulled in to get serviced, did she?"

He looked the number up on a card, dialed, and waited.

Mac spoke into the phone. "Steve Zajac. You killed him. I can prove it. You know who I am: Mackinley Fontana. Go ahead, hang up. . . . He wouldn't tell you what you needed to know. You tried to torture it out of him and maybe he told you most of it. I have no way of knowing. But he left information under the house. I know he didn't tell you about that or you'd have taken it.

"I know all about the fire department bribes. The fire at the Eldorado Arms. What's more, I think I can wrangle something out of one of those two dumbbells the San Francisco shyster is protecting. Wanna get in touch with me, darlin', phone the fire station in Staircase."

He dropped the receiver into its cradle.

"Why'd you hang up, Mac, for godsakes?"

"They'll call back. Thinking somebody's got the goods on you is like sitting on an anthill."

"Pooh. You've done it now, Mac, my boy. By golly, you've done it. You'll never hear from them again. Right now they're destroying evidence."

"They'll want a powwow."

"Why not just have em arrested?"

"I can't prove a thing."

"Who, Mac? Who is it?"

"I tell you and you'll claim you knew it all along.

"That's not fair."

He grinned. "So who said life was fair?"

When he got home the mayor was waiting for him in the living room. Sleepy-eyed, thick hair disheveled, Brendan sat in pajamas on the other end of the sofa. It was difficult to tell if he was awake or asleep. It looked as if the boy and Mo had shared the sofa a couple of minutes.

"Sorry I took so long."

Nobody spoke. Mac reached down, took Brendan's hand,

and walked him to his room, helped the boy into bed, tucked him in, kissed his warm forehead, and sat. The boy mumbled, "Hadda wizz, Dad. That lady—"

"It's all right, Brendan. She was just visiting." He kissed the boy again, waited until he was asleep, switched off the light, and went back to the living room.

In the living room Mo said, "You haven't seen my chow, Freud, have you? I've got fliers up all over town."

"I . . . Mo, I couldn't say."

She blew him a perfunctory kiss and sailed out the door. It wasn't until she had motored out of the yard that he noticed the badge was missing from the mantel.

In a haze of stomach-churning anticipation, Mac packed a gun Saturday and Sunday.

Not a peep.

Monday morning, a week and one day after the church fire, they woke him up at quarter to five. The boys on the aid car had driven over from the fire station.

Dempsey, the nineteen-year-old, rapped on the front door until Mac answered, jumping when he saw the revolver in Mac's fist. "God!" Dempsey said.

"What is it?"

"Got a really funny phone call at the station. Thought you should know about it."

"What?"

"Somebody said your lady friend who was scared of heights was going to commit suicide if you didn't do something. Said she was going to leap from the highest point in town if you didn't get there right away and discuss things."

"Who said?"

"I was out of it when I answered the phone. You know how that goes. By the time they were finished I almost woke up."

"Male or female?"

"God. Now that you ask . . . I thought it was a man. I don't know."

"Tell me what they said. Word for word."

"The phone rang. I picked it up and answered, 'Staircase Station One, Dempsey speaking.' They said, 'Sheriff Fontana—tell him his lady friend who's scared of heights is going to commit suicide from the highest spot in town if he don't show up to discuss things.' "

"That it?"

"Then they hung up. I thought we'd better hotfoot it on over here—that's all—and tell you. Mackelroy thought it was a practical joke but I didn't want to take a chance."

"Thanks, Dempsey. I appreciate this."

In the yard the October chill grabbed socks of exhaust from the tail pipe of the aid car and trundled them along the ground. "I hope everything's all right, Chief."

"I'm sure it is. Thanks again."

Traffic was sparse. The closer he got to town, the more fog he encountered. Seattle wore a layer a thousand feet thick, two hundred feet off the ground in some areas, hugging the pavement in others.

Quarter to six. It was cold. Frost blindfolded car windows. He ran the heater and defroster. He hadn't shaved, combed his hair, anything.

Inexplicably, two unrelated stories intertwined in his thoughts. One involved Clyde Hopcraft. An old-timer when Fontana had joined up back East, Hopcraft was small and wiry, was known for his excitability. One night Hopcraft raced into a basement fire so wildly he struck his head on a low beam and knocked himself cold. Later, when they were ribbing him, they discovered the nameplate from the front of his helmet was embedded in the beam.

The other tale involved Mac's great-grandfather who'd fought in the Civil War, creaky old Grampa Scott, who died when Mac was still a boy. He had entertained Mac and his cousins repeatedly with his war tales, called them "sprouts," said it was the "sceerdest" he'd ever been.

Eighteen sixty-four.

Grampa Scott had been a young private in the Union Army. As the Federals massed to attack a strongly fortified Rebel line at Cold Harbor, Virginia, Grampa and his bedraggled camp cohorts, hypnotized by the weaponry stacked against them, scrawled their names on scraps of paper and pinned them to their chests. Each had a dread of dying anonymously, of being buried in a nameless grave. In less than half an hour, seven thousand of Grampa's compatriots dropped. That single day dominated his life.

Mac had penned his note and left it in the desk in the sheriff's office. Now all he had to do was keep an eye out for the low beams.

34

One Foot in the Grave

FROM MID-SPAN on the Mercer Island Floating Bridge, Fontana couldn't see a single brick or signboard on the skyline. Not a jot of color disturbed the monotonous smog pudding.

Toting one gun under his navy-blue jacket, he had strapped a second small revolver to his left ankle. Both .38's. Satan sat at his side.

All the gates in the construction areas of the three towers were padlocked.

Were anybody to jump from the highest point in town, it would have to be the occupied building. Except for a teenage streetwalker who'd probably dozed in a doorway all night, nobody loitered inside the atrium-lobby of the completed Attwood Tower. His throat was dry and he realized he hadn't been this jittery since his first visit to Linda in ICU.

Ninety-six stories. An impossible fire to put out if the unthinkable ever happened. He wondered whether they were skimping on fire suppression systems in the four towers: risking twelve thousand lives per tower. When a whistle-blower like Zajac got under the wheels of this much money, he was bound to get squashed. Men ranted and whooped and squawked. Money killed.

Before the elevator opened on floor ninety-six, Max bent over and said, "Bad guys, Satan. Gonna help me find some bad guys? You and me? Bad guys?"

Instantly the curious dog began skidding around in circles on the polished floor, whining, triangular ears upright. The dog was game for one last ruckus. Mac shushed him. Nose to the tiles, the dog padded up and down the corridor on the ninety-sixth floor. It didn't take him long to pick up a scent that led to a navy-gray door recessed up a short set of stairs.

Printed letters in scarlet said EXIT TO ROOF. PRIVATE. KEEP OUT.

Unholstering the gun at his waist, he dropped the weapon into his jacket pocket.

"Bad guys," he said sharply. When he stroked the dog's muscular flank, a gob of loose hair came off against the perspiration on his hand. He wiped it nervously on the thigh of his jeans. "Bad guys."

Twisting the doorknob, Mac stepped out onto the roof of the completed Attwood Tower. His hand was in his jacket pocket, index finger curled on the trigger.

The smog was almost impenetrable.

The dog beat him through the opening, buzzed around his feet, then trotted off into the grayness. Mac didn't dare whistle. The roof was flat, the tar coating impregnated with tiny shards of gravel.

Behind him, the door hissed shut on a self-closer. Realizing he should have inspected it before making himself into a target, he reached back with his free hand to try the knob. To his chagrin, his hand trembled.

The door was locked.

He peered into the murk, began feeling his way along the roof.

Before he left Staircase that morning, he'd made a tele phone call to April. She hadn't answered. He dialed the Seattle fire dispatchers and was told she was scheduled to work that day. Might have already left for work.

She might be dangling from a window ledge somewhere.

She might be training a pistol on his back.

Feeling his way carefully through the grayness, Mac discovered the rim of the roof, found it protected by a waist-high steel railing. He traveled along it. The air was cold and clammy. He could have been walking in a gigantic cooler. He zipped his coat to the neck, disgruntled over the fact that his hand continued to tremble.

Except for the vacuum-cleaner sound of a bus ninety-six stories below, the morning was quiet. A steel clip on a rope banged lightly against the hollow flagpole. There was not much wind. Not at first.

Midway down the edge, he neared a corner, saw her on the next edge, facing away from the building.

Barefoot, she was dressed in a damp white nightshirt that clung to her shoulders. She looked demented, was standing on the edge of the building outside the railing.

Hands bound behind her back with thin cotton clothes-line, she was tilted out at a forty-five-degree angle. Every muscle in her body shivered. Her cat-gray eyes bulged in terror, as if some fiend were running an electric current through her. He didn't want to guess how long she'd been in that predicament.

The mist had beaded her red hair, frizzed the ends, bestowing upon her the eerie disguise of a crazed faerie queen about to launch into the empyrean.

The arrangement was ingenious.

It took a moment for Fontana to appreciate just how ingenious.

It was all one long piece of rope.

A skimpy piece of cotton line was strung from the whiteness somewhere in the center of the roof to the railing, where it was tied with a bow, then strung to tether her hands together, the second arrangement secured with a bow also. Her life depended on that short stretch of taut rope between her hands and the railing; it was the only barrier between April and the street.

The section of the rope that ran off to the center of the roof hung slackly. Were she to make a sudden movement, the bow at her hands would come undone.

A siren keened in the distance, raking up the morning, ricocheting against the buildings of downtown Seattle. An ambulance. A breeze began to stir. To the east, the first rays of the sun were brightening the mist, coming quicker and warmer than he would have suspected. Things were beginning to clear.

Had he accidentally tripped over the rope, the bow on the railing would have unknotted, she would have dropped the four or five feet necessary to take up the rest of the slack, and the momentum from that short drop would have straight-lined the bow at her wrists. She would have ended up on the sidewalk.

Nobody would ever know she'd been bound. The perfect suicide-murder.

"Mac?"

The instant she spoke, the slack portion of the rope bobbled and went tight. Somebody was pulling on it, not hard, but hard enough to stir up a horde of butterflies in Mac's stomach. When he took a step toward April, the rope grew tighter.

Her neck arched toward him, muscles straining as she brought her eyes to bear.

"Mac? Is that really you? Don't come near me. Mac? I'm right on the edge. Mac?" She tried to say more but it came out in gargling shudders. None of her words had been pronounced cleanly, and now she deteriorated into gibberish. Her body shivered so violently he was afraid she'd unknot the rope herself.

When he stepped closer he saw that her left eye was swollen shut, purple, bruised, her lips puffy, split and bleeding. A ribbon of blood laced her incisors. She hadn't stepped outside the railing willingly.

She hadn't even stepped out of her apartment willingly.

He wanted to move closer, but one stiff jerk and she would be airborne.

He wondered if the fog made it easier for her. Even as he wondered, she gasped, peered down, and seemed to stop breathing. She hadn't been looking down until then. Her shivering grew progressively worse. Her knees seemed about to buckle.

The cloud was lifting, a breeze had picked up, and April Falwell could suddenly see halfway down the side of the structure, forty stories. So could he. She made a dry, spitting sound, tried to puke, failed, and sobbed. If he'd had breakfast, he would have done it for her.

A breeze swept the roof.

Bundled in a black raincoat, a three-piece suit under that, he sat under the flagpole in a six-dollar lawn chair and sipped steaming liquid from a thermos at his side. Three helium-filled foil balloons were tied to the chair, bumbling gently against each other in the sudden gust. The thin cotton line was cradled loosely in his hand, the end of the line anchored around the flagpole: three wraps and a granny knot.

He said, "Howdy." The look on his face wasn't quite a smirk.

Mac didn't see any weapons. Just the rope. The lawn chair. The thermos, tendrils of steam wafting from it. The three helium balloons playing giddily on their leashes.

"Mac? I don't want to die," said April.

"Don't even think about it, darlin'. We'll straighten it out." He noticed the toenails of her left foot were painted vermilion, the nails on her right bare. The skin had been scraped off her right ankle.

A movement scuffed gravel behind Mac.

He turned and spotted Dahlia Grimm twenty feet away, weaponless, clad in black sweatpants, a black sweatshirt, bareheaded. Her inky eyes met his calmly and she said, "I knew we were going to have to meet like this someday. You just had the look of one of those persistent ones."

"Now, you just drop whatever guns you're carrying on your person," shouted Neil Attwood from his lawn chair. "We've only got a few minutes before that building next door fills up to eye level with the lunch-bucket brigade. You took a long time showing. Missy over there caught a slight chill." Attwood twirled the line in a large circle. "Weapons. Give them to Dahlia."

"Not bloody likely."

Attwood tweaked the line and Mac saw the largest loop on the railing shrink.

"You send her over and I'll kill you both before you can say boo. You been researching me for two days like I think you have, you know that."

Attwood's lips curved upward at the ends and his cheeks knotted, but it was by no means a smile. Dahlia looked somber, crouching for the attack. Fontana spotted Satan in a three-point stance thirty feet behind the lawn chair, waiting for a signal from him. Neither Attwood nor Dahlia had noticed the dog.

Fontana wanted to short-circuit the negotiations, pump bullets into Neil Attwood. But he was afraid. Almost as afraid as he was angry. A spontaneous jerk, a sudden spasm in the death throes would unleash April into the abyss. It was one time in his life when he knew he had to rein in his temper.

Behind, Dahlia's footsteps came closer, the gravel underfoot sounding off like a kid chewing gum with his mouth open.

"Your weapons," said Attwood. "Give them to Dahlia."

"Stand on your head and sing 'Dixie.' You hired Draper to torch the Eldorado Arms."

"Weapons." Using his fingers, Attwood began to roll up the slack in the line. Suddenly, an amorphous patch of blue spread above them. Fontana heard the sleepy drone of a traffic spotter flying above the smudge.

Removing the .38 from his jacket pocket, he snapped open the cylinder, dropped six bullets onto the roof, then tossed the pistol thirty feet away. To make it believable, he reached into his inside jacket pocket, retrieved the handcuffs and a fistful of bullets, and sprinkled them at his feet.

During the forty-five-minute drive in he had debated phoning the Seattle police. The debate had spurred a vision of the building being surrounded by SWAT teams, of bullhorns, flashbulbs, news crews, microphones, hyped commentators; television cameras panning the site from noisy helicopters.

Amidst it all he saw a falling woman. Shoes sliding through the sky beside her, hair yanked straight by the flight, eyes watery with the descent.

35

Zip Codes in Hell

"Now we can talk like civilized men," said Attwood, his face reduced to frigid inelasticity by the cold. "What proof do you have?"

"Don't play God, Neil. Let me help her back."

"I do wish I could oblige."

"You're getting off on this, aren't you?"

"Of course I am."

Fontana saw no option. If he could convince Attwood the swindle was over, perhaps he'd set April free. "You controlled the dummy company that owned the Eldorado Arms. Renaldo Pardew was a neighbor of your mother's. You set it up, had him sign papers. After he died you used his name like a stolen credit card."

"So we *have* been rooting around in musty old files."

"It could be that he's got another weapon on him," said Dahlia. "He could be chock full of weaponry."

"Too true," said Attwood. "Tell you what, Sheriff. Strip to your skivvies just so we know you're on the up and up."

"That'll be the day."

Attwood fiddled with the rope, transmitting gentle see-sawing sine waves along it. Any one of them could have ruptured the knot and thrown April over the precipice. "Do it."

April nodded in tiny stiff movements that encompassed only her head.

"Say what you've gotta, Attwood."

"Do I detect a glimmer of rebellion in your voice?"

"It's all written down. Every name, fact, theory. You kill us and it'll be in the newspapers tomorrow. County cops'll be crawling up your nose with questions and out your ears with indictments."

"Doubtful. You two had a lover's spat. Off you went. Double suicide. Or a suicide and a murder. My security officer will help puzzle out the story when the police arrive. Anything you wrote will be suspect."

"Three people knew where I was going this morning. One of them's a county cop."

"I very much doubt there is anything written down. I've done a thorough job of research on you, Fontana. Been a renegade all your life. In high school you blew your cool and punched out a gym teacher who was trying to discipline you with a paddle. You nearly picked up a court-martial in the army. You did pick up a Bronze Star along with a Purple Heart. You were having a seamy affair with a prostitute when your wife got into a fatal car accident."

"A *former* call girl," Fontana interjected angrily.

"Some of your colleagues think the coincidence of your wife's death and your affair accounted for your idiosyncratic behavior afterward. Quitting your career. Moving out here. There are other things."

Mary Gilliam was baby-sitting—didn't have a clue to where he was. The only thing he'd left was a short note on the sheriff's desk addressed to Brendan.

The wind stirred. To the southeast, the top third of Mount Rainier appeared, sun-dappled. The snowy Olympics. Mount Baker. Everything below was whited out. No water, no ferries, no city. Nothing except the roof of the dark Columbia Center a few blocks away.

"Tell me this," said Attwood. "How did you know we killed Steve Zajac? Dahlia was quite surprised to get your call. Seems to me, any number of people might have done it."

"You admit killing him?" Fontana asked.

Attwood paused. "I may as well. The only people you're going to tell are people who've already got zip codes in hell."

"Zajac was blackmailing somebody. The crisp new hundred-dollar bills indicated that, along with the guns, and the manner in which the murder was committed. He never would have let Max Draper get the drop on him. Wouldn't have let his old buddy Don Reinholt get the drop on him, either. Nor you. He was too distrustful of you three. Crews? I doubt if Fred Crews would have survived beyond the front stoop. And April? He wasn't going to let her in the door. He'd proved that already. Yet whoever visited Steve that night conned him into letting his guard down. It wasn't until I found out she'd been asking around Staircase that I thought of Dahlia. Before the Episcopal Church fire."

"I'm afraid you've lost me," said Attwood.

"Some peckerwood redneck out there told me a black woman had been making inquiries about whether I liked going into fires. When the Drapers hit that church and set off that fireball, I knew she'd instigated it. Under your orders.

"She showed up at Steve's door, gave him a suitcase heavy with bills, tried to dicker with him, then, when she got nowhere, clobbered him. After that, my guess is you came in. From the look on your face when you play with that rope, you get a sick thrill out of torture. Let her back over the railing."

April sobbed.

"How did you come to this conclusion? About us going to his cabin?"

"Zajac was a racist. He also thought women weren't strong enough to do a man's job. It wasn't until after I got to know him that I realized how he'd react to seeing Dahlia at the door. Thought he could manhandle her. Didn't realize she was the bodyguard who'd slammed him through a plate-glass window last June. He'd been drunk then and didn't recognize her when he was sober.

Dahlia was closer now. "The county said it was drugs. Zajac's murder."

"Been bribing fire department officers for a while, haven't you, Neil? Working with Fred Crews. I visited Freddy that first day and he called you afterward, didn't he? Said I'd no doubt be up at Sixes a few minutes later. He's a better judge of people than I gave him credit for. That's when you sicced Draper on me."

"You're almost as devious as me," Attwood said softly. "I almost believe you when you tell me it's written down. Too bad the way things turned out. You could put away a lot of money, you set your mind to it."

"You offering a bribe?"

"Would you accept if I were?"

"Let her back and I won't tell anybody. It's written down. You kill either of us and your mother reads about it in tonight's paper."

"Don't believe him," said Dahlia. Within striking distance now, she crouched.

Attwood snickered. "Look at it from my vantage point. Set her free and ten minutes later the world knows of my indiscretions. Or, I watch the two of you have an accident and take a chance that you're lying about putting this all on crib sheets. Certain ruin versus possible ruin. And whatever happens, nobody'll ever pin your deaths on us. There's only one right choice."

"Right choices don't involve murder."

Working his jaw muscles, Attwood stared about forty miles beyond Fontana's shoulder, slapped the cup down on the roof beside his lawn chair, and knotted his necktie one-handed. The tie was gaudy, like a Christmas present from a child, and didn't match his expensive suit

Nightgown ballooning out around her ankles, April shivered with less violence than previously. Dahlia inched closer. Mac knew he was too far away to reach out and drag April to safety. The more he contemplated the situation, the more his blood boiled. It angered him almost beyond the pale of reason. He knew he was losing control, yet was powerless to stop himself.

"You the sailor?" Fontana said to Dahlia.

Dahlia shot a quick glance at the knots. "I saw it in a spy movie in Mexico."

"Pays to have an education."

As he spoke, Fontana feinted at Dahlia, forcing her to retreat a step, then reached down and withdrew the .38 from his ankle holster.

Without looking in Attwood's direction, Fontana raised the pistol, pointed it at the lawn chair, and squeezed the trigger.

Pop.

It was too late.

Attwood, deciding to move simultaneously, had whipped the cord, sent a bulge of rope rolling toward the railing. The knot on the steel rail flipped into a straight line.

April lurched forward.

Screamed.

Tipped.

Fell face first over the rim.

Vanished.

He'd miscalculated. She was gone!

Turning from the horror, he fired a second shot at Attwood. Fleeter than he looked, Attwood had already overturned the lawn chair and scrambled away, was sprinting for the door that led inside the building. The dog gave chase.

Then the pistol arced through the air in a looping spiral, a pair of black sweatpants flashing past his face. Dahlia Grimm had kicked his hand.

Before she could make another move, Fontana planted a

fist in her face. The blow knocked her on her fanny and sprouted a bouquet of blood beneath her nostrils. She dragged a finger across her surprised face, tonguing the red off her fintertip.

He feinted with a left, popped her over the eye.

Two more jabs and her nose gushed like a winepress.

Now she got to her feet, had better balance than he, defter moves. He'd caught her off guard, was all. When he made another feint, she slammed the back of his elbow, nearly broke it. He backpedaled as she came in. When they moved between the railing and the lawn chair, he almost tripped over the cord.

It was tight.

The cord was still tight!

April might be hanging on it. Out of sight. Hooked. Damn, it was still tight!

36

Ollie-Ollie-Oxen-Free

TICKLING THE AIR WITH her long-nailed fingers, Dahlia moved in and gestured for him to quit shying off.

Mac couldn't stop thinking about the cord, the taut, still-thrumming cord.

Perhaps it had snagged on a piece of the building, was threaded tightly through a cornice, giving the illusion that she hadn't glided a thousand feet through the smoggy morning to freak out a busload of commuters. Or perhaps she was just beyond the ledge.

Taking advantage of his confusion, Dahlia nailed him with a powerful kick across the thigh. He folded and she kicked him in the ribs, her blows forcing ugly bagpipe sounds out of his diaphragm.

She was good.

Then he was down, rolling across the roof, banging elbows, knees. She pursued. She pistoned a foot into his kidneys. He rolled faster.

Then he was rolling free and all he could hear was a ripping sound. Urgent footsteps. Gravel splattering his face. He continued to roll but she was gone.

Growling.

Satan. The dog had turned away from Attwood, had her by

the britches, tugging, had already stained her brawny rump with misshapen splotches of crimson. The seat of her sweatpants was shredded.

"Kill," shouted Fontana, regretting the word even as he shouted it.

The dog released her buttocks, and before she could make tracks, snagged a loose arm, working her, yanking, had her immobilized. A hundred and five pounds of belligerent animal. Incisors that could snap a broomstick. Dahlia had turned into something pitiable; wide-eyed, mouth yawning, pink tongue dancing in consort with her shrieks, face furrowed so deeply somebody might have drawn the lines with a black felt-tip pen. The arm in Satan's teeth was broken.

Dragging himself along on his stomach, Fontana shimmied to the edge where the line ran over the railing. The greater part of his intestines seemed to ride in his mouth. The lip of the building had already begun chewing on the cord, spurts of fuzz marring the integrity of the cotton.

Mac smelled relatively fresh tar on the rooftop. He smelled fear, too.

The cord made sounds.

He grabbed the aluminum flashing on the raised rim of the rain gutter and peered over the edge. A dirty breeze slapped him in the face. His guts reacted like pinwheels.

"Christ!"

Just out of reach, April was suspended three feet below the rim by the cord at her wrists; nothing else. Instead of coming loose and releasing her into free flight, the bow at her wrists had cinched into a knot.

"Oh God oh God oh God oh God," April stammered.

Her left flank had scraped along the rough concrete side of the building. Her hip and shoulder were abraded. He glimpsed just enough of her face to realize it was peeled severely on one side. Her hands were swollen and reddish-purple, nightgown ensnarled.

"April, don't move."

"Oh, God, it hurts. Move? How could I move? Get me out of here, you mother . . .!"

Behind him Dahlia lay on her back, blood spilling onto her breasts from her arm. The dog watched. Attwood was nowhere to be seen, yet Mac sensed he was still on the roof.

The cord emitted a singing noise. Mac sensed it was about to snap, that he had mere seconds to effect a rescue. He wrapped his left arm around a stanchion on the railing, reached down with his right, and lowered everything above his waist beyond the edge. The slightest nudge from behind would be an express ticket to the lobby.

Only by lowering himself could he ball up enough of her nightgown to get a grip. Even so, he didn't know if the material would last, if the crook of his elbow against the stanchion would support their combined weight. The tented aluminum flashing on the building chewed into his rib cage. He took one wrap around his wrist, two. He was entirely vulnerable—if the cord snapped now, before he'd fully anchored himself, they'd both go.

Dutifully, he focused on her and her only, shrank his universe to a roof edge, a railing stanchion, and a woman; left the other one thousand feet in front of him to God.

Using the side of the building as a mooring, pulling her tightly against it, he heaved. She moved upward an inch.

Suddenly the knot in the cord sucked in on itself and she was loose, hands free, slapping and clawing at the side of the building. Certain that she was about to fall to her death, she let out a series of hysterical yelps. Her body did a slow somersault, was heavier than he thought. Her sudden swing and momentum nearly caused him to let go. If he hadn't wrapped the nightgown securely around his wrist he'd have lost her.

The steel stanchion dug into his arm. Blood pounded in his head. He felt his shoes beginning to slide in the flecks of gravel.

How to get out of it? He couldn't just let go, though the

thought intruded itself, along with a strange and sudden craving for a drink of water. Nor could they stay gripped in this deadlock forever. His fingers were weakening. An icicle of saliva launched out of his mouth and dropped past April.

Her yammering ceased, replaced by hiccuping sobs. Her swollen fingers clasped the rim of the roof feebly. He had her nightgown high over her head, twisted tight, supporting under her shoulders. She might slide out of it any second.

For over a minute, he tried to reel her in. It wasn't until she got some of the strength back into her hands, enough to reach around the stanchion and get her own purchase, that they were able to make any headway. She raised a scraped knee beside his face, fighting to get a better grip on the dew-beaded stanchion, clawing her way over him, swearing obscenely. Then she was on the roof from the shoulders up. A weaker woman would never have made it.

After she wormed her way to safety, April sat cross-legged in the gravel taking deep breaths. She held her disfigured hands limply in her lap, staring at the range of discoloration. Fontana glanced at the neighboring tower and saw a group of cheering hard hats on an upper floor. He pulled the nightgown down around her legs. He placed a shaky palm on either of her shoulders and she gave him a look of hatred.

What had seemed an eternity couldn't have totaled more than two minutes.

37

Aftermath

SIRENS SQUALLED BELOW.

April wouldn't walk or talk, had to crawl on hands and knees to the flagpole before she felt safe. She moved as if the roof were a rubber raft on a windswept lake. Dahlia Grimm hadn't budged, though she was beginning to mumble.

Mac left April near the door and walked to the far edge where he'd last seen Attwood. The dog, after dispatching Dahlia, had disappeared again, presumably to look for Attwood.

Sirens?

Attwood's deserted black raincoat lay near the far rim. It was ripped along one hem. The dog had torn it. Mac picked it up. A weighty 9mm pistol was snagged in a pocket.

Suddenly afflicted with a fear of heights, he stood away from the edge, glanced down at the street. He took three deep breaths before he could force himself to the corner. A set of red lights zippered the thinning fog below.

Looking like an ant that had been tromped with a boot, something lay on the sidewalk a thousand feet below. Several people stood in a wide semicircle around it. Was it the dog? Or a man? Or both? An aid car was beside them, light bar winking. A fire engine pulled up with a throaty roar that tunneled up between the towers. A chief's car. Another aid car. And then two police cars. It was a man.

"We're under the big top now," said Fontana.

The sirens would be for Neil Attwood. He had somehow gone over the railing.

And for Satan.

A tragedy.

That dog had been something.

Without Satan's help, Dahlia would have heaved him off the roof. And April as well.

They wouldn't have any trouble from the grand jury. Dahlia Grimm might try to lie, but he didn't see it making a difference. Wait—where was the dog's body? Mac glanced over the railing again. A second, smaller roof stood one story lower than the first. Attwood had missed that roof by twenty feet.

The dog hadn't, was gazing up at him. Without thinking, Mac let out a cheer.

Removing his jacket, he draped it over April's shoulders She said, "I thought you were going to let go of me You're pretty strong for a man."

"Thanks."

"Why did you do that to me? What's wrong with you? I never did anything to you."

"What are you talking about?"

"You got Attwood after me somehow. You bastard."

When Mac had retrieved his Smith & Wesson cuffs, the .38 shells strewn about, along with both revolvers, he knelt beside Dahlia and patted her down for weapons. He found a knife in a sheath in the center of her back.

"I'm sorry," she said.

"What?"

"I'm glad you stopped us. Somebody had to stop us. I made a mistake. I guess it was all the money that turned my head. Neil kept giving me bonuses. Like after I went up to Staircase and found out you went into a lot of the big fires yourself. Neil gave me a bonus. Man, I need a doctor. I'm really sorry about this whole thing. I've *never* hurt like this before."

"I'd splint it for you, but I think you're better off holding it yourself."

"I'm glad you put a stop to it all. I couldn't sleep anymore. In Staircase, dancing with you, I almost spilled it all then."

"I was right about Steve Zajac, wasn't I?"

"I gave him the briefcase stuffed full of money, and when he was counting it I sidearmed him across the throat. He was blackmailing Neil. Neil did all kinds of wicked things, just for the sake of the pure mean pleasure of it. We tied him up and made him walk out in the woods. And we found this spot. The moon was glowing through the treetops and it was so peaceful. I thought . . . something about the place . . about the nighttime and the moonbeams and all . . . that it would stop Neil. It didn't. In fact, it seemed to aggravate him. He wanted to kill that fireman. I didn't have anything to do with it."

"You were there."

"I did nothing."

"That's what I mean."

"Those kids in that other fire? I knew nothing about them until Zajac called Neil a baby killer. It scared me. Scared me worse when Neil stuck that knife in his back. The blade hit a bone or something and he kept hammering it in with the heel of his hand. And Zajac was hollering. I talked Neil into leaving. I told him I thought I heard someone in the trees. I was hoping somebody'd find that fireman. I even picked up the phone and started to dial 911 but I chickened out. You know I didn't sleep for two days. I'm glad you stopped us. I didn't want to see her die. You have to believe me. Tell me you believe this."

"Who's the fire department connection?"

"After you pulled the gun I reacted on instinct, thought you'd shoot us all. God, that hurts. Look, a lot of what happens to me from here on out depends on how you tell it. You do believe me?"

"Give me the names."

"You mean the SFD people? There's only one name."

"Crews?"

"Fred's been working with Neil since before I became head of security. I knew about it but I never figured it would lead to anybody dying."

"Was Zajac right? That Crews stopped city units from responding because he knew about the arson?"

"You believe me, don't you? You've got to believe me. I didn't want anybody to be hurt. I hired on as a bodyguard, not an assassin. Are you listening? I need you to believe."

"Dahlia, sweetheart, five minutes ago you wanted my ass for a Frisbee. Now you expect miracles. There wasn't a lady present, I'd throw you off the roof myself. Talk and I'll see what I can do."

"Sounds fair," she said compliantly. "More than fair. Crews knew. Of course he knew."

April, alert now, caught his eye and said, "You caused the whole damn thing. Why did you ever include me in any of this? I didn't have to be in it. You and Steve were two peas in a pod. That's why I was mad at him in the first place."

She had been squatting on her haunches but she popped up, gritted her teeth as her cold feet pressed into the gravel, hobbled over to Dahlia, and stared down at Mac without sympathy. "You did it! They would have left me alone, safe, if you hadn't come up here meddling, firing guns and shit."

"April?"

"It's true. You forced him to pull that rope. Do you have any idea at all what that felt like? And what the hell took you so long? I musta hung there ten minutes."

Dahlia said, "Wasn't his fault."

Mac said, "What are you saying, April?"

"You did it to me. Don't you know the whole thing was a joke?"

"A what?"

"Of course. They were going to let me back until you forced the issue. You should have called in the police. That would have killed the joke. I know why you didn't. You were mad at him. You wanted to do it yourself. Revenge. That's what you men are all about."

"What are you talking about?" snapped Dahlia. She looked at Mac. "Crews is a silent partner. I think he owns fifteen percent. Neil cut him in because of all the help he's given us over the years. Of course he knew in advance."

"Can you prove it?"

"If it'll help save my ass, I can prove Nancy Reagan popped out of a cake at a KKK meeting."

A few minutes later a security guard opened the door to the roof, the Seattle police directly behind. April had to be coaxed into an elevator. Escorted by a pair of paunchy uniformed cops, an SFD aid crew went to the roof with a stretcher and hauled Dahlia away. Mac retrieved the limping German shepherd, then took the elevator to the lobby.

Satan didn't appear to have broken anything, but Mac thought it wouldn't hurt to take him to the vet anyway.

In the street Fontana took advantage of a lull in the interviews to saunter over to the platoon chief's auto. He leaned an elbow against the roof.

Fred Crews looked up, cranked the window down, snagging his sleeve in the mechanism. "What are you doing here?"

"Lucky your shift was working this morning. See that lump in the middle of the street?"

They both looked at the dead man. One of his shoes was sixty feet away, sitting upright on the sidewalk. A bum would find it later in the morning, wonder who would be foolish enough to lose one shoe, and toss it into a dumpster. A fireman had shrouded the corpse in a yellow-backed, disposable emergency blanket. Strangely, not a single drop of blood soiled it.

"You just mosey on out of here," said Crews. "This is a Seattle Fire Department operation. We're in charge until somebody says different."

"Maybe you recognize the suit." Crews squinted and straightened a red suspender on his bunking pants. All of the firefighters wore bunkers, which meant they had been roused from bed. Which meant it was not yet seven. "It's Attwood."

Wordlessly, Chief Crews opened his door, climbed out, waddled in his bulky bunking pants across the barricaded street, and conferred with a pair of medics in white smocks. The focus of the huddle was a billfold. He turned, plodded back, his pants making a sound like cardboard being folded, and sat heavily in the auto, staring at the radio on the dash.

"You've been helping Attwood for years, haven't you? He needs a favor from the department and you hand it over. I wonder what sort of shortcuts you people have taken in the Towers project here. What'd the fire supression systems cost? Thirty million? It wouldn't take too much cheating to make it worth somebody's while, would it?"

After almost a minute of silence, Crews said, "What do you want?"

"Me? I just want to see you squirm."

Crews gave him a long, weary look. "You done?"

"For now. I'll catch the rest in court."

38

Dirty Looks from a Retarded Cat

MAC DECIDED HE WAS NO crazier after solving Zajac's murder than before.

They were on the upper fork of the river. Mac, Mrs. Kilpatrick, and the two boys, Brendan and Bobby Kilpatrick. Mrs. Kilpatrick had recently evicted her husband for the third and, she boasted, final time. His lameness long since healed, the dog traipsed after them, now lay curled on the bank, off-loading fleas and twitching his sharp ear occasionally at the gossip of a Steller's jay.

Four miles upriver from Staircase, Mac had discovered the secluded glen on one of his solitary walks. It was early January, and frost lingered in the shadows.

The sun was at its zenith, warm and cozy. They had hiked, the boys taking point, Mrs. Kilpatrick scarcely completing the trek. Her brow was shellacked with sweat. All morning she'd been churlish toward her boy, and Mac found himself hanging an entire coat of dislike on the peg of that small habit.

Brendan and Mac parked themselves on a wind-toppled log eight feet in diameter. Mac picked at the bark. Brendan studied his line in the deep pool. Bored with fishing, Bobby Kilpatrick chased frogs in a stand of ferns. In blue jeans and electric-raspberry sweatshirt, the woman lay on the far side of the creek, recuperating.

Brendan said, "You 'spose there's any big ones in here?"

"Monsters."

"You come out here when I'm at school?"

"Sometimes."

The boy pulled some line in, the chartreuse yarn on the hook just visible. He stiffened, unsure if a steelhead was bumping the hook. "Mac?"

"Yeah."

"Dillon at school said you killed a man."

At the far side of the pool, a fin grazed the surface from below, was gone. "What did he say, exactly?"

"Said when you were sheriff you caught the guys who set fire to the Episcopal Church and you shot one dead."

"Fired at him once. Bullet hit him and he died."

Brendan reeled in some line.

"What do you think?"

The boy shrugged.

Mac wanted to give him a squeeze, but sensed the timing was wrong. "Maybe I should have told you about it earlier. Brendan, I did it only after he tried to kill me and some others in that fire. He shot a gun at me. I was protecting myself and the dog. I never wanted to kill anybody."

"But you did?"

"Any time you point a gun, you take the blame for the results. He was a human being. Lot of people say he deserved it. But I still feel terrible."

"As bad as when Mom died?"

"I could never feel that bad again."

Brendan fished for ten minutes and got a couple of nibbles. An insect, sprung from his larval hibernation by the unseasonable sunshine, scratched the glassy surface near the tip of his pole.

"You know, Brendan, when you kill somebody, a piece of

271

you dries up. You never get it back. It's the worst thing you can do."

"But he was a bad man."

"He was a man. God created him. I killed him."

Sunlight angled through a gap in the trees. Rummaging mindlessly through his pockets, Mac discovered a crumpled note he had penned two months earlier.

In the event of my demise:

Dearest Brendan,

I love you more than anything. Always remember that. Your grandparents will take care of you. Respect them. Obey. I wish you a life of peace. Don't run somebody else's race the way I did for too long. Be important to yourself, not others.

Your old man,
Mac

He tore it into bits and dropped the pieces into the stream.

Since the fogbound morning on the tower, he'd been grilled in exhaustive sessions by the city police, county cops, the special prosecutor in Seattle, and others. The affair debauched the city. The media fought to get their hooks into him, but he weaseled out of it each time. One article branded him a hermit. Outside of Tens one morning he "accidentally" lost the guts of a soft ice-cream cone down a shrewd lady interviewer's blouse as she jockeyed a microphone in his face.

Dahlia Grimm had been charged in the abduction of April, as well as the murder of Steve Zajac. When the news broke, a day after Neil Attwood's fall, the city government came loose from its moorings. Fred Crews was charged with conspiracy and subpoenaed to appear before the grand jury so they could decide if they might not add murder charges. Before he could keep the date, he inserted the muzzle of a shotgun into his mouth and pushed the trigger with a stick.

Seeking a plea-bargain arrangement, Dahlia became the state's prize witness. Charlie Dexter and Rafe Draper were charged with arson, attempted murder, assault and battery, conspiracy, and various other felonies.

For ten years Attwood had been bribing inspectors: building, electrical, and fire. He'd gotten his start buying buildings, jacking up their price, setting fire to them, and collecting the inflated insurance dollars. Because he'd switched jurisdictions on almost every deal, nobody had doped out the pattern. Using Chief Crews as his inside man, he had installed a cheap and illegal fire suppression system in the Attwood Towers and it had saved him six million dollars.

In a news interview, Attwood's beautiful widow blamed the entire scam on his cocaine habit.

The chief of the fire department got canned. A new man was imported from Houston, the department reorganized.

The three unfinished skyscrapers in the Attwood project remained skeletons. National TV networks jetted in news anchors. It became commonplace to see choppers with television cameras circling the project for aerial views. The tenants who had moved into the first tower vacated because of safety considerations.

In death, Steve Zajac was reinstated into the fire department, editorial paeans were written to him, his pension was restored and handed over to his estate. Movie types from down south put out feelers, determined to shape the material into a movie of the week.

April Falwell came out to see Mac. She'd fattened up a bit, in fact had become quite plump, had told him she was posing for art classes at the University of Washington in her spare time. Though she'd toned down some, she continued to blame everything on him, had resigned the fire department, was handing tools to a dentist for a living.

She said, "I've got nerve damage in my left hand. Did you know that? I can't go above the ground floor in a building. Me and James Stewart. If you'd stripped down to your skivvies when Attwood said, everything would have been copacetic."

"I'd stripped down when Attwood told me to, darlin', we'd both be staring at velvet liners until our eyes dried up."

Later on, he learned she had retained a lawyer and was suing the fire department. At least she hadn't sued the dog.

Reinholt had been innocent of everything but philandering.

Mo Costigan eventually ripped the flyers for Freud off the phone poles, fireplugs, and out of the Exxon station's men's urinal. She had a cat now, a cat that seemed retarded and gave Mac dirty looks. Mo bitched every time they met. She'd gotten it into her head that he was sheriff material. He told her he'd sooner work in a parking garage and sniff exhaust all day.

Staircase's Engine 1 had driven into a ditch on the way to a chimney fire, denting the right side. Brendan lost a front tooth. Things went on. Life remained just as dull as Mac could make it.